airplane mode

elliott downing

For Tracey, who waited with unprecedented patience

1
planespotting

FROM HER VANTAGE POINT six miles above it, the gray, moonlit world undulated and folded upon itself like the surface of some massive brain, its curvature and finer structure lost to the hazy distance. Cassandra sat with her neck craned and watched the fleeting, isolated lights of little hamlets she'd never visit or see again pass beneath her. The moon's reflected face flashed up at her from the waters of some far-off lake, mountains and craters a quarter of a million miles from her eyes suspended for an instant within a perfectly positioned patch of liquid, but the sense of wonder such a sight would once have evoked in her remained stubbornly absent tonight. After a year and a half of flying on more days than she'd remained on the ground, Cassandra rarely spent much time looking out airplane windows anymore.

She could still remember the initial allure of flight, the awe she'd felt as the vastness of the visible world uncoiled and revealed itself beneath her, but the view outside had long since become a part of her daily routine, pressed inward by the numbing repetition of travel until it dwindled to the unvarying bubble of her laptop's screen and the knees and elbows of her fellow passengers. She'd learned aisle seats offered simpler access to the restrooms, no risk of being pinned in by sleeping seatmates, water from the flight attendants when she needed it. The window seat she occupied tonight, however, had been the last seat open when she'd checked in for her flight that afternoon, and the world seemed to have been conspiring ever since to take away anything else she might have used to occupy her mind.

The battery in Cassandra's laptop had died unexpectedly half an hour after takeoff, killing her hopes of finishing her article on the Jacobys and their augmented toilets while she was in transit, and also cutting off access to all her music and the half-read book she'd downloaded in Pittsburgh two days earlier. The same mischief seemed to have crept into her phone's battery this evening: Although it still showed a tiny sliver of remaining charge, she'd need that to navigate to her hotel when she landed. The phone was all but useless to her in airplane mode anyway, so she'd switched it off and returned it to the canvas messenger bag she'd stowed beneath the seat in front of her. Cassandra spent most flights scrupulously avoiding the visual blare from seatback screens, but she would have considered it a welcome distraction tonight if the seats on her puddle-jumper jet had been equipped with them. This lone daily flight from Helena to Reno seemed designed to cater to midnight gamblers, or those who wanted an early start on losing money in the morning. The overhead lights had been switched off as soon as the plane reached cruising altitude, and most of the passengers around her were napping, the dark of the cabin broken only in a few spots by the glare of a reading lamp or the more diffuse glow of a screen in someone's lap.

Cassandra didn't sleep among strangers. She'd tucked her feet beneath her on the seat and stretched up on her knees to switch on her own reading lamp, resigned to enduring the banality of the in-flight magazine, but found that some earlier, even more desperate traveler had left with it. The seatback pocket in front of her contained only a crumpled Three Musketeers wrapper, a glossy safety card, and a barf bag. Asking her seatmate to loan her his copy of the magazine would have felt like some sort of public confession, and might also have prompted attempts at conversation she'd feel somewhat obliged to entertain. She unfolded the safety card instead and flipped through it grimly, willing herself to take an interest in the emergency features of the Embraer E-175 passenger jet and the hand-drawn escapees from the uncanny valley who populated the card's illustrations. As in all official depictions of life-and-death procedures, these figures exhibited an almost laughable calm, plodding straight-faced through disaster in orderly ranks, their eyes fixed upon some distant vanishing point while smoke filled the cabin or water rose around them. No shouting, no shoving, no discernible expressions on their faces at all, as if someone had summoned an army of the dead to extinguish onboard fires and operate inflatable escape slides.

Cassandra located her seat at the left end of row 22 on the aircraft map and went through the drill: The nearest exit was five rows behind her at the rear of the plane. Should her jet end its journey over the desert by crashing into a large body of water, a steel ring on the underside of her seat—she reached down and located it with her fingers, shaped her hand to the curve of its metal and tugged until she felt the first hint of tension in its strap—would transform her cushion into an awkward-looking flotation device. If the baby-faced, bearded stranger in the aisle seat next to her were unable to don his oxygen mask after a loss of cabin pressure, she should secure a mask over her own face and tighten it with the pull tabs before helping him to attach his. She managed to kill five or six minutes this way before she exhausted the safety card's possibilities, which left switching her reading lamp off again and gawking out the window like the wide-eyed newcomer to the sky she'd once been as her sole remaining entertainment option.

She had little to look at, now, along this section of the Idaho-Nevada border. Mountains alternating with pine forests had furnished her with some variety earlier in the flight, but they'd finally given way to this endless, generalized grayness—lighter below, darker above—and the rippling pattern of the landscape that never seemed to change. Cassandra stared down into the gray until it defeated her. When she turned away from the window at last, she saw from the corner of her eye that the bearded man in the aisle seat next to her was staring in her direction, head at a slight tilt, eyes apparently unmoving.

Here was another recurring joy of air travel that only became amplified when she sat in a window seat, pinned between the fuselage and a seatmate intent on working out the details of her body through her clothes. Cassandra made a minor bet with herself before she turned her head to face him. Usually a single, sharp glance directly into the eyes of a man doing this would prompt him to find business for them elsewhere, but there was a smaller set of men who'd take the eye contact as the sign of a successful overture and flash that sickly, on-demand smile they always mistook for an escalation in charm. This one, she decided, would be the kind who looked away.

Cassandra composed her face into the most dispassionate expression she could muster, snapped her head toward the man to deliver the look, and found he wasn't staring at her after all, but at the window beside her and the world beyond it. Even when she looked directly at his face, his eyes didn't turn to meet hers. Discomfited to find she was now the one staring, she turned back toward the seat in front of her. Perhaps she could make another run through the safety card, brush up on the French she hadn't practiced since high school.

"Did you see it?" the man asked. He had a voice made for a microphone, surprisingly low and modulated, given that in all other respects he resembled an oversized schoolboy who'd somehow finagled enough hormone treatments to grow a beard. She'd had this same thought about him an hour ago, she realized, when the flight attendant had come by with the beverage cart and he'd asked for a cup of ginger ale, but she'd forgotten it immediately. She glanced at the man's face again, just to confirm he was speaking to her, but his eyes hadn't shifted from the window. He lifted one hand and pointed past her through the glass. "F-22. Been sitting fifty, sixty yards off our wing for about ten minutes now. See it?"

Cassandra turned back to the window and scanned the dark space beyond it until, with the silent mental shock of an optical illusion springing into focus, the unlit profile of a gray-painted fighter jet resolved itself abruptly from the surrounding grays of earth and sky. "Holy shit," she said. It was matching their speed almost exactly, appearing to hang perfectly still beside their plane as both aircraft hurtled through the upper troposphere at five hundred miles per hour. "Has it been out there this whole time? I was looking right past it."

"Running dark," the man said. "It's supposed to have its position lights on when it's operating in civilian airspace. Anti-collision lights, too. The FAA will bend the regs sometimes if somebody's flying a surveillance op, but it's not the kind of thing you'd do in the middle of an aviation corridor."

Cassandra had gone with her father when she was nine years old to watch the Blue Angels perform aerobatics over San Francisco Bay, during the two weeks she'd spent with him every summer, and that had been the entirety of her previous experience with fighter jets. In the fourteen years since, her memories of the day had compressed into a highlight reel of noise and grace and astonishing speed, smoke trails crisscrossing the sky in patriotic colors, the atmosphere-splitting roar the bright-blue jets produced when they passed directly overhead. She'd ducked at the force of that noise and then laughed as it receded, clapping along with the crowd after each new stunt as if the pilots in their cockpits could hear them.

This jet outside her window seemed to be of a newer, more angular generation, and it differed from the ones she'd watched that afternoon in several other respects: the way its drab paint job blended with the sky rather than standing out from it for the entertainment of crowds; the illusion that it flew in perfect silence. Above all, this uncanny persistence of its physical relationship to her, not swooping overhead and roaring off elsewhere an instant later, but hanging against the sky with its canopy seemingly locked in position alongside her window.

Nose to nose with this creature, she saw the inescapable truth that had lain concealed from a child's eyes beneath all the air-show pageantry: This was a machine built for death. Its sleek shape cold, alert, almost vulpine, awaiting only some signal entirely outside her control to trigger it into violent action. Heights had never bothered Cassandra, but she felt her lungs beginning to constrict as she contemplated the miles of empty air separating her from the ground, thought of all that could go wrong between here and there. The figures on the safety cards were never depicted burning alive or tumbling helplessly out of the sky, never revealed what expressions their faces might acquire if they found all their practice and protocol had failed them.

"Do you know a lot about fighter planes?" she asked the man beside her.

"Well, planes in general. But yeah."

"Should this scare me?" She was embarrassed by the way her voice nearly squeaked these words, the air barely able to pass her throat.

The man leaned closer to the window and studied the jet again. "It's scaring the living heck out of me," he said.

Cassandra had been a child the last time she'd used the word *heck* unironically, and she had to look more closely at the man's face to work out whether it denoted something serious in his world. The set of his jaw as he looked past her said it did. He was younger, she realized, than his looming bulk in her peripheral vision had led her to assume, perhaps a year or two older than she was. He reached down between his knees abruptly to fish a vinyl windbreaker from the underseat storage space at his feet, unzipped one of its side pockets and withdrew a small pair of folding binoculars. In a detached way, Cassandra recognized how odd this would have seemed to her under ordinary circumstances, but the darkened jet hovering outside the window was consuming all her capac-ity for worry. "Would you mind leaning back for a second?" the man asked. "I want to get a look at something."

"Go for it." She pressed herself dutifully against her seatback so he could lean across her and bring the binoculars nearer to the window. She heard his breathing close beside her, rapid at first, then slowing as his finger adjusted the focus knob set into the binoculars' hinge.

"The external hardpoints look empty," he said. "On this side, at least. No missiles mounted on there."

"Okay," she said. "Good?" Still that timbre to her voice, half an octave higher than she'd aimed for, turning her words into unintended questions.

The man made a noncommittal motion with his shoulders, keeping his face perfectly still against the lenses. "Raptors have a couple of internal missile bays, too. No telling what could be in those." He straightened again and lowered the binoculars. "And to be honest, he wouldn't need a missile to take us down. His cannon could chew our wings off in a couple seconds, if it came to it. That's the little bulge under the right wing." He extended his finger past her nose again, like a tour guide pointing out a feature she'd be sorry to have missed. "Vulcan A2. They're nasty."

"Do you think that's what he's here to do?" Cassandra didn't like the way she was hanging on every word her seatmate spoke now, but somehow, by dint of exhibiting more knowledge of the topic at hand than she possessed, this man she'd diligently avoided meeting until two minutes ago had been transformed into The Expert, keeper of all wisdom, knower of all answers. He didn't reply immediately, but she could see the wheels turning in his mind, knew he was taking her question seriously, and she found it comforting.

"He's beside us, not behind us, so I guess this is a visual inspection for now. Checking if we've been hijacked, maybe?"

Cassandra unbuckled her seatbelt and rose on her knees again to see over the tops of the seats, scanning the motionless cabin and the sleeping passengers. Nothing in here seemed remotely out of the ordinary. All the weirdness was outside. She settled back down on her heels. "I always assumed if my plane got hijacked, I'd know about it."

The man nodded. "I saw the flight attendant up in first class bringing somebody a drink a few minutes ago. No one's acting like anything's wrong. Maybe we just lost radio contact and they sent a bird to check up on us."

"Wouldn't it turn its lights on to do that?" Cassandra asked.

"You're right," the man said. "Especially if our radio was down." He looked crestfallen, whether because of the manifest logic in this or because she was the one who'd thought of it. "That can't be the reason."

Still the gray jet hung beside them, silent and inscrutable. Having exhausted every unpleasant possibility she could think of offhand, Cassandra set about coming up with worse ones. "There was a pilot who crashed a flight full of people into a mountain a few years back, right?"

"That Germanwings jerk. Yeah. Decided killing himself all by himself wouldn't have enough gravitas or something, so he took a whole plane full of people down with him."

"If they found out our pilot was planning something like that, what would they do?"

"What could they do? They can't stop us from crashing by shooting us down."

"I mean if we were going to crash into a city or something. Like a 9/11 thing."

She'd hoped her seatmate would have some piece of information immediately at hand to rule out this possibility, and was disappointed to see how long he thought about it. "If they were a hundred percent sure that was going to happen...then, yeah, they'd probably shoot us down over the desert. Save the people on the ground." The man glanced around the quiet cabin again, as if he were trying to talk himself out of this. "It was only the co-pilot who crashed that Germanwings flight, though. He had to wait until the pilot went to the bathroom and lock him out of the cockpit. The pilot was trying to break back through the door right up until they hit the ground. Everybody on that plane knew something was wrong."

"Maybe our pilots are in it together?" Cassandra thought about the voice she'd heard over the intercom during the announcements from the cockpit earlier in the flight: female, calm, nothing more alarming to be discerned in it than a hint of tiredness. She wondered if there would have been more than that to go on, something that could have tipped her off if she'd been paying closer attention. She realized her seatbelt was still unbuckled and snapped it around her upper thighs again, for all the good it might do her.

"I can't think of any better reason for that thing to be up here with its lights off," the man said. He peered up the aisle toward the cockpit door, found no answers in that direction, and resumed looking out at the jet. "If you see him drop back and get behind us, that might be a good time to say good—"

The F-22's pilot chose that moment to bank sharply and accelerate, giving Cassandra a glimpse of the undersides of swept-back wings as the jet surged forward. Her seatmate's head nearly collided with hers as they both lurched reflexively closer to the window, trying to keep it in view. Then Cassandra felt textured metal brushing against her knuckles and realized he was pressing his binoculars into her hands. "Can you track him?" he said. "You've got a better angle on him than me."

She lifted the binoculars to her face, found the eyepieces set a little too wide for her eyes and folded them inward. Her hand bumped the focus knob as she did so, knocking the world beyond the lenses into a useless blur. "Fuck." She found the knob with a fingertip, tried to adjust it, but her hands were shaking, her fingers having trouble with small movements. She twisted too far in the opposite direction, back again, again, until the horizon resolved into a sharp, solid line once more.

"Do you see him?" the man asked.

"No..." A moment of desperate scanning, until she picked out the shape of the jet against the sky ahead of her, flying level again and looking much smaller now. "Yeah! Got him."

"Does it look like he's circling?"

Cassandra watched a bit longer to make sure her eyes were interpreting the jet's motion correctly. It seemed to be moving considerably faster than their plane now, accelerating forward and away at a constant angle. She let a few more seconds pass, just to be sure. "It looks like he's leaving," she said.

She watched its shape dwindle, fearing it would bank again at any moment and come sweeping back around toward her, but it didn't deviate from its new course. Just as its outline began to blur and merge with the dark of the sky, she saw two small, white dots appear on the backs of its wings, like eyes opening in the night to stare back at her. A moment later, a pair of brighter red dots began to strobe above and below them.

"Um, he just turned some lights on," she said, "if that means anything."

"What color?" the man asked.

"Two red ones that are blinking, and two white ones that aren't."

"Can you see a green light or a red light? That's not blinking, I mean?"

"No. Just the white ones."

"Heading straight away from us," her seatmate said. "Good deal. You mind watching him a little longer and making sure he doesn't turn back?"

"I'll try," Cassandra said. "He's getting pretty far away, though. I can't really see which way he's pointing anymore."

"That part's easy. There's a steady red light mounted on the front of his left wing and a steady green light on the front of his right one. If you start seeing either of those, it means he's turned. The two white ones you're looking at are mounted on the back."

"Do the blinking lights mean anything?"

"Just *Here I am, don't run into me*. The steady ones will tell you which way he's facing."

Cassandra kept watching. She saw no change in the lights: steady white, blinking red, all growing closer and closer together as the jet receded. A minute passed, maybe more. She felt as if she ought to continue giving updates, but nothing new seemed to be happening. "Why do you carry binoculars around with you?" she said. "If you don't mind me asking."

"I do some planespotting." She heard a timid note in the man's voice for the first time, a slight waver to its basso rumble. "It's kind of a nerd thing. Don't judge."

"My whole job is talking to people about nerd things. I won't. What's planespotting?"

"You watch the traffic coming in and out of airports. Note down the tail numbers of the planes you see, look up who they're registered to, where they flew in from, where they're going next. I have a YouTube channel where I talk about it. It's been doing pretty well."

"People watch videos of you talking about planes you've looked at?" She wondered if her promise not to judge had been too hasty.

"Well, I mostly talk about stuff other people have seen. We don't get that much traffic up in Helena. But once you get tapped into the community, you realize there's a whole lot going on. Covert stuff, military stuff, experimental stuff. That's why I'm going to Reno, actually, to talk to some people about those things. And I've never been through RNO before, so..." It took Cassandra a moment to parse this, remember the airport designation she'd seen on her laptop's screen when she booked her ticket. "...I figured I'd look around a little when we get there. See if it's any more interesting than up where I live. *If* we get there," he added.

Cassandra didn't want to dwell on that. "What's the most interesting thing you've seen so far?" she asked.

"This," the man said immediately. "And thanks to my stupid phone dying on me, I couldn't even get a video of it."

"I mean on the ground, watching an airport." It was hard for her to imagine what *interesting* might mean in this context, but the man's voice was soothing, and her hands were growing tired holding the binoculars, and she found she wanted him to keep talking. As it happened, getting people to open up about dull hobbies was one of the primary skills by which she earned her living.

"I saw Air Force One land a couple years ago," the man said. "Saw Harrison Ford's Cessna the year before that. Rich people on hunting trips, mining executives with private jets, stuff like that. I was hoping I could learn to fly myself, maybe fly people like that around for a living, but..." She heard a faint rustle of shirt fabric against his seatback which she took to be the sound of a shrug. "Too poor."

"Seems like you know a lot about fighter planes. Could you fly for the military?"

"I don't really want to kill people. Or get killed by people. How are we looking on that front, by the way?"

"So far, so good," Cassandra said. "I can barely see the jet anymore. No red or green lights, though, so he hasn't turned." She threw in that detail just to reassure him she'd been paying attention. "I guess now I know why you have the colors of all the wing lights on an F-22 memorized."

"Oh, those are the same on every plane in the world. Red on the left wing, green on the right wing, white in the back. If pilots see another plane flying in the dark, they need to know which way it's facing."

Casandra risked lowering the binoculars to peek out the window at her own plane's left wing, a few yards ahead of her. Sure enough, as she tracked her eyes along its leading edge, she spotted the steady glow of a red light mounted near its tip. "Huh," she said. "I fly all the time and I never noticed that."

"I guess it doesn't matter so much when you're a passenger," her seatmate said. "On a normal day, anyway."

Cassandra returned the binoculars to her eyes, but found only varying shades of gray and black beyond the lenses. She worried she'd lost track of the fighter jet, lowered the binoculars an instant before it had changed course and come roaring back to kill them at last. She picked up the minute, flashing red pinpricks again, far in the distance. Squinted and was just able to make out the two white lights shining between them, their orientation unchanged. "It doesn't look to me like this guy's paying any attention to us at all anymore," she said. "Maybe he checked us out and decided we were okay?"

"Let's hope."

Finally, the jet reached a distance even the binoculars could no longer comfortably bridge. "He's gone," Cassandra said, and lowered them. Her eyes ached from staring into the dark. She handed the binoculars back to her seatmate. "I'm glad you had these with you. When you took them out, I wondered if you were a peeping tom or something."

He gave her a sheepish grin and shook his head. "Only if you're an airplane."

"Do you think we're okay now?"

The man's eyes strayed to the window again before he answered, and she couldn't help glancing in that direction herself—checking whether a second jet might have appeared to relieve the first one, checking for monsters clambering over the wing, checking for who knew what, at this point—but the space outside remained empty.

"We're still breathing," he said. "It's a start."

2
tagalong

THE REMAINDER OF THE FLIGHT passed like a tense, surreal dream, neither Cassandra nor her seatmate able to keep their eyes off the window for long. When the pilot's voice finally returned to the intercom, it was only to make the same closing announcements she'd heard on hundreds of other flights: Their aircraft would begin descending shortly; anyone needing to use the restrooms should use them now; garbage should be given to the flight attendants rather then left in the seatback pockets; the crew was grateful they'd chosen to fly this route on the only airline that flew this route. No mention of broken radios or mysterious visitors lurking off the port wing. No mention of death, impending or narrowly avoided.

Soon afterward, the rim of the world ahead began to brighten, like a lantern shining beneath a blanket someone was slowly drawing back. The glow grew nearer, broader, and the lights of outer Reno began to pass beneath her, thickening as the plane flew on: all the reassuring, orange-lit circuitry of streets and buildings, houses and parking lots. Cassandra swung her legs back down into a sitting position and tightened her seatbelt. Her new traveling companion leaned over to get a better view of the lights, his upper body crossing the armrest in what would normally have been a serious breach of airplane etiquette, but under the circumstances, she couldn't fault him for it. "I'm pretty sure we're home free," he said. "Be too late for anyone to shoot us down now."

As much as she appreciated his confidence, Cassandra watched intently as the lights on the ground drew nearer. The plane banked and left her looking nearly straight down upon the roofs of a cul-de-sacced neighborhood, its ground-level illusion of natural, haphazardly winding streets rendered geometrical and calculated when viewed from above. When her aircraft leveled out a few seconds later, she heard the whir of the landing gear extending, felt the disconcerting thump they made as they locked into position jolt up through the metal struts beneath her seat and into the backs of her thighs. She kept watching until she could make out the models of cars on the roads, read the signs on the fronts of buildings as they approached their normal scale again. A brief interlude of darkness followed, the ground beneath her seeming to vanish as if her plane were crossing over some final abyss. Then the white-striped edge of a lighted tarmac came rushing up to meet her, and she felt that moment's last, weightless lull before the wheels touched down.

Deceleration felt like an act of violence as always, the roar of the jet's engines rendered abruptly audible and palpable as she tipped forward in her seat. She heard the collective exhalation of the passengers throughout the cabin as the jets cycled down and the plane began to roll along at ordinary ground speeds, although she doubted most of them had experienced anything close to the tension she now felt draining from her body. Low terminal buildings appeared in the distance. Her seatmate met her eyes and gave her a clenched-mouthed nod of relief, but the other aircraft parked along the tarmac outside drew his attention an instant later. He twisted in his seat and scanned them as they passed, picking out details invisible to her.

They taxied for a couple minutes more before easing into a berth facing the concourse. The engines cut off and the cabin lights switched on and the *Fasten Seatbelts* signs went dark all at once, and the passengers around her began to move as if sprung from a hundred jack-in-the-boxes. After spending the previous forty minutes with her body tensed to die suddenly in the dark, this all felt utterly discordant to Cassandra, as if she were a time traveler who'd been transported from a hushed, nighttime world where predators crouched at the edge of sight into the center of a brightly-lit, modern cacophony of competing voices, chiming phones, people jostling for places in line.

Beyond the window, an articulated walkway maneuvered out from the concourse wall and fastened itself to the side of their jet. Cassandra sensed a shift in the tension of the line shortly thereafter as people at the front of the plane began to exit, although she couldn't see them from where she sat. Habit and muscle memory began to reassert themselves at last. She extended one foot down beneath the seat in front of her, hooked the strap of her messenger bag with the toe of her boot and tugged it up into her lap. She confirmed that her phone and her laptop were both inside it, then took a quick peek into the seatback pocket to make sure she hadn't left anything in there. She hadn't put anything in there, but this routine was what staved off disasters on the road, and she stuck to it as always.

When the people waiting in the row just in front of hers began walking toward the front of the plane, Cassandra's seatmate swiveled sideways in his seat, extending his legs across the aisle to clear a path for her without getting up. "You can scoot past me if you want," he said. "I'm going to wait and talk to the pilot about the..." He motioned toward the window with one hand, though not at anything currently visible beyond it.

"I'll wait with you," Cassandra said. "If that's okay. I'm curious about it, too."

"Cool." The man swung his legs forward again and motioned the people in the rows behind them to pass by. When he and Cassandra were the last two passengers remaining at the back of the aircraft, he gathered up his windbreaker and clambered out into the aisle. He moved forward a couple rows, then looked back at Cassandra and hovered awkwardly, uncertain whether their relationship was now such that he should wait and walk with her or just head that way on his own.

She pulled the strap of her messenger bag over her head, stepped up onto the cushion of the seat he'd just vacated, angled one arm up into the mouth of the bin above her and felt for the handle of her little rolling suitcase. She found it and tugged it forward to the bin's lip.

"Need a hand with that?" the man asked.

"I do this every day, just about." Cassandra swung the suitcase out and down, realizing as it dropped that the man had moved up the aisle toward her again. The falling bag missed his face by inches as he lurched back out of its path. Cassandra caught its weight at hip level, lowered it to the aisle floor and hopped down in front of it. "All good," she said. Her seatmate turned and started toward the front of the plane once more. She extended the pull handle at the top of her suitcase and rolled it down the aisle after him.

Their pilot stood just outside the cockpit doorway, her hair bound up in a set of short, tight braids that ringed the crown of her head. A co-pilot and the two flight attendants flanked her, mouthing a series of rote goodbyes to the last of the departing passengers. Cassandra's seatmate took a step past the exit door and said, "Excuse me, Captain Gates?" Cassandra found a spot to hover a few feet behind him. "I noticed we had a visitor up there for a while."

"You saw our little tagalong?" The pilot made a faint smile that could have meant anything. "I was waiting for someone to ask me about that. I guess you were the only ones who noticed."

"What was that all about?"

"I have no idea," the pilot said. "Air traffic control said we'd have company for a little while. Told us not to worry about it, asked us not to make any announcements about it. Just maintain course and act like nothing was happening."

"Did they tell you why?"

"Routine training maneuvers, supposedly."

Cassandra remembered what her seatmate had mentioned about the jet's lack of lights. "Did anything about that strike you as routine?" she asked.

"I've been flying for twenty-two years, and I've never heard of anything like that happening. Not to anyone I know, not to anyone they know. If it had, we all would have heard about it. They'll be hearing about it as soon as I get online tonight, I'll tell you that." Cassandra thought she recognized the expression on this woman's face, a look of profound stress only now beginning to dissipate. She imagined her own face looked much the same.

"Scared you too, huh?" she said.

"They don't pay me to get scared," the pilot said. "But I've got 76 passengers, two cabin crew, First Officer Hansen and myself to look out for, and none of us signed up to have some dipshit fighter cowboy flying that close to us. Pardon my language. If they have some kind of training they want to do on a scenario like that, I say great. Lease a jet. Do it over a military base. Hire a pilot who's getting *paid* to participate. Don't drag us all into it."

"They didn't mention anything about what they were training for, though?" her seatmate asked. "No idea why they picked our plane?"

"If they'd told me more, I'd tell you more. Honestly, we're no more clued in up here than you all were back there."

"Thanks. What does the 'R' stand for, by the way?" Cassandra's seatmate motioned to the pilot's nametag, *CAPTAIN R. GATES* embossed in dark letters across the brass.

"Rashida," the pilot said. "Why?"

"I'm going to be posting a video on YouTube about this in a couple days. Just want to make sure I get your name right."

Cassandra noted the way the pilot took an unconscious half-step away from him, her expression shifting back to its original configuration of spokesperson-friendly neutrality. "I'd appreciate it if you didn't mention my name at all in anything like that."

"It'll just be a factual account. Nothing that'd make you sound—"

"Look, we had something happen tonight that was out of the ordinary, it gave me some concerns for the safety of my passengers, I think my concerns were justified, but we all did our jobs and it turned out fine. That's where I stand on that. If you want to quote me, that's my quote."

"I'm honestly not looking to get anybody in trouble."

"I'm happy to hear that."

"We should probably let you finish up," Cassandra said. "I'm sure it's been a long day for everyone. Thanks for keeping us safe." She maneuvered the wheels of her suitcase around the toes of the nearest flight attendant and stepped off the plane into the rolling walkway, hoping her seatmate would follow. After a moment, his footsteps behind her signaled that he had.

"Enjoy your stay in Reno," one of the flight attendants called after them.

Up the hollow-sounding floor of the walkway now and out into the emptying nighttime concourse. One of the ugliest carpeting patterns Cassandra had ever seen stretched away toward the terminal, flanked at intervals by banks of blinking slot machines. This carpet looked as if a thousand graphs illustrating principles of advanced chaos theory had been chopped into squares, dyed the wrong shade of brown, and arranged so none of the lines and curves jittering across any one square would harmonize pleasantly with those on any of its neighbors. Still, it was a floor that didn't echo beneath her feet when she walked, incontrovertible evidence she'd lived through whatever had just happened.

Her seatmate emerged from the gate a few yards behind her and hurried to catch up. He stood at least a foot taller than Cassandra and outweighed her by perhaps a hundred pounds, and his footsteps clomping behind her proved to be one test too many for her fight-or-flight reflexes this evening, so she slowed her pace and let him draw along-side her, taking two steps for every three she did. "I know a few people online who specialize in tracking military flights," he said. "I'll see what they can find out about that Raptor."

"Great," Cassandra said. Now that she had a semblance of solid ground beneath her feet, she found her interest in this topic waning by the second.

"The people I came down here to meet with might be able to dig up something about it too. They're pretty connected, supposedly. If I hear anything, I can let you—"

Cassandra spotted a sign for a ladies' room on the wall ahead and veered toward it. "Listen, I'm going to need to stop in here," she said.

"Okay," her seatmate said, and paused just beyond the doorway. "See you down at baggage claim, maybe?"

Cassandra wiggled her suitcase back and forth on its wheels and tried to make her smile look regretful. "This is all I ever carry."

"Well," the man said, "I guess we survived our whole adventure together, then. I'm Graham." He stuck a hand across the space her suit-case occupied between them, and she disengaged her own hand from its handle long enough to shake it.

"Cassandra."

"In a really messed up way," he said, "it was nice meeting you."

"Let's never do it again," Cassandra said. She'd meant that as a joke, but as soon as she said it, she wondered if he'd take it that way. Then she remembered it didn't matter. Her favorite thing about the people she met on airplanes was that if she made a bad impression, she'd never see them again. "Have a good night." She trundled her rolling suitcase around the divider and onto the clacking tile of the restroom, where she could exhale fully, where she could allow her hands to trem-ble, where her own face could emerge at last.

3
fortress

THE HOTEL WAS A MINOR VARIATION on all the hotels, the standard set of elements arranged in a slightly novel configuration, as if someone kept hitting a button marked "Randomize" in a piece of architectural-design software and building the results. Here was the unnecessarily high atrium, in this case topped with translucent skylights after rising through all eight floors of the building, lined on three sides by walkways fronting the guest rooms, with a glass-walled elevator idling at ground level. Here was the poorly-utilized space just off the lobby she wouldn't want to be alone in late at night, in this case occupied by a pair of tired-looking vending machines and an unattended mop in a bucket, its handle reclining against a long, empty counter that appeared to serve no function at all. Here was the restaurant with the puzzling decor, in this case occupying the rear half of the atrium and adorned in some incomprehensible cyber-Western motif featuring varnished tree limbs held together with gleaming chrome joints. Cassandra wheeled her suitcase past a scattering of couches and chairs at the near end of the atrium and turned toward the elevator. Its doors slid apart with a faint metallic scrape, startling her, just as she reached for the button to open them.

She tugged her suitcase inside and watched the atrium grow small beneath her as the elevator carried her up six floors. She made her way around two segments of elevated walkway and into her room at last, where she was greeted by a wall of dead-smelling, too-warm air and a painting of a cattle drive for which someone had seemingly scoured the globe to locate the most perfectly wrong frame imaginable, surfaced once again in polished chrome. She hoisted her suitcase onto the nearer of the room's two beds, lay her messenger bag beside it, and went to figure out the controls for the air conditioner.

She hadn't remembered to turn her phone on and take it out of airplane mode until she'd followed the chaos carpet down to the airport terminal, descended an escalator, waited in line at the rental-car counter, and handed her driver's license over to an attendant in a vest and a bow tie for scanning. Three separate cameras were mounted on motorized spindles at various places along the thick exterior wall that backed the rental office, and all three, she noticed, seemed to be aimed straight at her. When her phone connected to the network and came to life, she found a text waiting from Georgina, sent to her mid-flight, already a couple of hours old: *The Rasmussens had to move their interview to Sunday. We'll need you to stay in Reno until then.* Tonight was Thursday. Cassandra had planned to drive out to Sparks and meet the Rasmussens at noon tomorrow, then take a late flight home to Los Angeles in the evening. This plan suited her better. She liked to be as far from home as possible, liked eating room-service dinners at odd hours and waking up between sheets someone else was being paid to change and clean.

No problem, she texted back, and asked the attendant to extend the return date on her rental agreement by two days. She'd reschedule her flight home once her laptop had charged in the morning.

Her phone chimed with a reply before her paperwork had finished printing. *Sorry we're taking up your whole weekend. Expense everything while you're there, obviously.* It was unclear to Cassandra whether Georgina ever slept, or when. She couldn't recall sending her any message, day or night, from any time zone, that had gone more than five minutes without being answered. Cassandra texted a happy face in response, took the sheaf of papers the attendant handed her and walked out to the garage on the far side of the terminal's access road to collect her car.

She'd chosen a four-door Honda she knew would have seat-height and tilt-wheel controls to her liking. She stowed her suitcase in the trunk, made the necessary adjustments to the driver's seat, and pulled up the navigation app on her phone. She located her hotel on the map first, nestled into the curve of a westbound on-ramp along Interstate 80, then searched for all-night drugstores in its vicinity. She found one only a mile farther up the highway and plotted a route that would take her to the drugstore first, then loop back to her hotel. She hit "Begin," started the car, showed her papers to one more attendant in a booth guarding the garage exit, and drove where the blue line told her to drive.

It guided her a couple miles north along Interstate 580, then around a long cloverleaf and west onto 80. Downtown Reno, rising to her left, gave her a pleasant sensation of viewing chaos from a safe remove: tall buildings floodlit in theme-park colors, with frantically pulsing lights at their bases. Shortly after she'd left them behind, she noticed a vague, soft light glowing in the sky to the right of the highway, which proved to be the glass roof atop her hotel's atrium. She studied the building and its grounds as she drove past, looking for the simplest path in when she returned.

The hotel occupied an acre or so of land on a rise above the interstate, alongside a four-lane boulevard that ran downhill past the freeway's on- and off-ramps and vanished beneath the overpass she was crossing. A condo complex spread across the hillside just above it. The front of the hotel faced across a fountained, circular plaza, with a view consisting primarily of its own parking garage. Oddly, the garage appeared to have had several times more artistic effort applied to its design than the building it theoretically existed to serve. The hotel's exterior had been fashioned in the style Cassandra thought of simply as

American Hotel, a self-contained entity referencing only itself and its thousand other exemplars. The garage, conversely, had somehow been turned into a fanciful architect's playground, each of its four levels painted a different primary color and cantilevered out several feet beyond the level below it, like an untidy stack of building blocks forever on the verge of falling into the boulevard behind them. Cassandra marked the spot where the hotel's access road wound down past the lower side of the garage and connected to the main boulevard, since she'd need to turn in there later, then drove another mile west along the interstate to make her post-flight supply run.

The drugstore looked brightly lit and all but deserted at this hour. An aging Chevy Blazer and a neon-colored hatchback, reminiscent of a melted gumdrop, sat side-by-side in an outer orbit of the lot that suggested both cars had been parked there by employees hours earlier. She drove past them, cut across several rows of empty parking spaces, and pulled in a few slots over from the only other vehicle in the lot: a delivery truck backed up near the store's front door with a metal ramp extending like a tongue from its bed. Inside the store, apart from herself, Cassandra saw only a middle-aged female clerk hunched over her phone on a stool behind the register and a man kneeling beside a hand truck ten or fifteen yards away, stocking a refrigerated case at the head of one aisle with cans of soda.

A large security monitor hung from the ceiling directly above the clerk's head, its camera mounted on a bracket atop the screen like a selfie cam writ large. As Cassandra angled past the counter, she noticed the camera swiveling silently to face her. When she glanced in its direction, it reversed its motion and centered itself again, the image on the screen beneath it stabilizing as it came to rest. Cassandra walked on toward the aisles, feeling as if she'd just encountered the electronic equivalent of the men who stared at her on airplanes. "Let me know if I can help you with anything," the clerk said behind her, and bent over her phone again.

Cassandra had come here with two purchases in mind, one a necessity in her eyes, the other contingent upon whether a man or a woman would be ringing her up this evening. Both items were difficult for her to carry on airplanes from one city to the next without a piece of checked luggage in which to stow them. Neither, Cassandra assumed, was the sort of purchase Georgina intended for her to put on the company credit card, although she'd never asked.

She found the pepper spray first, in a glass-fronted case whose shelf space was mostly devoted to phones and handheld game consoles. Both of the case's sliding panels had padlocks attached to their lower corners, but one of the locks had been left hanging open this evening. She pulled it loose and swung it by its hasp from her index finger while she trundled the glass door aside and considered her choices. Of the two pepper spray options on offer, the more functional-looking one came in a squat, wide canister that appeared too large for her to handle comfortably in one hand. She chose its companion, absurd-looking but sized appropriately for her fingers: a slim metallic tube whose entire surface was lacquered in strident, hot-pink gloss. Cassandra slid the glass panel closed again, slipped the open padlock back onto its latch, double-checked that the female clerk was still the only employee at the checkout counter, then began scanning the signs overhead for the word "Feminine."

She found it marking an aisle just past the man stocking the soda case, who shot a furtive look at her legs as she stepped around him. Down at the far end, beyond several yards of shelving filled with tampons and pads, she found a corkboard rack proffering condoms and lube, surrounded by items that would make one think twice about any situation where they'd be needed in the first place: pregnancy tests, spermicidal gels in assorted colors, medicated vaginal suppositories, ointments for labial chafing. She discerned a certain brute, masculine logic at work in this product arrangement—*If it goes in your pussy, it's on Aisle Five*—but it struck Cassandra as poor salesmanship, like displaying weight-loss pills on the same shelf as the brownie mix. Some connections, she thought, were better left implicit.

This straightforward stocking scheme proved a reliable guide, however. On a floor-level shelf below the condom rack, she found what she was looking for: A plain, opaque white box with VIBRATOR written across its front in a small, vaguely embarrassed-looking font. There appeared to be only one model for sale, and family-drugstore considerations precluded offering any illustrations of what she'd be buying, so she simply grabbed the box in front and hoped for the best.

She returned to the head of the aisle and held the vibrator box against her outside leg as she stepped past the man with the hand truck once more. She dangled the pepper-spray package from her other hand with its label facing him as he stole a second glance at her, then made her way back past the mouths of the aisles toward the checkout counter. The security monitor directly ahead gave her a live view of her own progress toward it, and also of the kneeling man turning his head for a more comprehensive inspection of her ass as she walked away from him. She shifted both of her packages to one arm and waved at his image on the screen, hoping he'd take a hint, but the clerk waved back at her from directly beneath it and she never saw if he noticed or cared.

"Hi, there," the clerk said. "Find everything you needed?"

"Yep." Cassandra lay her two purchases on the counter, set her messenger bag beside them, and fished out her wallet while the clerk rang her up. She thumbed past the company credit card in its place up front, pulled out her personal card from behind her driver's license and slotted it into the chip reader. The vibrator and pepper spray totaled just over fifty dollars. Expensive though it was to keep throwing these items away and replacing them each time she flew to a new city, the fact that she only paid for her own meals on the rare days she ate at home more than covered the cost.

"Get you a little bag for these?" the clerk asked.

"I'll just put them in here." Cassandra opened the mouth of her messenger bag and slipped her wallet back inside. "Actually, do you have a pair of scissors?"

"Should." The clerk found a pair of black-handled scissors in a drawer beside her knees, and Cassandra used them to hack open the fortress of clear plastic encasing the pepper spray. It would do her no good locked in there. "I can recycle that for you if you want," the clerk said.

Cassandra glanced at the image of the man with the hand truck on the monitor above her, found him intent on his work again, and used the scissors to slit open the seal on the white box containing her new VIBRATOR brand vibrator. "I might as well give you this, too," she said. She opened the box, pulled out a white plastic tray nestled inside it, found the vibrator enclosed in a semi-opaque foam sleeve inside that, and unwrapped it. The clerk began gathering up all the packaging. "I'm leaving you with a lot of garbage here," Cassandra said. "Sorry."

"I like knowing it's all getting recycled," the clerk said. "When people take it home with them, you never know."

The aesthetic philosophy of the vibrator was the diametric opposite of the pink pepper-spray canister beside it. It looked knobby and ruggedized, its latex tinted a murky cream-yellow Cassandra associated with bulldozers and off-road vehicles. If these two items' color schemes and finishes had been swapped, she thought, both of them would have made infinitely more sense.

"Whoop. Don't forget your batteries." The clerk pulled two cellophane-wrapped double-A's out of some overlooked hideaway within the white box. Cassandra reached across the counter for them, thinking she'd just slip the little packet into her bag and assemble everything later, but the clerk cracked the plastic open and dropped the two loose batteries into her hand. "Go ahead and make sure they're working, as long as you've got it unwrapped," she said. "If not, I'll find you a different pair."

The clerk carried the armful of empty packaging over to a recycling bin a few feet behind her, leaving Cassandra to work out how to open the plastic battery cover set flush with the base of the vibrator. She found a tiny inset catch with her fingernail, popped the lid open, squinted at the raised diagram embossed on its underside, and slid the batteries home. She clicked the lid back into place, gave the button on the side an experimental press and heard the motor hum gently to life. All in order. She pressed the button a second time to switch the motor off, but this increased its speed instead, the hum growing louder and rising in pitch. She checked the opposite side of the vibrator to see if it had a separate Off button, but this was it. A third press and the thing practically bucked in her hand, its vibration shifting to an aggressive roar that echoed through every corner of the store. On the monitor, she saw the kneeling man's head lift from his soda cans and turn her way again. She stabbed at the button once more, frantically, and it finally went silent.

"Pro tip," the clerk said, returning to the counter. "Electric toothbrush." She held Cassandra's eyes, raising her eyebrows and flashing a conspiratorial smile whose meaning took a moment to register.

Cassandra looked down at the vibrator in her hand, back at the clerk. "Yeah?"

"Cost you half as much, battery'll last you just as long. Go for the one with the soft bristles. Do you up just fine."

"Thanks," Cassandra said. "I'm going to have to replace this in a few days, actually, so that'll—" She stopped, wondering what she'd just implied about how she intended to use this beast in her hand. It looked indestructible, eternal, like it could be hurled against a cliff face from a speeding train and keep humming without interruption. "I mean, I fly a lot, so I'm always needing to—" She decided, belatedly, that this explanation was serving no one. "Anyway. Good to know."

On the security monitor, she watched herself watch herself slip the vibrator into her messenger bag, followed by the pink tube of pepper spray.

"Don't grab the wrong one in the dark," the clerk said.

In the hotel room, Cassandra plugged in her phone and her laptop, hung up the few clothes in her suitcase that needed hanging, and brushed her teeth while she stood by the window watching cars and eighteen-wheelers pass on the interstate below. When she pressed her forehead to the glass and looked out to the left, she could see one protruding upper corner of the parking garage where she'd left her rented Honda. The boulevard descended to the overpass at the base of the hill just beyond it. To the right, the highway stretched away toward a line of mountains, two far-off, snowcapped peaks lifting into the moonlight from behind the shadowed bulk of their front ranks. She drew the curtains, rinsed her mouth out in the bathroom, pulled the bedspread off the bed her bags weren't occupying and climbed up onto it. Quiet now, and a whole day tomorrow without a single person she'd be obliged to talk to. Cassandra fell back against the blanket with her arms spread and closed her eyes. She'd planned to take the ugly vibrator on its maiden voyage once she was settled in, but the stress of the flight had wrung more out of her than she'd realized. Sleep came for her almost immediately, the purr of the air conditioner deepening as she went away, merging with a half-heard memory of jet engines.

4
panopticon

SHE WOKE TO A RINGING PHONE on the nightstand and dragged herself across the bed to pick up the receiver. "Yes?"

"This is the wake-up call you requested for...seven...fifteen...A.M." A computerized female voice that fell a bit short of passing for human, but still managed to sound several times more enthused about making this call than Cassandra was to be receiving it. "If you'd like me to give you another call in...ten...minutes to make sure you're awake, press one or say 'Snooze.'"

"I didn't ask for this one," Cassandra said.

"*One*," the voice said. "Great. I'll call you back in...ten...minutes."

"Fuck," she said. "*Cancel.*"

"Thank you for choosing the...Reno...Grand—"

She hung up. She'd crawled under the covers at some point during the night, although she was still wearing the clothes she'd flown in. Fortunately, she'd be staying here long enough to drop them with the hotel's laundry service and let Georgina foot the bill. Cassandra considered trying to sleep for the nine or so minutes until the phone would ring again, but the damage had been done. She was also, she began to realize, ravenously hungry.

She found a room-service menu at the back of the nightstand, spent a couple minutes looking over her breakfast options, picked up the phone again and dialed the three-digit number printed on the menu's front page. A harried-sounding male voice answered on the second ring.

"Room service."

"Hi, I'd like to order a garden skillet and a—"

"I'm sorry, but our ordering system is down this morning. Would you mind just coming down to the café? It'll be the same menu down there. And you can still ask them to send the food up to your room, if you want."

"Can I just tell you my order, and have you ask them to send it up?" It occurred to Cassandra that the function she'd just described might be called *room service.*

"I wish I could," the man said. "I'm in an office in the basement, and I have to stay by the phone. Normally I just put the orders in my computer and the kitchen gets them, but—"

"No problem," she said. "I'll head down there. Thanks."

She pushed the covers off and swung her legs over the edge of the bed, committed now. She weighed her grooming ambitions against her hunger and decided the flying-and-sleeping clothes she was wearing could function as breakfast clothes this morning, too. She crossed to the desk beneath the cattle-drive painting and swiped a finger across her laptop's trackpad to confirm it had charged during the night. The screen lit up and displayed the single sentence she'd managed to type before her battery had gone dead on the plane the previous evening: *When Stan and Irene Jacoby of Helena, Montana were both diagnosed with type 2 diabetes within four months of one another, Stan had an inspiration.* Cassandra read this sentence over by reflex, deleted *within four months of one another*, then snapped the laptop closed and slid it into her messenger bag. Its battery was at full power again, and she could write more while she ate. She made a similar check of her phone and dropped it into the bag too.

She went into the bathroom and tried not to study her reflection too closely while she wiped goo from the corners of her eyes and tugged her hair into a vaguely symmetrical arrangement. She straightened her bra, slung her bag over her shoulder, rode the elevator down into the well of the atrium and entered the shadow of the stylized cyber-forest that overhung the café, reminding herself that travel rules applied to the people she encountered in hotels as much as they did to those on airplanes. She didn't know any of them, so there was no need to impress them.

She hadn't taken three steps beyond the entrance to the café when a voice said, "Cassandra?"

She glanced around the nearby tables. Inside the small, circular booth nearest to the café's entrance, she saw a bearded face peeking over the upper edge of a phone nearly as large as her laptop's screen. The phone dipped a few inches and one of the arms holding it waved to her, tracing out a perfect semicircle as if drawing the shape of the rising sun. Graham, her seatmate from the night before. A plate containing the remnants of a sausage-and-eggs breakfast rested on the table before him. He waved to her again, the second wave an exact replica of the first one, and there was nothing for her to do but go over and say hello.

"Are you staying here too?" Graham asked. Cassandra gave him the brief nod-and-smile combo she reserved for questions whose answers seemed abundantly obvious. Graham appeared well rested, freshly showered, dressed in a t-shirt that looked like he'd ironed it. She suspected he'd trimmed the ends of his beard since she'd seen him last, too. If he noticed she was still wearing the clothes she'd flown in, he gave no sign.

"How are you?" Cassandra said, hoping to get through the rudiments of small talk quickly and find someone who could take her food order.

"Feeling a little paranoid this morning," Graham said, which wasn't among the rote, scripted answers she'd hoped to elicit. "Apparently I attract airplanes. Got a different one following me today. Check it out." He spun his phone around to face her, bumping his breakfast plate with one elbow, and Cassandra realized she might not get out of here so easily. "This is the plane that made me famous. YouTube famous, anyway."

The image on Graham's screen looked like a section of a low-detail map on which someone had scrawled a series of ragged, overlapping freehand circles with a green crayon. Near the center of the map, two winding gray lines formed a cross shape which looked vaguely familiar to her. Markers near the spot where they crossed identified these as Interstates 80 and 580. She'd recognized their layout from the map she'd followed on her phone screen in the rental car last night. This pattern of green loops, whatever it signified, had been drawn over Reno and its surroundings. All the circles appeared to have been formed by a single, continuous stroke, originating at a point north and west of the city. Cassandra located its other end at the terminus of a half-completed circle, not quite touching the south side of Interstate 80. As she watched, the leading edge of the line extended itself by a few pixels to the opposite side of the highway, continuing a long, counterclockwise curve.

"It's been flying in circles up there for a couple hours now," Graham said, and she realized the looping line was mapping out a flight path. "Came down from Helena last night, about an hour before we did. Landed up at Reno-Stead and took off again first thing this morning. Now it's right above us. It's freaking me out, let me tell you."

Cassandra tried to perceive the menace depicted here, but all she could see on the screen was this mishmash of green arcs. "What do you mean, this plane made you famous?"

"I started doing videos on aerial surveillance about three weeks ago. The government spying on civilians just because they can, you know? This plane here is like the crown jewel. Seriously advanced surveillance platform. Some of the equipment on it's better than we're using in wars right now. But it only flies over cities in America, and no one's ever admitted they own the thing. Not the military, not the FBI, nobody."

Cassandra looked at the green circles with a bit more interest. "Why do they have an app to let you watch it fly around, then?"

"This is just a flight-tracking website." Graham saw this hadn't clarified much for her. "Public data. If you're flying over cities and you don't want other planes flying into you, you need to have a transponder turned on, and that means you can be tracked. Can't stop people from receiving radio signals. Can't stop them from posting the data on the web, either, so far. And the data from this plane is seriously weird."

"How so?" She was beginning to tune out again, imagining breakfast in her belly and her article in progress being more than a single sentence long.

"It just keeps jumping around the country, circling over one city after another. I couldn't figure out any pattern to it until it showed up in Helena and then followed me down here. Before that, it was just these random cities. Pittsburgh, Charlotte, all over the place." Cassandra was staring at Graham now, but he didn't notice. "It ticks me off. They're sucking up massive amounts of data on millions of people, and no one will even say why. You just step outside your door and somebody's watching you? It's messed up. And if the people in my comments are right about the gear on this thing, you might not even have to step outside. We've got this total Panopticon nightmare going on that nobody signed up for, and there's no way to even find out who to complain to about it." Graham's hands had risen from the table and begun to swing about in increasingly animated gestures as he spoke. He calmed them, lay them alongside his phone again. "Anyway, I guess people like watching me angry. I picked up a whole lot of subscribers since I started doing videos about this."

"That plane hasn't been to Atlanta, has it?" Cassandra asked carefully.

"Yeah. Right before Charlotte."

"How about Albuquerque?"

"Yeah..." She saw the question forming in Graham's eyes, but the one thing she was certain of right now was that she didn't have an answer for it.

"Seattle?" she asked.

"There, too," Graham said. "Have you been watching my videos?"

"*No*," Cassandra said. A little too vehemently, perhaps. Graham looked as if she'd smacked his nose with a rolled-up newspaper. "Are you able to find out the dates it was in all those places, by any chance?" she asked.

"You can see that on this same page, actually," Graham said, flipping his phone back around and hunching over it. "Let me just switch the date range."

"Will you be joining him this morning?" said a voice behind Cassandra's shoulder. She turned and found a tall young woman in an apron looming several inches above her. She had straight dark hair and a prettier-than-thou affect, with a smile that came nowhere near her eyes.

"Well, I was planning to—" She glanced at Graham, torn between the need to get her article written in peace and the mystery that had just presented itself on his screen.

"I don't mind if you sit here for a bit," Graham said. "I'll have to head out in a few minutes anyway, when the guy I'm meeting with shows up. You can have the table after that."

"Okay." It sounded like a tolerable compromise.

"I'll get you a menu and some silverware," the waitress said, and hurried away.

"I already know what I want to—" But the woman was gone. Cassandra slid onto the opposite end of the semicircular bench from Graham.

"Here's all the data for the last thirty days," he said, turning his phone to face her again. The map on his screen now encompassed most of the country. The surveillance plane's travels appeared as a series of long green lines stretching from one city to the next, connecting densely filled dots depicting the circles it had flown above them. The series ended with Helena and then Reno, its own dark dot still being filled in as she watched. "All the flight dates are in a table under the map if you scroll down," Graham said. But the map itself had already told Cassandra most of what she needed to know. The lines tracing out this surveillance plane's path around the country were also an exact map of her travel itinerary for the past thirty days.

"I don't think this plane *is* following you," she said, wondering what this could even begin to portend. "It looks like it's following me." She scrolled through the table of dates and places below the map to make sure, but all the information seemed to match up. "I was in Pittsburgh the day before yesterday. Before that, I spent two days in Charlotte. Here's Atlanta before that." She noticed something discordant. "That's weird, though. I flew back to L.A. for two days after Atlanta, but this says the plane just went straight on to Charlotte, right?"

Graham peered at the row she was pointing to in the table. "Yep."

"And then it just sat there for two days until I caught up again. Like it knew where I was going before I did. What the fuck is going on?"

"That's what I've been asking in my videos, in so many words," Graham said. Cassandra wondered if he'd stop bringing them up if she promised to watch one. "The guy I'm meeting with this morning is hooking me up with another guy who can tell me, supposedly."

"Here you go." The dark-haired waitress materialized beside Cassandra a second time with no audible warning. She set a glass of water and some silverware wrapped in a paper napkin down on the table, then pulled out a menu she'd been holding tucked beneath one elbow.

"I just want to get a garden skillet and a glass of orange juice," Cassandra said quickly, before the waitress could set the menu down and teleport away again. "No ice in the orange juice."

The menu snapped back into its spot against the waitress's side. "I'll get that started for you. And you're all set, right?" she said to Graham.

"Yeah. I can go ahead and give you this. It's all signed." He passed the waitress a plastic-covered check presenter that had been lying by his plate. She took it from him, scooped up his plate too, and hurried away.

Cassandra pulled her laptop out of her messenger bag, set it on the table in front of her, raised the lid and opened a new tab in her browser. "Would you mind giving me the link to that web page you're looking at?" she said.

"Want me to email it to you?"

"My email address is kind of complicated. If you can just read the link to me, I'll type it in."

The link turned out to be significantly more complicated than her email address, but Cassandra didn't want a pen pal. After the name of the flight-tracking website and the first slash, Graham recited a long, arbitrary jumble of letters and numbers, which Cassandra typed in carefully one by one. She hit Enter when he'd finished and saw the map of Reno appear on her screen. "Got it," she said. The green flight path showed the surveillance plane had now completed another circle somewhere overhead.

Graham scooted partway around the bench and pointed at her screen. "You can pick whatever date range you're interested in here," he said. "And if you hit where it says *More details*, it'll show you altitude, airspeed, that kind of... Hang on. I think this is my guy."

He was looking out past the café entrance now, where a man in dark jeans and an army surplus jacket stood scanning the faces of the people seated on the chairs and couches in the atrium. The man had close-cropped hair on an oddly shaped head, and shoulders that seemed to tilt permanently forward. The pockets of his army jacket bulged strangely, as if he were smuggling an entire family of cats inside it. Graham stowed his giant phone away somewhere at hip level and slipped out from the far end of the bench. "Let me see if he wants to talk to you before we go. I think he might."

"I don't really want to—"

Graham hurried out of the café and across the atrium. He seemed dressed more for a nature walk than a business meeting, Cassandra saw. Below his t-shirt, he wore khaki cargo shorts and a pair of brown hiking boots laced up to mid-shin. The way he approached the other man and extended his hand told Cassandra this was the first time they'd met in person. As the man's arm rose for the handshake, she saw a portable radio on his hip, extending below the hem of his jacket. They exchanged a few seconds' pleasantries, then Graham leaned close to the other man, speaking more softly and pointing toward the café. Cassandra looked down at her screen and focused on the green arcs of the flight path unspooling across it, uncomfortably aware she was being talked about.

When she glanced up next, she saw the other man gesticulating angrily, though he was keeping his arms close to his sides and his voice low. He turned and looked Cassandra directly in the eye, then turned back to ask Graham a question. A moment later, he was striding briskly in her direction, with Graham bobbing worriedly along behind him. The man's face seemed all eyes and browbone, tapering to a mouth like a struck-through 'V'. Graham managed to scoot around him as they entered the café and arrive at the table a second before him.

"He...has some questions for you," Graham said.

The other man pushed in beside him and glared down at Cassandra. "My question is, who the fuck are you?"

Cassandra let a little silence linger, for the period of time she thought most likely to annoy him. "Cassandra," she said. "Who the fuck are you?"

"Call me Lem," the man said. "Or Lemontail, if you like using more syllables."

Cassandra rolled that around in her mind, but was unable to make it signify anything. "What does Lemontail mean?"

"It means I'm not using my real name. Just a second." Lem reached into one of his jacket's many pockets and withdrew a device that looked like a miniature speaker mounted on four plastic insect legs. He twisted a knob on its face and plunked it down on the table. The noise that emerged from it reminded Cassandra of the hiss from the overhead air conditioners during her flights. Lem adjusted the volume higher and scooted the thing toward her. "White noise generator," he said. "Don't mind it. Keeps people from listening in if you happen to have a bug on you."

"I don't have a bug on me," Cassandra said, wondering what sort of person would assume she did.

"Have you got a phone in there?" Lem asked, pointing to her messenger bag.

"Yeah. Why?"

"Then you have a bug on you. Now, Graham's telling me he just met you recently—like, very recently—and that's worrying me. You two met each other how?"

Graham kept trying frantically to catch Cassandra's eye while Lem spoke, nodding encouragingly to indicate that she should answer his questions. "We were on the same flight last night," she said.

"Sitting right next to him, too, I hear," Lem said.

"If you've already heard that, why are you asking me?"

"I want to see if the version you tell me matches his."

"Graham and I met each other...on our flight last night," Cassandra said slowly, "while I was sitting...right next to him. Happy?" The pattern of faint lines surrounding Lem's frown made her think he'd been an unpleasant ten-year-old about twenty-five years earlier, and had primarily grown taller since.

"What made you choose that particular seat?" Lem asked. "I assume you got to pick one when you checked in. Why'd you take the one next to him?"

"I didn't have a choice. It was the last open seat on the plane."

"No, I got the last open seat," Graham said. Lem's eyes flickered toward him.

"If your seat had been open, I would have taken it," Cassandra said. "I always grab an aisle seat if I can get one."

"I wanted a window seat, and yours was already gone. All the other seats were gone. Trust me, I looked. I don't get to fly very often. I wanted to see out."

"Isn't that interesting," Lem said. His head tracked between the two of them a moment longer and settled on Cassandra. "Why didn't you just trade seats with him after you sat down?"

"I didn't know he wanted mine," Cassandra said. "I don't really talk to people on planes."

"And yet," Lem said, "you decided to talk to him."

"It was me who started talking to her, actually," Graham said. "After I saw the fighter jet."

"Yeah, your mysterious dark jet. I've already heard about that part, so let's skip ahead. I'd love to know how you both came to be staying at this hotel."

Graham gave an annoyed exhalation. "Dude, you booked me the room here."

"I'm asking her," Lem said. "Out of all the hotels in Reno, why'd you decide to stay in this one?"

"My boss asked me to," Cassandra said. "Our company gets a discount here."

"When did he ask you to do that, exactly?"

"She," Cassandra said, but Lem's eyes told her this was one detail of her life he didn't care to hear about. "It was yesterday afternoon."

"What time?"

"I don't know," she said. "Two, maybe?"

"And how did *she* ask you to book a room here? Email? Phone call? Face to face?"

"She sent me a text."

"How about you check the timestamp on that text, then, and tell me the exact time she sent it to you."

"Why?"

"Because then I'll know the exact time she sent it to you."

Cassandra was getting fed up with everything about Lem, but Graham looked stricken, and this information seemed harmless enough. She fished her phone out of her bag, opened her list of messages, tapped her finger on Georgina's name at the top, and scrolled past their brief exchange from the previous evening to find her text about the hotel.

"She sent it to me at 1:13 P.M.," Cassandra said.

Lem seemed to relax a little. "That was Montana time?"

"Oh." Cassandra looked at the timestamp again, realizing why it had seemed off. She'd still been wrapping up her tour of the Jacobys' toilets at 1:13 yesterday, and Georgina hadn't texted her about flying to Reno until she was on the road afterward. "We switched time zones last night. I guess it would have been 2:13 Montana time."

"See, Graham, that's a problem," Lem said. "When I booked your room here, it was 2:05 in Montana. She got a text from her boss telling her to stay here eight minutes later." Lem looked back at Cassandra. "You can see why I'm concerned."

"Not really, no," she said.

"A surveillance plane no one admits to owning has been traveling to every city you have for a month. I have associates in all those cities. Not the kind who like surveillance planes. I make contact with Graham and whoever's running this plane decides to fly it up where he lives, and they fly you up right along with it. I book him a room at this hotel and eight minutes later, you're booking one, too. Then he gets on his flight to come meet me and you're sitting right next him."

"Nobody flew me up there," Cassandra said. "I had people to interview in Helena, so I went to Helena."

"And Pittsburgh? And Charlotte? And Atlanta? You just fly around to random cities interviewing people?"

"That's my job," Cassandra said. "It's got nothing to do with whatever you two are up to."

"Seems like a staggering set of coincidences, then, doesn't it?"

It did, but Cassandra didn't want to dwell on that. Particularly since Lem seemed so eager for her to dwell on it. "It's a big world," she said. "Shit happens."

"Shit most certainly does. Someone diverted a fucking Air Force jet to fly along next to your plane last night, and as far as I can tell, the *only* thing it did while it was up there was get Graham talking to you."

Graham looked at him sharply. "You think that's what it was there for?"

"You like to look out the window when you fly, right? You're certainly a person who'd notice a fighter jet sitting next to his plane. But guess what, you're over in the aisle seat, so if you want to get any kind of decent look at the thing, you'll have to talk to her about it. Neat little conversation starter, seems to me."

"That's insane," Cassandra said.

"Everything we've been talking about is insane, if you haven't been listening. And we haven't even talked about all of it yet. Because the very next morning, here you are again, at a meeting I only invited Graham to. Kind of hard not to see the pattern developing."

"I'm not here for your meeting. I'm here to have breakfast." Cassandra thought of her unrequested wake-up call, the computer failure that had brought her down here when she would have preferred to eat in her room. She decided against bringing those things up now, or thinking too hard about them at all.

"I don't see any breakfast. What I do see is you sitting at Graham's table, on the day I'm supposed to introduce him to someone who'd very much like to stay hidden from prying eyes. So pardon me for repeating my question, little Miss Cassandra, but who the fuck are you?"

"Could you watch your mouth?" Graham said. "I get that you guys need to be cautious, but you don't have to be a jerk about it."

"You're so right, Graham," Lem said. "Let me start over. It's been a pleasure meeting you, Cassandra, at this little get-together no one invited you to. And now that we're all friends, would you mind telling me, pretty please, exactly who the fuck you are?"

She began to wonder whether Lem might be not just annoying but dangerous; what sorts of items might be concealed in all those bulging pockets of his. "I'm not anyone," she said. "Not like you're thinking. I fly around the country and write articles for a website."

"Articles about what?"

"Smart homes."

"*Smart,*" Lem said. "Of course. What could be smarter than putting yourself under 24-hour surveillance inside your own house? 'Alexa, record every fucking word I say and store it in somebody's database forever'? That's what you do for a living, and you're telling me I shouldn't be worried about you?"

"I don't cover commercial stuff like that. I write about custom things people have made for themselves. Hobby projects, basically. Build a sensor array, make it do something useful in your house. Turns out a lot of people like to do that. Some of them call it Homebrew. Because ha-ha, *home.*"

Lem had been staring closely at Cassandra's face while she spoke. "Are there any photos of you on the web?" he asked, and the question landed like a grenade being dropped in her lap.

Cassandra felt her face reacting in a way she couldn't control and didn't like, but she found no immediate way to countermand it. Part of her subconscious, a large part, had been waiting for someone to ask her this question for the better part of two years. She forced herself to keep her eyes steady on Lem's, keep her breath moving in and out of her body. "Why do you ask?" she said.

"Just looking for some faint shred of evidence that you might actually be who you say you are. Do you have a Facebook page? Snapchat, Instagram? Anything?"

"I'm not on those anymore," Cassandra said. But that, too, was connected to topics she'd rather avoid.

"Good idea, generally speaking," Lem said. "Bit of a pain in the ass for me today, though. Is there anything out there at all that might show me you're you?"

Graham's eyes still darting in her peripheral vision, terrified she might say the wrong thing. "You can go to the website I work for," Cassandra said. "Smart Home Journal dot com. Click any article on there, click my name at the top, and you'll see a photo, my bio, whatever the hell it is you're hoping to find."

"Do you mind if I look at that site on your laptop?"

"You can use my phone," Graham said. He pulled it out of his shorts pocket and slid back into his previous spot on the far side of the booth, laying it on the table. "Come on around and—"

"Let's assume for the time being that I'm picky about what we do with your phone, Graham. If this site's going to be dropping any clever little trackers, it can drop them on her." Cassandra still appreciated Graham's attempt. Lem motioned to her laptop. "May I?"

Reluctantly, Cassandra slid aside and made room for Lem to sit in front of her laptop, keenly aware that she was now stuck between him and Graham in the center of the booth. "I have some work going in those open tabs," she said. "Don't fuck it up."

"I don't browse in public mode," Lem said. "Not even on your computer. I'll be doing this in a completely different window." He unleashed a flurry of keystrokes, leaving Cassandra feeling as if she'd just failed some litmus test she hadn't known was in progress. A moment later, the familiar front page of the Smart Home Journal website appeared on her screen, with its list of her recent articles. Lem scrolled through them quickly, looking at the bylines. "Cassandra Holt Davies? That's you?"

"Like I said."

He kept scrolling, looking at her name under every headline. "Are you the only person who writes for this thing?"

"On the U.S. site, yeah. I think they have some other sites for other countries. I've never really looked at them."

Lem opened a random article and clicked on her name below the title before she had a chance to see which one. Cassandra's own face appeared on the screen then: the winning selection from among the thirty-odd headshots she'd taken on an afternoon eighteen months ago, after Georgina had written to tell her she'd been hired. Getting a usable picture had taken her a long time, trying to maintain an expression that said *friendly but professional* while angling her right arm to hide the fact that she was also the person holding the camera. Lem snapped his head toward Cassandra for a brief, sharp, searching look at her face, did the same thing to the photo, and nodded. He read over the bio text she'd written later that same afternoon and returned to the article he'd opened previously. Cassandra was able to glimpse its title this time: *Sensors that Benefit the Environment and the Pocketbook*. Lem scanned the first paragraph of the article, then began scrolling through it restlessly, pausing here and there to peer at the photos she'd embedded amid the text. As in all her articles, some of the pictures showed her interview subjects' smiling faces and others showed their sensor gear. "Tell me what I'm looking at here," Lem said.

"These are the Melmans," Cassandra said. "They live in Osceola, Wisconsin. They installed a bunch of temperature sensors around their house, analyzed the way air flowed between the rooms under different temperature conditions, and came up with a spot-heating system that brought their utility bill down by about 60%. It only changes the air temperature in a few key places at a time, and those differences generate air currents that carry the heat through the rest of the house."

Lem continued scrolling up and down the page at random. He jumped to the bottom, glanced at the copyright notice in the page footer, whipped back upward again. "That's nice," he said. "Who gives a shit?"

"It's good for the Earth. It's good for the Melmans."

"But besides them, you, and whoever your boss is, who gives a shit about any of this? It doesn't look like they're selling their little thermostat system. They don't give you any instructions on how to make your own. You can stick all the DHT sensors you want around your house, but somebody's still got to write the code to make them talk to each other. There's not one word in here about the code." It began to dawn on Cassandra that Lem had absorbed far more information from the article than his random jumps around the text suggested. "So why do these people want you to interview them? And why is your boss flying you all the way to wherever-the-fuck, Wisconsin to do it?"

"I think people just like the idea of somebody writing about them. People they don't know reading about them. They get to feel famous for a day."

"Because *that's* always a good idea." Lem scrolled through the article again, pausing to look at each of the photos Cassandra had taken. "Seems like Mrs. Melman wears a lot of jewelry around the house."

"People get dressed up for their interviews, usually. They know I'll be taking pictures, so—"

"Do you publish their home addresses?" Lem asked.

"Of course not."

"But you do give their full names and what town they live in. Finding the address would take me about ten extra seconds. I assume this is their front door, yeah?" Lem pointed to a photo of the Melmans standing side by side in their living room, the house's entryway visible in the background. "I notice one thing they *didn't* include in their little home automation setup is a burglar alarm."

Cassandra didn't like the turn this was taking. "It's a small town."

"It's a big internet. It only takes one person to notice they have nice things in their house. No alarms, free jewelry…"

"Would you do that?" Graham said. "Seriously?"

"It's not something I'd go back to prison for myself, no," Lem said. "Just making everyone aware of the possibilities." He opened a new tab, typed a web address more quickly than Cassandra could read it and hit Enter like an exclamation point at the end of a sentence. "Let's see how many people *are* looking at their stuff."

Lem had a way of using her computer that made Cassandra feel like it was being violated, possessed by an unfriendly spirit and forced to act against its will. He eschewed touching the trackpad unless he absolutely had to, relying on keyboard shortcuts she'd never taken the time to learn for most of his navigation. Cassandra was a fast typist, but Lem's speed was freakish. He pasted the address of her website—she hadn't seen him copy it, but here it was—into a box on the page that appeared next, smacked the Enter key again, scrolled down the instant he got a result. Cassandra saw the word "Analytics" flash past on the screen, then a graph and a table of statistics. Lem's hands finally went still while he looked these over.

"Your site gets shit for traffic," he said. "The Melmans have that going for them, at least. I'm not big on security through obscurity, but I've got to admit, this is pretty fucking obscure." He spent another half second looking over the numbers. "Okay. Let's see what the Wayback Machine says about you."

More rapid-fire navigation, and then Lem was pasting the address he'd copied into yet another box on another website. The page he summoned this time had a horizontal timeline running along the top, marked with dates from the late 1990s to the present, empty until a few colored tick marks appeared in the area representing the past two years. Lem clicked on one of them, and Cassandra found herself looking once again at the Smart Home Journal front page, only subtly wrong now: the layout of the articles somehow less tidy, the font a little more cramped. The titles of the top few articles on the page were ones she only vaguely remembered writing.

"What is that?" Cassandra asked.

"Internet archive," Lem said. "Snapshot of your site from a year ago." That had been before the redesign Georgina had commissioned last fall, Cassandra realized. This page looked wrong in the way older versions of things always came to look wrong, once you'd grown accustomed to their replacements. "Just wanted to see if all those timestamps on your articles are legit. Make sure someone didn't fake up this whole site yesterday to give you a cover story."

"Who would do that?"

"I don't know, Cassandra. Who'd do any of this? Has it ever occurred to you that your job doesn't make the slightest bit of sense?"

"Just because you're not interested in this stuff, it doesn't mean other people don't want to read about—"

"Your site doesn't have any ads. Do you get that? It isn't selling subscriptions. It barely gets any traffic. No one's *reading* this shit. But somebody's flying you all over the country, putting you up in hotels like this one, just so you can talk to these assholes about their little hobby face to face? Who's paying for that?"

"My company pays for it."

"Ah, yes. The vast multinational empire that is Automation Journalism, LLC." Cassandra only ever saw that name on her paycheck deposits, and she wondered how Lem knew it. Then she remembered it also appeared in tiny print in the website footer, part of the copyright notice he'd glanced at for a fraction of a second. "And where do *they* get the money for it, exactly?"

"Maybe they have deals with the companies that make the sensors. I don't know."

"You never asked?"

"Why should I? I get paid well to do something I don't really mind doing, and I get to live in hotels like this. I never saw a need to question it."

"When was the last time you talked to your boss?" Lem asked.

"She texted me last night."

"And in person?"

"We never have," Cassandra said. "We exchanged a bunch of emails when she first hired me, and we've mostly texted since then."

"Well, *that* sounds totally normal," Lem said. "How did she manage to hire you in the first place?"

"She found my resume on LinkedIn. Asked me if I'd write a trial article for her, see how it went. Flew me out to interview this couple in Ohio, liked what I wrote about them, and that was that."

Lem had already turned back to her computer by the time Cassandra had finished speaking. He typed *cassandra holt davies linkedin* into the search bar and clicked on the top result. Cassandra found the experience of watching Lem type her name inexpressibly creepy. "There you are," he said, and a moment later he was scrolling through her resume, scanning up and down the text in the same quick, restless way he seemed to read everything. "Three years at the UCLA School of Journalism. 3.8 grade-point average. Hired straight out of college. Congratulations." He scrolled down through the sections about her job at the bakery and the work she'd done for her high school newspaper. She didn't want him to know these things about her, but she had no way of preventing it now. She'd posted her resume because she wanted people to see it, of course. Just not him. Lem scrolled back upward. "Only three years of college, though. Did you graduate early?"

"I didn't quite graduate."

"Why not?" He stared her full in the face again, unblinking.

"None of your fucking business," Cassandra said.

Lem smiled. It didn't make him any more pleasant to look at. "That's the first smart answer you've given me since this conversation started," he said. "That's the correct answer to every question in the world, just about. But people never learn." He closed the browser window he'd opened with a final flourish of keystrokes, leaving her original window with its still-updating map of the surveillance plane's flight path sitting in the foreground of her screen once more. He swiveled the laptop around to face her and slid to the edge of the booth. "Graham, we're going to have to postpone this for at least a day. I need to talk to my client about this, and our mail doesn't travel too fast. How about we meet back here at the same time tomorrow? I'll put you up for the extra night and eat the cost of changing your flight, but don't be too surprised if he decides to cancel. And do try to come alone tomorrow, like I asked you to."

"Wait," Graham said. "We're just blowing the whole day off? Are you serious?"

"I'm afraid I have to be," Lem said.

"I took time out of my life to fly down here. You specifically said I had to be here today if I want to talk to Crimson. And now you're just going to—"

"Thank you," Lem said, "for blurting out *that* name while we're all together."

"Isn't that why you've got your little bug jammer on the table?" Graham poked at the white-noise generator with one finger.

"It works on electronics," Lem said evenly. "Not so much on her. And no offense, but you spend your life making YouTube videos. It doesn't sound to me like you're all that busy."

"You think posting a twenty-minute video every day means I spend twenty minutes making it? I have to research them, write the scripts, edit them, post them, write the descriptions, plug in links. I spend another two, three hours every day just answering people's comments. It's my livelihood. Yeah, I'm busy."

"Your livelihood, as such, was selling pet food up until a month ago, according to the information I've got. Not so much of anything since then."

"I get paid for my videos," Graham said. "The recent ones, I've gotten paid."

"Then don't fuck this up tomorrow, and maybe you'll learn some things that can keep that going. Your odds just got a lot worse, though."

Lem pulled the handheld radio from under his jacket and switched it on. He turned off the white-noise generator in front of him before he hit the transmit button. "We're a no-go today, kiddies," he said. "Everybody head home." He returned the radio to his belt and clicked the white-noise generator back on immediately.

"I can't just sit here doing nothing for an entire day," Graham said.

"Then you should have followed my instructions. I told you we needed to meet alone. I told you to keep every bit of this a fucking secret. If you're going to drag in any random twit you pick up during a plane ride, this isn't going to—"

Cassandra slammed the lid of her laptop shut. "How about I make this simpler for both of you?" she said. "Seeing as how I didn't care about any of it in the first place. You can put your minds at ease, because

I'm leaving. Okay? Now *you* can have your super-secret Boy Scout meeting," she said to Graham, then turned to Lem, "and you can go fuck yourself." She slid toward Lem and the exit from the bench, but he remained immobile, blocking her. "*Move*," she said.

Lem looked back at her impassively. Cassandra thought of the pepper spray in her bag and wondered if using it on him now would qualify as self-defense. She suspected it wouldn't, but she also suspected she might not mind. Graham pushed himself up from the other end of the bench, clearing a path for her. Cassandra reversed direction and slid around to that end, snatching her laptop off the table and stuffing it into her bag as she went. "Sorry about this," Graham said quietly as she angled past him.

Cassandra waved to the waitress, who was approaching with her breakfast. "Hi. Can you send that order up to my room, actually? I'm in 706."

The waitress didn't look pleased. "What's the name on the room?"

"Cassandra Davies." She shot a glare at Lem. "If that's my real name."

The waitress glanced at Lem, but sensed this exchange wasn't worth pursuing. "I'll have this sent up to you." She carried the plate of food back the way she'd come.

Cassandra turned in the other direction, toward the exit. "I'm not very impressed with your taste in friends," she told Graham as she passed him.

"Neither am I," Lem called after her. Cassandra crossed the atrium to the elevator and passed through the doors, upward, away from them.

5
legend

WHEN STAN AND IRENE JACOBY of Helena, Montana were both diagnosed with type 2 diabetes, Cassandra wrote, Stan had an inspiration. The Jacobys, avid gardeners living in an arid climate, have spent the past five years designing and perfecting an automated plant-watering system controlled by more than 300 wireless moisture sensors laced throughout the grounds of their home. "Some of our neighbors call it the Miracle Garden," Stan tells me, as he walks me through the startlingly green oasis he and Irene have coaxed from the dry Montana soil. "But it's really just a matter of letting technology guide your decision-making. Anyone could do this."

This year, grappling with the new logistics of a life-changing medical diagnosis, Stan wondered if similar sensors, installed in each of the home's four toilets, could monitor sugar levels in the couple's urine and alert them whenever

Cassandra stopped typing, took a bite from her cooling breakfast, and found herself staring at the last word she'd written, unable to remember what she'd decided the next one should be. Her difficulty focusing this morning had nothing to do with Lem, she told herself. She didn't care about Lem or any of his accusations. It was the feeling of being watched, of being followed, that had burrowed into her mind: no longer as a thing she assumed happened in the abstract, all the time, to everyone in the modern world, but as a thing happening here, today, directed specifically at her. A thing she could now see happening as it happened, traced across a map in a pattern of green loops with her hotel at a point near its center. She switched away from the browser tab she was using to compose her article and watched the surveillance plane's path for a few more minutes, still drawing its endless circles somewhere high above her.

When in doubt, work, she told herself. It had carried her through her first rough months in this job, when Georgina's offer of full-time employment had felt like passage onto a lifeboat she was terrified might be revoked if she didn't continue earning it every hour. It had carried her through the better year-and-some that followed, as she'd grown accustomed to the idea that the entire country was her workplace, airplanes and hotels her true home. It helped far less, she discovered, when it was the nature of the work itself she doubted. Lem's words had dug themselves a space inside her head after all. *No one's reading this shit.*

Cassandra opened a new browser tab and searched for "Automation Journalism, LLC." She had a faint memory of having done this once before, just after Georgina had hired her, and what she learned about her employer this time was no more memorable than it must have seemed to her eighteen months ago: incorporated in Delaware; privately held; between zero and ten full-time employees; headquartered in Tucson, Arizona. She Googled the address listed for the corporate headquarters and found a strip-mall packaging store that rented out post-office boxes by the month. She considered texting Georgina a list of questions about the company and its business model, asking who determined her travel itinerary and how, but pulling Georgina into this now would have been tantamount to admitting Lem had won.

The article that should have taken her two hours to finish took all day. She had long stretches of time she wasn't able to reconstruct in her memory afterward, typing a few sentences and then staring at the walls of her room, examining every detail of the horses and men and cattle in the painting above her desk: the bristly mustache of the nearest cowboy, the way another had half-risen in his stirrups, one upflung elbow jutting against the sky like a ship's prow as he clutched his hat to his head. She realized she hadn't rescheduled her flight home yet, so she spent a few minutes changing her reservation from tonight to Sunday evening. She wrote a little more. She switched tabs again and monitored the spy plane's progress until it reached a spot she thought should be visible from her window, then went and stood before the glass, staring up into the sky across the interstate, searching for a wink of paint or metal against the blue. She saw a white jet descending a few miles off to her left, but it was facing in the wrong direction, heading toward the airport south and east of her. She didn't know what color the surveillance plane was, or even what size it was. Graham could have told her, but she hadn't thought to ask him. She'd have no way of recognizing this plane if she did see it.

The day went by. She flipped through the spiral notebook she carried to interviews, read over the quotes from both Jacobys she'd written in it the day before, plugged them into her text and rearranged them and took them out again. By sundown, she finally managed to produce an article of the usual length—if not, she suspected, the usual quality—then scrolled through her phone's camera roll for photos to accompany it. She selected the greenest, most lush-looking image of the Jacobys' garden she'd managed to capture; another of Stan and Irene posing in front of it. She dumped both pictures into her Dropbox and continued scrolling. Cassandra wasn't much of a photographer, didn't even own a proper camera, but Georgina had never complained. Perhaps because no one was expected to look at these pictures? She pushed the thought away. When in doubt, work. She was flipping through two dozen marginally different photos of the Jacobys' sensor-equipped toilet bowls, trying to devise some fathomable set of criteria by which she might select a best one from among them, when a light knock sounded at her door.

She walked barefoot across the thin carpet, rose on her tiptoes to look through the peephole, and found a nervous-looking Graham shuffling his feet on the walkway outside. Cassandra returned to her chair just as quietly and continued flipping through toilet photos, although her mind was even less engaged with the task than before. Another, louder knock came. "Goddamn it," she said, hoping her voice would carry through the door, and rose again. She snapped open both locks on the door but left the swinging security bar in place as she jerked it open.

"Sorry," was Graham's first word when the door smacked against the limit of the U-shaped bar.

"How did you get my room number?" she asked him, through the gap between door and frame.

"You gave it to the waitress at breakfast," Graham said.

"So you...what? Memorized it, just in case?"

Graham looked miserable. "Lem did," he said.

"And?"

"I need to ask you a favor." Only one of Cassandra's eyes was visible to Graham, but the look she gave him still made him step back a pace. "I know I'm in no position. I still need to ask."

Cassandra waited.

"The person I flew down here to talk to—" Graham glanced quickly in both directions along the walkway, lowered his voice. "What the heck. You already heard his name. Crimson. I was supposed to take a drive and see him today. Talk about that surveillance plane, talk about a bunch of other stuff too. You heard that got put off, I guess."

"Mm-hmm." Her face giving him nothing.

"Lem sent Crimson a message this morning after we— After what happened. I'm not really sure how they talk to each other, but whatever they're doing, it has a long turnaround time. Lem told him about you, how I'd met you, how that plane's been going to the same places you have, all of that. He told Crimson you'd compromised me—that was his word—and he should call the whole thing off."

"I already wasted my time this morning trying to convince Lem I'm not involved in this. And I only bothered doing that because you looked so fucking *morose* about it. You want a favor from me, I did you one. I'm not doing it again. I'm sorry your meeting got canceled, but—"

"That's the thing," Graham said. "Crimson got back to Lem tonight, and he doesn't want to cancel. He wants to have the meeting tomorrow. And he wants you to come too."

Cassandra was silent a moment. "Why?"

"He says you're important. In whatever's going on. Actually, he said he won't meet with me unless you're there. Which is kind of why I'm—"

"I'm not important. I've got nothing to do with any of this."

"It seems like you might. Whether you know it or not. You saw the places that plane's been flying. Don't you want to know what that's about?"

She did. She just wasn't certain she wanted to find out this way.

"First of all," Cassandra asked, "who the hell is Crimson?"

Graham took another furtive look around him. "Would you mind opening the door for just a minute? I shouldn't really be saying this stuff out here."

Cassandra pressed her eye closer to the doorframe, peered out at the little of the walkway she could see on either side of Graham. "Is Lem with you?"

"No. He left the hotel this morning. He hasn't been back."

"Hang on." Cassandra closed the door, stepped over to the bed where her messenger bag lay, retrieved the hot-pink pepper-spray canister from inside it, and stuffed it into the back pocket of her jeans. It sat awkwardly and dug uncomfortably into her ass, but she could pull it out in a hurry if she needed it, and Graham wouldn't see it in the meantime.

She swung the security bar aside, opened the door, stepped back to let him in.

"Make this quick," she said. "I'm working."

Graham stopped just inside the doorway, letting the door close behind him. "This wasn't my idea," he said. "Sorry I'm asking."

"Noted," Cassandra said. "Who's Crimson?"

"He's...this hacker legend, apparently."

"Legend in which sense of the word?"

Graham thought about that. "A little of both, I guess. No one claims to have actually met the guy, but they all say he's great at what he does. And according to Lem, he can tell me everything. Who's running that spy plane, why it's been flying around to all those cities, what it's looking for. All of it."

"And where's this conversation supposed to happen?"

"They haven't told me," Graham said. "Somewhere out of the city. Understand, this guy is, like, way off the grid. No one meets him, no one sees him. But he wants to meet me. And he wants to meet you. I don't know if your day's free tomorrow, I don't know if you'd even consider doing this, but just on the off chance—"

"How are you supposed to meet with him if you don't know where you're going?"

Graham hesitated. "Lem's driving me."

"Nope," Cassandra said immediately. "I'm not going anywhere with Lem."

"Look, he's a jerk. Okay? Agreed. But he's a source. You're a journalist. You know how this works. You get the information."

"I'm not a journalist," Cassandra said. "I ask people how they made their toilet bowls smarter, and I write down what they say."

"You went to journalism school, right? It sounded like you did pretty well there." Graham said this a bit warily, as if Cassandra might view any knowledge he'd acquired about her during Lem's interrogation of her this morning as tainted. He wasn't wrong about that. "You must have had some kind of ambitions."

"*Had*," she said. "Correct. Life didn't turn out that way."

"Do you ever wish it had?"

The annoying thing about Graham, she decided, was this utter earnestness with which he asked his questions, as if he genuinely cared to know the answers. It made dodging them feel ungracious, even when she could see full well where he was trying to lead her. "I used to, sometimes. What difference does it make?"

"Well, there's got to be some kind of interesting story to be told in all of this. And no offense, but it doesn't sound like you necessarily love this job you're doing."

"I love everything about my job," Cassandra said. "Maybe not the job part, but so what? Nobody loves the job part. It gives me a good life. That's the whole point, isn't it?"

"What if it's a lie? What if it really is just a front for something you don't know about?"

"Then why would I want anybody to tell me? Seriously, why am I supposed to care about any of this?"

"Because it affects you. Even if you were just a random person on the street, a surveillance plane like that would affect you. But this actually affects *you*. It's followed you city for city, date for date. There's no way that's a coincidence."

"Lem made that pretty clear already, thanks."

"I'm not Lem!"

"When you keep saying the same things he does, it gets kind of hard to tell which one of you's talking sometimes."

"Look, I saw your face," Graham said. "When I showed you where that plane had been. I don't think you were trying to fool me. I don't think you're some kind of infiltrator. I don't think you knew about any of this before today. But that plane *is* following you, and it has been for at least a month. Either you're suspected of something you don't know about, or you're being used for something you don't know about. Either way, it seems like you might want to find out what it is."

"And this Crimson person knows what it is?"

"He says he does." Graham frowned, and admitted, "Lem says he does. But I don't get the feeling Lem's been doing this all on his own."

"How would you know? Have you talked to anyone besides him?"

"No. But I don't think he'd be so ticked off right now if he was the one running the show. Someone's giving him instructions he doesn't like."

"What kind of instructions?"

"To bring you with us," Graham said. "That really bothered him. If you do come, it'll bother him even more. You'd get that out of it, at least."

"How do you know he's not planning to just drive you out in the desert someplace and rob you? What do you actually know about this guy?"

"I know he already spent more money flying me down here than he could possibly make back by robbing me. I'm not really worth the trouble on that front."

"He was talking about breaking into people's houses. Spending time in prison. I don't want to be alone with him."

"You wouldn't be alone."

"Great," Cassandra said. "So if I just put my trust in you, the complete stranger I met on a plane twenty hours ago, everything will turn out perfectly fine?"

"It worked okay for us on the plane. Trusting each other. At least I thought it did."

Cassandra sighed. "You know what made me decide I kind of liked you last night? After you handed me your binoculars, you didn't hover. You didn't pester me every five seconds to find out what was going on.

You assumed if there was something I needed to tell you, I'd tell you, and you sat back and let me get on with it. Most people aren't like that with me. It scored you some points." She saw Graham ramping up an *Aw, shucks* smile and kept talking before it could bloom. "What you're doing right now is the exact opposite of that. What you're doing right now is being manipulative and hoping I'm too dumb to see it."

Graham lowered his eyes. "Look, I don't really have a choice here. Lem's coming back tomorrow morning, and it's going to be the last time. Either we're both on the bus, or I go home with nothing."

"Why is this so important to *you*?" Cassandra asked. "You're not the one this plane's following."

"First of all," Graham said, and then he went silent for several seconds. "You know, I could give you my big speech about the importance of civil liberties, and how angry it makes me to see them being violated on a massive scale, and the threat I think this surveillance plane poses to everyone in the country, and it'd all be completely true. But the other thing is, I got laid off from my job about a month ago. I didn't have much else going on, either, not at first. I'd been running my YouTube channel in my free time for a couple years, but it was nothing big. The only audience for the stuff I talked about was other dorks like me, and there just aren't that many of us. Then I found out about this surveillance plane that had been spying on millions of people, with nobody willing to say why. I did a couple videos about that, and people started paying attention. Some major news sites ended up writing articles about this plane, and they embedded links to my videos in their articles. I got a huge number of views out of that. Got a whole bunch of new subscribers. And, biggest news of all, those two videos got watched enough times that YouTube started running ads in front of them, and I got paid. Not a lot, but I got paid actual money for talking into a camera. So I rolled with it, and I did a whole series of videos about this plane. Where's it flying today? What exactly is in these cities that might explain what it's doing there? Why won't anyone tell us who owns it? What are people's latest theories? Blah, blah, blah, blah, blah. Those videos did pretty well, too. But at some point, the people watching them are going to notice that I don't have anything else to offer. How many different ways can you keep saying 'Gee, guys, this seems really bad and nobody knows what's going on'?

"Then Lem got in touch with me and said he knew a guy who *could* tell me what's going on. Said he was willing to put me on a plane to come meet him, too, which is something I haven't gotten to do since I was thirteen years old. But mostly, he said he could get me answers. I said yes. If I can come back from this with actual information, tell people something they don't already know—something even the news sites don't already know—then maybe I'm not just some guy spouting off on the internet. Maybe I start looking more like an investigative journalist. Maybe there's even some kind of steady job in that. But I had to promise Lem I wasn't going to talk about any of this in the meantime, or post any new videos until I'd flown down here and back. So now my channel's been dead for three days, right when it was starting to take off, and I'm still sitting here with nothing. I got right up to the edge of having something this morning, and then it died."

"Because of me," Cassandra said.

"That's not what I'm saying."

"No," she said. "You're not *saying* it."

"Look, you aren't the one who sent that Raptor chasing after our flight. You didn't ask for some spy plane to follow you around. None of this happened because of you. It happened because of whoever's doing it to you. And I think it'd be pretty sad if them messing with you was the reason no one ever got to learn the truth about them."

She could still see Graham working her, but she didn't entirely disagree with him. "When is this meeting of yours supposed to happen?" she asked.

"If you come, then we'll meet Lem downstairs at 7:30 tomorrow morning. He says we're supposed to wear shorts. I'm not sure why. We can bring our phones with us, but no laptops. Then we all drive to wherever we're driving, we spend two or three hours talking to Crimson, and we drive back. It should all be finished up sometime in the afternoon. If you come."

"I'll think about it," Cassandra said.

"You want to grab some food, maybe? Think about it there?"

Cassandra shook her head, but decided to be gentler with him this time. "I do find you to be a reassuring presence," she said, "and that's a feeling that makes me very nervous. Plus I've still got work to do tonight."

"Okay." Graham shifted toward the door. "Any recommendations on where I should go for dinner around here?"

"It's my first time in Reno, too," Cassandra said.

"But you live like this all the time, right?" He gestured around the hotel room. "Waking up in a different city every couple days? How do you figure out where to eat?"

"Most of the time, I eat at my hotel. Otherwise, I just look up what restaurants are close by and pick one. Sometimes it's good, sometimes it's not."

"This might be the only night I ever get to do this," Graham said. "I'm kind of hoping mine'll be a good one." He looked up at her. "What's the best meal you ever had while you were traveling, and how did you find it?"

"Room service," Cassandra said. "Waffles in bed."

Graham looked dubious. "I'm talking, like, *very* best meal."

"Waffles in bed," she said. "It might have been the context more than the food, I don't know. I'd only had this job for about three months then, and I was still kind of a mess about it. It didn't feel real yet, I was constantly afraid it was going to be taken away from me, that type of thing. I'd been going through a really shitty time before I got the job, too, so it all kind of blended together. And one day I was in Chicago, and I was working on this article until about 11:00 at night, and I hadn't remembered to eat any dinner, so after I finally posted the thing, I had some waffles sent up to my room. I'm realizing," she added, "that this story's going to seem really dumb and pointless to anybody who isn't me."

"I think we agreed last night that we're operating on the not-judging plan," Graham said.

"I think I was the only one who agreed to that."

"Well, I'm in."

"Fine. I'll make this short: My waffles arrive. They have strawberries, they have whipped cream, they have butter, they have syrup, they have I don't even know what else, but they certainly have it. They are *really* tasty waffles. And I'm sitting there in my room, way high up in this hotel, looking out at the buildings all around me, eating this extremely non-nutritious but tasty breakfast, for dinner, in bed, going on midnight. And I just had this realization, like, *I'm free*. You know? Nothing can touch me up here. I'm going to be okay now. And there were some caveats to that, and I'm not saying I've felt that way every minute of every day since or anything, but things got better."

"Maybe I'll give that a shot," Graham said. He reached for the doorknob. "Oh, and Lem said I should let him know tonight if you're coming. If you decide you are, just give me a call. I'm down in room 214."

"214," Cassandra repeated, and Graham let himself out. She waited for the door to close, snapped the bolts and the security bar back into place, fished the pepper spray out of her back pocket and put it in her messenger bag again. She returned to her camera roll with its collection of nearly identical toilet photos, closed her eyes, pointed to one of them at random, and saved that one to her Dropbox alongside the other two pictures she'd chosen. Close enough. She returned to her laptop, embedded all three pictures into the text of her article, typed up a brief caption for each one, then hit "Publish" and closed the tab without rereading it further. Few other people were destined to read it either, it seemed.

She called room service and found their order-entry software was functioning perfectly well this evening. She ate a Greek salad in bed while she read a couple more chapters of her book on her laptop, then set the dirty dishes out on the walkway. She returned to her laptop and was preparing to start her next chapter when her reading app glitched and crashed. Its window vanished, leaving her looking at the flight-tracking page in the browser behind it. The surveillance plane was drawing a straight line to the northwest now, leaving behind the pattern of circles it had been tracing all day and moving toward the airfield where it had begun its flight early that morning. She watched it fly a little beyond the airfield, make a 180-degree turn, draw its green line back to within a pixel or two of the place it had started, and halt there. The day seemed to be ending for everyone.

Cassandra changed the date range on the page as Graham had done that morning, switching her view to the plane's full itinerary for the last 30 days. She looked at the spiderweb of green lines spanning the continent, at the circles this plane had drawn above her head, unnoticed, every day she'd spent on the road for a month. Where would it go when she left Reno? Follow her to Los Angeles? Wait here until Georgina texted Cassandra her next destination, then fly there ahead of her, to resume its vigilant, unexplained circling when she arrived? How would it feel, now, to go on living in the shadow of this thing, knowing it was up there and not knowing why?

Cassandra picked up the nightstand phone, dialed the front desk, and asked to be connected to room 214. Graham's sleepy-sounding voice answered on the second ring.

"It's me," she said. "I'm in."

6
adversarially perturbed

"HELLO, CHILDREN," SAID LEM. "Here we are again."

Cassandra had set her phone's alarm for 6:00 AM, showered, dressed in one of the jeans-and-V-necked-blouse combos she normally wore to interviews, put on a little of the makeup she only wore to interviews, and slipped her phone into her bag. She peeked at the still-open browser tab on her laptop and found the surveillance plane already airborne again, drawing its counterclockwise circles around the same center point as yesterday. She lost a couple minutes standing beside the desk, watching its silent, hypnotic churning. Then she snapped her laptop shut and, with more than a few misgivings, maneuvered it into the safe inside her closet, tilting it at an awkward diagonal to fit it through the opening. She stuffed its power brick into the triangular gap beneath it, programmed a keycode derived from a locker combination she'd had during high school, locked the safe and shouldered her messenger bag, which felt strangely light and flimsy now. When was the last time she'd left a hotel room, any hotel room, without her laptop in her bag? Probably never. She closed up the room, reprised yesterday's elevator ride to the atrium floor, secured the same round booth at the front of the café, and ordered breakfast from the same waitress. She watched the people passing through the lobby while she ate, and left the waitress a doubled tip afterward to make up for walking out on her yesterday.

Her phone said 7:25 when Graham came hurrying across the atrium and spotted Cassandra at the table. He stopped and made that odd semicircular wave to her before he approached, which she'd now decided was a perfectly Graham thing to do. "Waffles," he said. "good call."

"Tastier at night, right?"

"I ate mine like half an hour ago," Graham said. "But they're good here." He slid into the booth. "Listen, I want to say thank you. I know you didn't have to do this, and I just... Thank you."

He'd already said this to her on the phone last night, and Cassandra had nothing new to offer in reply, so she was almost relieved to see Lem crossing the atrium and entering the café. The feeling faded quickly when he lowered himself uninvited into her side of the booth, leaving her wedged between him and Graham yet again. In a reversal from the previous morning, Cassandra appeared to be the only person at the table wearing fresh clothes today. Graham had on the same shorts, hiking boots and t-shirt he'd worn the day before, and Lem looked more or less identical in his voluminous army jacket with its bulging pockets.

"It's going to be a busy day, so let's get started," Lem said. He withdrew the white-noise generator from his pocket and reached for the knob to switch it on. The waitress chose that moment to appear beside him.

"Can I bring you gentlemen some menus?" she asked.

"I already ate," said Graham.

"All I need is a peanut butter sandwich to go," said Lem. "Lots of peanut butter, please."

"I don't think we have those on the menu," the waitress said.

"It's peanut butter and bread. You must have those two things in the back somewhere. Little kids eat here, don't they?"

"We probably do have them. I'm just not sure how much they'd want me to charge you for—"

"Tell you what." Lem fished two bills out of a pants pocket and fanned them out so she could see them: a twenty and a five. "If you bring me my sandwich in the next four minutes, I'll leave both of these on the table and you can keep however much of it you decide was the change. Fair enough?"

"I'll get that right out to you," the waitress said, and hurried away.

"Lots of peanut butter," Lem called after her. He lay the two bills down on the table, pinned them in place with the insect legs of his white-noise generator and twisted the knob on its face. That air-conditioner hiss filled the air again. He leaned forward and lowered his voice. "We're going to be heading over the mountains into California this morning. It'll be about a three-hour drive each way."

"Where in California?" Cassandra asked.

"You'll see when we get there. Until then, you both need to follow my instructions exactly. If I say to do something, you do it. No hesitation, no questions. Timing's going to be critical on this, and it'll start the second we walk out of this building." Lem leaned back and glanced down at Cassandra's legs. "My very first instruction was to wear shorts, by the way."

"I'm traveling for business," Cassandra said. "I didn't pack any shorts." She no longer owned any shorts, but Lem didn't need to know that.

"Whatever," Lem said. "That part we can work around."

"Why *are* we supposed to wear shorts?" Graham asked.

"I have no idea." Lem looked uncomfortable admitting this. "Crimson just said to tell you to wear shorts. Nothing I can do about it now, is there? Can't really shoot him a text and say hey, that girl you asked me to work into this thing at the last second showed up with pants on, should I call the whole thing off? You can ask him why yourself when you see him."

"It's fine," Graham said. "I just wondered."

"I'm going to be checking you both for weapons and transmitters before we go," Lem said. "No bitching about it when the time comes. For now, I need you to take your phones out and turn them off."

Graham wrestled his head-sized monstrosity of a phone out of a pocket of his cargo shorts, and Cassandra pulled her own phone from inside her bag. She made a final check of her messages and email, found nothing new in either of them, and held down the power button until the shutdown prompt appeared on her screen. She hesitated before she swiped it to confirm. She felt as if she were severing her last link to normal life, however tenuous a concept *normal* might have become since she'd boarded her flight to Reno.

Lem produced two thick, black pouches from his jacket, with Velcro flaps at their tops. He ripped the Velcro on one pouch open with both hands, lay it on the table in front of Cassandra, and started peeling open the other one. "Faraday bags," he said. "Your phones will stay in here until this is over." He pushed the second pouch across the table to Graham. "They block any transmissions from coming in or going out. Especially from going out."

"What transmissions?" Cassandra said. "My phone's turned off."

"How do you know?"

"Because I just turned it off."

"You hit a button and you watched the screen go black. If I had the right exploit on your phone, I could simulate that shutdown sequence and transmit every word you said afterward. Broadcast your location, do anything I wanted." Lem nudged the pouch an inch closer to her. "Remember what I told you about needing to do what I say and not ask questions? That part's started now. Let's go."

Cassandra slid her phone down inside the pouch, folded the flap over the top and sealed the Velcro. The pouch's material felt heavy and alien, the way she imagined Kevlar might feel. She prodded its unyielding surface with a fingertip, then Lem plucked it from her hand. "I'll hang onto this for now," he said. At Cassandra's look, he added, "You'll get it back after the meeting. I can't have you deciding to pull it out and call somebody halfway through." He double-checked that the Velcro was fully sealed, then reached across the table and collected the second pouch from Graham. Both went back into the jacket pocket from which they'd come. "Neither of you's wearing a Fitbit or anything like that, are you? Nothing that transmits a signal, as far as you know?"

They both shook their heads.

"We'll make sure of that before we go. Here's the lay of the land: Our adversaries are light on manpower but extremely heavy on passive surveillance. I've been told to assume every camera, every microphone, every sensor is being compromised in real time. If it connects to the internet, it's our enemy."

"And who are our adversaries, exactly?" Cassandra asked.

"People who can mess with airline reservation systems and reroute an Air Force jet. People who can get surveillance flights authorized anywhere in the country. Let's assume people we don't want to meet."

"What are they after, though?"

"That's what you're going on this little field trip to find out, isn't it?"

"Well, if they can already see us sitting here, why don't they just send somebody to arrest us?"

"For one thing, we're not doing anything illegal right now. For another, they don't want us. They want the person we're going to see. My job is to make sure they don't find him."

"Sandwich with extra peanut butter," the waitress said, arriving beside their table with a clamshell Styrofoam box in her hands. She set it down in front of Lem. "Handmade," she added, prompting Cassandra to wonder whether there was any other way to make a peanut butter sandwich. "I put some potato chips in there for you, too."

Lem cracked open the top of the clamshell and peeked in. The layer of peanut butter on the sandwich inside looked nearly as thick as the slices of bread containing it. "That's beautiful. Thank you." He plucked his money out from under the legs of the white-noise generator and passed it to the waitress.

"Enjoy," she said as she turned away, both bills vanishing into a pocket of her apron.

"Planning to," said Lem. He watched her walk away for a few more seconds than seemed strictly necessary, then rose from the booth, holding his sandwich container in one hand and scooping up the white-noise generator in the other. He didn't switch it off. "If either of you need to go to the bathroom, now's the time. After this, you stay in my sight for the duration."

"What if I need to pee again during the drive?" Cassandra asked.

"I'll loan you a thermos," Lem said. "If you don't like that idea, I suggest you squeeze it all out before we go."

Cassandra turned her head at an angle that removed Lem from her sightline altogether, and asked Graham, "Do you have any idea where the bathrooms are?"

He pointed beyond the fake, chrome-accented trees surrounding them and out across the atrium. "Back behind the elevator over there."

"Keep an eye on my phone until I get back, will you?"

She left the booth and made her way between the chairs and couches in the atrium, realizing these might well be the last moments she spent alone today. As she neared the elevator, she wondered what would happen if she just rode it back upstairs, returned to her room, locked the door, and lay in bed until Graham and Lem were gone. Lem would leave with her phone in his pocket, for one thing. She'd already passed the point of making such stands. She kept walking until she found a door tucked back under the second-floor walkway marked "Ladies."

When she returned, she found Lem standing by himself in the middle of the atrium, balancing his still-hissing white-noise generator atop his sandwich box. "Where's Graham?" she asked.

"Bathroom," Lem said. "He went right after you did." He yawned, tried to stifle it, gestured toward the messenger bag at her hip. "No laptop in there today, I hope?"

"I left it in my room."

Lem nodded. "You've got a good eye for gear," he said. "That laptop's small, but it's got power. Great battery life, too, from what I've read. Same thing with your phone."

She opted against telling Lem that both her phone and her laptop had been furnished and paid for by Georgina. "If my batteries are so great, why'd they die on my flight down here when I'd barely used them all day?"

"If you're asking me, it's because someone wanted them to die. Keep you bored during your flight. Put you in the mood for conversation with the people around you."

"They must not know me very well," Cassandra said.

"You can't argue with success," Lem said. "Here comes your boy."

Graham hurried across the atrium and joined them. Lem motioned for them to follow him and headed toward the lobby. "Thanks for watching my phone," Cassandra said as they fell in behind him.

"Three hours is a long time to sit in a car," Graham said. "I decided I ought to go too."

"You couldn't wait until I got back?"

Graham glanced at Lem's back and lowered his voice to a whisper. "I didn't think you'd want to be alone with him that long."

"If you have any questions you need to ask me," Lem said over his shoulder, "try to be standing within three feet of this while you do it." He held the white-noise generator up where they could see it. "Otherwise, please don't talk." He veered toward the little alcove off the lobby with its pair of quietly wheezing vending machines, as deserted now as it had been the night Cassandra arrived here, although someone had collected the mop and bucket in the meantime. "Last couple things to do before we go." Lem peered up at an innocuous bubble of reflective glass which protruded from the juncture of wall and ceiling above the vending machines. "We're going to be doing them on camera, but that's okay. I don't mind if they watch this part." Cassandra squinted up at the curved glass. If she focused her eyes to see past the reflections on its surface, she could just make out the boxy profile of a security camera mounted on the wall inside it. Lem set the white-noise generator on top of the vending machine directly beneath the camera and turned its volume all the way up. "They still don't get to listen, though."

Lem lay his sandwich box on the counter nearby, fished in his jacket and withdrew a squat, black, rectangular device with an LCD screen, a baffling array of buttons on its face, and four small antennas protruding from its top. The screen flickered as he powered the device on, then displayed a wavering, pixelated line that reminded Cassandra of an EKG readout. He reached under the hem of his jacket to unclip the radio from his belt and switched that on too. The line traversing the screen jumped slightly when he did so, and the device gave out a quiet beep. Numbers Cassandra didn't know how to interpret displayed above and below it. Lem squeezed the transmit button on the side of the radio and the device emitted a shrill screech, the line on its screen jumping like a seismograph during an earthquake. Lem nodded, switched the radio off again and returned it to his belt. The line on the screen settled down and the device went silent.

Next, Lem ran the scanner's antennas up and down the front faces of the vending machines. The device emitted another faint beep. Lem sighed and stabbed at a few of its buttons. "The snack machines are on wi-fi," he said. "I can filter it, but let's move a little farther away." He led them to the opposite end of the alcove, watching the face of the device as he went. "Okay," he said. "Let's see if anything on you two is broadcasting."

"Did you empty out a whole Radio Shack just for us?" Cassandra asked. She wondered how Lem was able to move with so many gadgets squirreled away on his body.

"Radio Shack doesn't sell the model with the explosives sniffer," he said. "I had to go a little higher-end for that. Graham, can I have you empty your pockets for me?" Graham rummaged in his shorts and withdrew a wallet, a ring of keys, a few one-dollar bills, and his binoculars. He spread these out on the counter. Lem ran the scanner over each of them. It remained silent.

"How much does one of those cost?" Graham asked, pointing at the scanner.

"About four grand," Lem said. "Plus shipping."

"Who's paying for all this?" Cassandra asked. After the way Lem had grilled her the previous morning, she couldn't resist. "What's their business model, exactly?"

"Your host is paying for it," Lem said. "How he's paying for it is another question you're welcome to ask him if we ever get there." He turned to Graham. "Stick your arms straight out for a minute." He ran the scanner along both of Graham's arms from shoulders to fingertips, back along their undersides, up his chest and down his back, then all around his shorts and his shoes. He set the scanner on the floor and stood again. "I need to check you for weapons, too. This part's going to get a little personal." Graham took a breath and raised his eyes to the ceiling while Lem patted his body down, then pressed the loose fabric of his cargo shorts flat against his inner thighs and ran his hands upward until they could go no further. He cupped one hand briefly over the front of Graham's crotch, wiggled it perfunctorily, and stepped away. "Good to go," he said, and turned to Cassandra. "Your turn."

"Um," she said, her body stiffening at the thought.

"I won't need to be that comprehensive with you," Lem said quickly. "Benefits of tight pants. I can already tell you don't have anything in your pockets, and I could see down the front of your shirt the whole time we were sitting in the booth. No worries there." Cassandra willed her hands to remain loose at her sides, not give him the satisfaction of seeing her adjust the neckline of her blouse. "I'll only have to pat you down around your waist and your ankles. Okay?"

"Okay," she said.

"So, just...arms up, if you could." It occurred to her that Lem was nervous about this, too. That was something. She set her bag on the counter and raised her arms. Lem ran the scanner over them as he had Graham's, waved it up and down her body and then her legs. He lay the scanner on the counter and stepped behind her. She felt the palms of his hands make a brief, brisk circumnavigation of her torso between her hips and the bottom of her rib cage, starting at her belly and ending at her lower back. It was over in seconds, but her muscles still recoiled at the unfamiliar sensation of hands on her body. Lem knelt and made a similar traversal of both her ankles, pulling back the upper edges of her boots to peer down inside each of them. He rose and turned toward the counter. "I just need to take a look through your bag, and we're all set."

Cassandra ran a quick mental inventory of its remaining contents and cringed, but there was nothing to be done about it now. Lem ran his scanner over the outside of the bag first, then pulled back the top flap and unzipped the small pocket hidden immediately beneath it. He glanced through the assortment of tampons and spare pens she kept inside there, gave them a wave with the scanner and zipped it shut again. On to the main area of the bag now. Lem flipped through the pages of her spiral notebook and set it aside on the counter, unzipped her wallet and peeked inside, opened her peach-colored compact and waved the scanner over its interior. He made a cursory dig through the jumble of keys, hair ties, lip balm and breath mints lying at the bottom of the bag, scanning them all *en masse*. His fingers brushed against the hot-pink canister of pepper spray that lay nestled among them, but she saw his eyes and his mind slot this into the same category of *girl things* as the items around it and move on without a second glance.

Lem seemed far more intrigued by the dull-yellow vibrator at the other end of her bag. He shot Cassandra a look somewhere between a smirk and a grin, then prodded its base with two fingers to stand it upright. Cassandra hadn't wanted to leave it lying out for the maid to find while she was away today, but it occurred to her now that she could have just stuffed it into the safe with her laptop. Lem ran the four antennas up the length of the vibrator's shaft and down the other side. The scanner didn't beep. "Rock on," he said, and stepped away.

Cassandra pulled the bag over to her immediately, stuffed her notebook back inside it and closed the flap. Graham, at least, had been standing too far away to see any of this, occupied with returning his own possessions to the pockets of his shorts.

Lem put his scanner back in one overstuffed jacket pocket, unsnapped another that had remained closed until now, and began pulling voluminous lengths of printed cloth from inside it, like a magician revealing handkerchiefs. Pink, then brown, then dark green. He shook the brown one out, and Cassandra saw it was some sort of hat, albeit a hat that appeared to have been made from several square feet of cloth scavenged from a secondhand curtain. A short brim protruded from one edge, an elastic band squeezed a portion of the cloth into a head-sized semicircle abutting it, and an absurd length of fabric trailed down everywhere else. "This one's yours," Lem said, handing the thing to Graham, who turned it over in his hands and frowned at it. "By *yours*, I mean you should put it on your head." Graham did so, and Lem arranged the descending cloth so it covered his shoulders and trailed down his back. He turned to Cassandra. "I picked out a pink one for you," he said, shaking it out.

"I'll take the green one," she said.

"You'll take the one I give you."

"I don't like wearing pink. I don't like you assuming I like wearing pink. I'll take the green one."

Lem opened his mouth to say something else and closed it again. "Whatever. Clock's ticking." He shook out the green hat and handed it over to her. Its fabric was dyed an iridescent color that made her think of seaweed drifting in polluted waters. "Make sure the cloth covers your shoulders, and keep the brim low on your face," Lem said. "We've got cameras in the sky again today." He pulled the pink hat onto his own head and arranged the fabric around his shoulders. Cassandra did the same with the green hat. It felt strange and heavy on her head, like wearing a shower cap with a cape attached.

"Where did you get these?" she asked. "Just so I can make sure never to shop there."

"I have a friend who sells them at music festivals," Lem said. "Keep the sun off your shoulders while you're outside all day, something like that. She makes money at it, believe it or not. People must do a lot of drugs at music festivals." He checked the way the green cloth hung around Cassandra's shoulders, then turned his radio on once more, moved to the corner farthest away from the white-noise generator, and raised it to his lips. "We're on our way out," he said. "Two-minute warning. Next check-in will be at 7:58. Repeat, next check-in at seven-five-eight. Radios off until then." He waited in silence a few seconds, then squeezed the transmit button again. "If you're still hearing this, I fucking mean it. Turn them *off.*" He gave Cassandra a rueful look she had no idea how to interpret, snapped his own radio off and returned it to his belt. "All right," he said. "Let's do this."

He picked up the Styrofoam sandwich box, returned to the alcove's entrance, rapped one extended middle finger against the mirrored glass covering the wall camera, and grabbed his white-noise generator off the top of the vending machine. He led them out past the reception desk, the pink cloth swaying around the shoulders of his army jacket as he went. A doorman stationed beside the two broad doors at the front of the lobby swung one of them open as they approached. Cassandra saw him look their headgear over and decide asking about it wasn't in his job description. "Have a nice day, folks," he said, over the hiss of the white-noise generator.

"You too," Cassandra said, trying to sound as if this were an ordinary morning and she didn't have half a prom dress hanging off her head. Outside, Lem turned left and skirted the edge of the hotel's circular driveway, leading them past an airport shuttle van parked along the curb. He veered toward the passenger door of a gray Subaru idling a few feet beyond it. A man in dark sunglasses sat behind the wheel. Cassandra assumed this was their ride, but Lem only leaned over and peered in through the Subaru's side window. The man in the sunglasses reached across and held a phone up to the glass, its screen facing outward. As Cassandra came up behind Lem, she saw the familiar pattern of green circles on its screen tracing out the surveillance plane's flight path. A square of black tape covered the phone's camera lens. Lem shaded his eyes for a better look, nodded, and resumed walking. The man inside the car returned the phone to his lap. As Cassandra stepped past the Subaru, she saw a handheld radio lying on the passenger seat, identical to the one that hung from Lem's belt.

Out from beneath the shadow of the pillared awning that overhung the hotel entrance now, Cassandra's eyes narrowing as the sunlight hit them. She hadn't been outside once, she realized, since she'd arrived here the night before last. "Everybody smile for the camera," Lem said quietly. "The plane's right above us."

"Good thing we're wearing our clever disguises," Cassandra said. "No way it'll spot us with these on."

"It's supposed to spot them," Lem said. "That's the whole point." He led them past the fountain toward the parking garage on the far side of the circular drive.

The nose of a large white pickup truck emerged from the dark mouth of the garage as they approached. American flags mounted on flexible poles jutted up from both of its side mirrors, missing the swinging height marker that hung from chains over the garage entrance by a fraction of an inch. Between the flags, a rectangle of plywood had been lashed to the truck's roof rack with bungee cords. It held three squat, round metal containers whose bottoms appeared to have been glued to the wood. Each pot had a stripe of color painted around its middle: one red, one white, one blue. The truck's occupants were hidden behind darkly tinted windows. As its back end emerged into the sunlight, Cassandra saw the truckbed was filled to the rim with something that bulged and shifted oddly beneath an olive-green tarp, held in place with crisscrossing yellow ties, like a vehicle-sized version of Lem's army jacket. The truck eased its nose past the near side of the fountain and turned onto the access road which led out to the main boulevard. Cassandra watched it until it passed out of sight behind the garage.

"Since the people who built this hotel didn't have the courtesy to cover their whole walkway," Lem said, "how about we not stand out here being filmed for longer than we have to?" He moved into the garage, and Cassandra and Graham followed. The ramp she'd seen briefly two evenings ago angled upward to her right, lined with cars. Her rented Honda was parked two levels above her. Farther inside the garage, a similar ramp led downward. Lem headed that way.

"Why *did* you pick this hotel?" Graham asked him.

"It has a Mormon owner," Lem said.

Graham slowed for half a step, his head turning. "Are you in the Church?"

"There's no casino here," Lem said. "It's one of the only hotels in town that doesn't have one." He moved toward the side wall of the garage, where a fire extinguisher hung inside a red steel cabinet. "Casinos have surveillance up the ass. You can never figure out where all the cameras are. This place is a little easier to manage." He set the white-noise generator atop the cabinet, then reached up and tapped on another bubble of mirrored glass which protruded from the wall a few feet above it. "The only camera on this whole level of the garage is right in here."

Lem set his Styrofoam sandwich container beside the white-noise generator, popped its lid open, and peeled the upper layer of his peanut butter sandwich carefully away from the lower one. Standing on his toes, he smeared the underside of the bread slowly and comprehensively across the left half of the mirrored bubble, coating every portion of its glass with peanut butter. He left the bread slice sticking to its side like a barnacle, then did the same thing to the other half of the bubble with the remainder of his sandwich. When he'd finished, not a glint of mirrored glass could be seen. "Their surveillance plane can't see us through this much concrete," Lem said, "so as long as we're in here, they're deaf and blind now." He picked up the Styrofoam clamshell that had held his sandwich and closed it again. "As soon as we shake off the plane, they'll be completely blind. Anybody want some potato chips for the drive?"

"I'll take them," Graham said, and Lem handed the container over.

"How are we going to shake the surveillance plane, exactly?" Cassandra asked.

"You'll see," Lem said. "We've got a two-in-three chance of doing it in the next five minutes. But if we draw the short straw this time, I have a plan 'B' set up once we cross over into California." He licked a stray glob of peanut butter from one of his fingertips. "Listen. There's going to be a little chaos breaking out shortly. You'll know it when it starts. If somebody hands you a different hat, you take it from them, you give them the hat you're wearing, and you put theirs on. Get your head and your upper body covered again as quickly as possible. No matter what color the hat is," he added, glaring toward Cassandra. "Understood?"

She rolled her eyes, but he continued staring into them until she said, "I heard you."

"This'll go quicker if you just nod." Lem gestured toward the descending ramp behind him. It seemed something of an architectural afterthought, descending only ten or twelve feet below ground level before flattening out and dead-ending against a blank wall. "We'll be getting in the van down there with the blacked-out windows. You two are going to sit in the back." Cassandra looked around the parked vehicles below her with morbid curiosity, thinking this sounded like precisely the sort of rolling murder factory she'd half expected Lem to usher her and Graham into all morning. She was almost disappointed to see it was just an ordinary minivan with an overabundance of window tint, parked about twenty feet down the ramp. "Don't put your seatbelts on. We won't be in it for long, and I'll need you to move fast when it's time to get out. After that...California, here we come." Lem turned and started down the ramp.

Graham picked up the white-noise generator Lem had left behind and called after him. "Do you need this?"

Lem looked over his shoulder and stopped walking abruptly. "If I needed it, I'd be carrying it. Leave it exactly where I put it, please." Graham set it back on the steel cabinet below the camera, and Lem resumed walking. Cassandra and Graham followed him down.

As Lem drew alongside the minivan, she saw his right arm lifting, fishing something from the interior of his jacket. He swung around to face them and held up a bent white cardboard sign in front of his chest with both hands. His stance reminded Cassandra of the hired drivers she saw in airports, holding hand-lettered signs with people's names written across them, except the letters on Lem's sign said:

DON'T SAY A WORD.
DON'T MAKE A SOUND.

Lem punctuated these instructions with a look so fierce Cassandra thought he might lunge back up the ramp and attack them if they disobeyed.

Throbbing, bass-heavy music erupted nearby, making Cassandra jump. The sound came from inside a black Audi coupe parked on the opposite side of the ramp, which also had heavily tinted windows. The music swelled abruptly as the doors on both sides of the Audi swung open. Lem continued aiming his sign at her and Graham with one hand while he released the latch on the minivan's tailgate with the other. As it swung upward, Cassandra saw some sort of heavy, quilted fabric rising with it. Its corners had been attached to the top of the back seat, then stretched like a tent across the cargo area and affixed to the tailgate. In the space beneath this covering, three people unfolded their limbs and climbed quietly out of the back of the van. The first was a thin man wearing an army jacket similar to Lem's. Behind him came a younger, rounder man with a reddish beard, then a small-framed woman with curly hair drawn back in a ponytail. All three had sweat trickling down their faces. Cassandra wondered how long they'd been hiding in there.

Lem unclipped the radio from his belt and passed it to the man in the army jacket, then pulled the pink hat from his head and handed that over too. He plucked the hat off Graham's head and passed it quickly to the bearded man; did the same with Cassandra's hat and gave it to the curly-haired woman.

Cassandra saw motion in her peripheral vision. Two more men stepped out of the Audi across the ramp. Another army jacket, another beard. A slightly bewildered-looking girl climbed out of the back seat after them and took hold of the bearded man's hand. She looked about thirteen and already stood a couple inches taller than Cassandra. All three of these people wore differently colored variants of Lem's absurd hats: one orange, one yellow, one sky-blue. They left the doors of the Audi hanging open and walked across the ramp toward the minivan without a word. The three who'd emerged from the back of the van headed toward the Audi, fastening the hats Lem had given them onto their heads and pulling the dangling cloth around their shoulders. Cassandra felt as if she were watching some obscure interpretive dance piece, the six hats and their wearers flowing past one another while Lem stood perfectly still in their midst holding up his sign. Nine people on the ramp altogether, including her and Graham. Three army jackets, three beards, and three young women who stood within an inch or two of five feet tall. Cassandra began to get an inkling of what Lem was up to, although the number of hats and vehicles present didn't quite make sense to her.

The man who'd come from the driver's side of the Audi lifted his arm to give Lem a high five as he approached, but Lem shook his head and raised a finger to his lips. The man looked in Cassandra's direction, his eyes running up and down her body as thoroughly as Lem's scanner had. He winked at Lem and moved toward the driver's door of the mini-van, followed by the other two from the Audi. The girl peered curiously up the ramp at Cassandra as she passed.

The bearded man holding her hand trundled open the side door of the minivan, ushered the girl inside and ducked in after her. The man in the army jacket opened the driver's door, slid into the front seat, then leaned his head and shoulders out again and looked back at Lem beside the tailgate. He held up three fingers, nodded to Lem, then lowered them one at a time. When his last finger dropped, Lem slammed the tailgate and the other man slammed his door, more or less in unison, the two thumps merging into one. The side door of the minivan rolled shut a moment later.

The three who'd emerged from the back of the van disappeared inside the Audi, although they left its doors standing open. The army-jacketed member of this group started the Audi's motor and stomped on the gas. The roar of the revving engine echoed through the garage, and Lem waved for Graham and Cassandra to follow him once more. He walked quickly past the minivan, whose own engine turned over and caught as they passed behind it, leading them toward the bottom of the ramp.

Down where the floor leveled off, Lem angled his body between two parked cars and hurried toward the outside wall. Cassandra saw a thick fire door there, a green EXIT sign glowing above it. The Audi's engine continued its deafening crescendo while Lem pressed on the steel push bar as gently as he could and unlatched the door. A wedge of light from outside spilled in across the floor of the garage, widening as he pushed it open. Outside, a concrete stairwell littered with cigarette butts led back up toward ground level. Lem waved Cassandra and Graham through the doorway and stepped out after them. The stairwell had no roof, but Cassandra could see slabs of concrete jutting out from the garage wall higher above them: the cantilevered sections of the upper parking levels, protruding over her head and blocking all but a tiny sliver of the sky.

Lem eased the door shut behind them as gently as he'd opened it, the engine noise from the garage dropping by several decibels as it swung back into place. He stabbed a finger at the block letters written across his cardboard sign once more, then raised it to his lips for good measure. From inside the garage, Cassandra heard two car doors slam. The music receded to a muffled throb, barely audible now.

Lem pulled a pair of black-framed glasses out of his army jacket's breast pocket and dipped his head to put them on. When he looked up, Cassandra had to stifle laughter. The glasses looked like part of a costume made by a child, with a piece of thin cardboard, cut roughly into the shape of a pair of glasses itself and printed with a pattern of blurry orange-and-black whorls, glued to the front of the plastic frames. The glasses had no lenses, Lem's eyes glaring out at her through the holes in the cardboard as steadily as ever. Cassandra's amusement died quickly when Lem produced two more pairs of glasses, one larger and one smaller, and handed them to her and Graham. The cardboard glued to Cassandra's pair had been printed with blue whorls; the pattern on Graham's was green. Lem's expression suggested terrible things would happen to her if she didn't put them on, so she did, adjusting them on the bridge of her nose a few times until she could see out of them comfortably.

A shift in the engine noise and a screech of tires from inside the garage told Cassandra the Audi was moving. Lem led them up the stairway, but halted them again a few steps from the top, with only their heads and shoulders protruding above the ground. From here, Cassandra could see the boulevard running down past the garage, toward the overpass she'd driven across two nights ago. The minivan rolled into sight on the hotel's access road, not far down the hill from them, and pulled to a halt when it reached the boulevard. The Audi roared up and stopped close behind it, muffled bass still throbbing from its speakers. The occupants of both vehicles were invisible behind their tinted windows.

The sharper sound of a honking horn approaching from the other direction drowned out the music. Cassandra looked that way and was reminded, for the second time in two days, of the fighter jets she'd watched twisting and swooping over San Francisco Bay with her father. The white pickup truck she'd seen exiting the garage earlier came racing down the boulevard from the hill above them, the flags above its side mirrors flapping so hard they were barely visible. Three streams of thick, colored smoke spewed from the pots mounted on its roof, blanketing the roadway as they swirled in its wake: one red, one white, one blue.

The truck's horn reached maximum pitch and volume as it rushed past them, dopplering down again as it passed the other two vehicles waiting at the hotel exit. A car headed uphill in the opposite direction honked its own horn at the truck, its driver extending a raised fist through his open window in what Cassandra took to be an expression of patriotic solidarity. The minivan and the Audi swung out onto the roadway behind the truck. Through the billowing smoke trails, Cassandra saw a woman's upper body leaning out through the pickup truck's sliding rear window, her hands working furiously at the yellow ties which anchored the tarpaulin in place over the truckbed. Another of Lem's curtain-like hats clung precariously to her head, this one in muted purple, the fabric of its long tail flapping wildly around her shoulders. Someone else's arm emerged from inside the truck and gripped the trailing end of the hat's fabric, steadying it against her back.

All three vehicles began to slow as they passed the interstate's westbound on-ramp and neared the overpass below. The woman leaning out the back of the pickup threw the yellow ties aside at last and yanked the tarpaulin swiftly toward her body, bundling it up in her arms. A shifting mass of red, white, blue, and silver erupted upward from the truckbed, widening and separating as it lifted through the haze of smoke overhead. The tarp had been securing a hundred or so mylar balloons, Cassandra saw, with a flag-and-eagle motif printed on one side and blank, reflective silver gleaming from the other. One of the final balloons to bob up from the truckbed brushed against the top of the smoke pot directly above the woman's head and vanished in an instant. Cassandra saw her flinch, and the sound of the popping balloon reached her ears half a second later. The cloud of remaining balloons rose above the smoke, tumbling into the air above the boulevard and the freeway. Cassandra pictured how the scene around the overpass would look from the perspective of a surveillance plane circling overhead, and found herself acquiring a grudging respect for Lem's ingenuity.

The pickup truck rolled into the shadows beneath the overpass and pulled onto the shoulder toward its far end. The minivan and the Audi stopped behind it. Doors swung open on all three vehicles as the smoke pouring from the truck's roof began to gather and eddy in the enclosed space around them. Cassandra could dimly perceive a flurry of activity taking place inside the smoke cloud: Figures running from one vehicle to another, headgear being removed and exchanged. The armada of silver balloons tumbled and flashed above it all. Cassandra glanced over at Lem, watching this unfold, and found an expression on his face that was the closest thing she'd seen him exhibit to unalloyed joy.

Car and truck doors slammed beneath the overpass now. The black Audi made a dangerous, screeching U-turn and emerged from the smoke cloud, speeding back toward them on the wrong side of the road. It swerved left through an acute angle and raced up the westbound on-ramp toward the interstate above, vanishing from view as it passed behind the corner of the garage. The white pickup truck accelerated out from beneath the far end of the overpass, back into the sunlight. The colored smoke had ceased billowing from its roof now. Either someone had capped the smoke pots or they'd exhausted their fuel. The truck made a left turn onto the eastbound on-ramp and sped out of sight. A few seconds later, the minivan pulled forward and took the ramp in the same direction.

The smoke cloud hung in a fading haze above the boulevard and the overpass. The balloons grew tiny overhead, drifting slowly to the southeast. Whatever was meant to happen here seemed to have happened, but Lem remained standing perfectly still in his spot on the stairway, one fingertip still resting against the handwritten letters on his sign.

They waited. Most of the smoke had blown away now. The balloons rose so high Cassandra could barely see them. She felt as if she were standing on a station platform after the train had come and gone, but still Lem didn't move. Another vehicle drove slowly into view down on the access road: the gray Subaru they'd passed outside the hotel's main entrance, which Cassandra had forgotten until now. It pulled to a stop at the edge of the boulevard, its right turn signal flashing. Cassandra saw the sunglasses on its driver's face blink in the sunlight as he checked for oncoming traffic, taking no apparent notice of the three of them huddled on the stairway. The Subaru turned right, drove down through the dissipating remnants of the smoke cloud beneath the overpass without slowing, and vanished southward.

With that, Lem turned and led them up the last few steps. Once out of the stairwell, they crept along the side wall of the garage and rounded its far corner, the highway noise quieting behind them as they emerged from the shadow of the garage's upper levels. Lem led them between a couple of scrubby bushes and angled across a drab-looking expanse of sunlit pavement occupied by four dumpsters and countless cigarette butts. "Walk fast, but don't look like you're hurrying," he whispered. Cassandra could make no sense of this instruction, so she simply matched Lem's pace and assumed it was what he meant. They passed beneath a spindly row of trees growing along the dirt strip that separated the hotel from the condominium complex up the hill, and emerged in a row of close-packed parking spaces in the complex's back lot. Lem pulled a car key from his pants pocket, unlocked the rear passenger door of an aging Volvo station wagon that had been parked there with its nose facing outward, and motioned for Cassandra to get in. The air inside the car felt hot and stale, as if no one had breathed it for days. On the floor behind the driver's seat, she saw a flat of bottled water wrapped in plastic, a six-pack of Red Bull, and a paper sack with a box of ginger snaps poking out the top.

Lem shut the door behind her and unlocked the front passenger door for Graham. He rounded the hood of the car, unlocked his own door, and climbed into the driver's seat. Cassandra tried to remember the last time she'd seen someone circling a car and unlocking its doors manually, a process so unfamiliar to her now it felt like some nostalgic relic of childhood. Lem closed his door gently and slid the key into the ignition.

"It should be safe to talk now," he said, "but keep your voices low until we're on the highway, just in case."

"Whose car is this?" Cassandra asked.

"Someone I know. You won't be meeting her."

Cassandra pulled off the glasses Lem had given her and flipped them around to peer at the inscrutable patterns ringing the eyepieces. They kept threatening to resolve into forms she could recognize, then failing to do so.

"Did the plane just film us getting in here?" Graham asked nervously.

"The plane's gone," Lem said. "Our main worry from here on out will be traffic cameras and dashcams. That's what the glasses are for," he added sharply, the moment he noticed what Cassandra was doing. "Put them back on." Cassandra squinted at the pattern a few seconds longer before doing as he'd instructed. "Adversarially perturbed," Lem said, and for a moment she thought he was referring to her, but he tapped a finger against the cardboard cutout fronting his own glasses. "The patterns are designed to screw up the classifiers in face-recognition algorithms. Make them read your face as a different shape than it actually is. It's great shit. You just 3-D print the frames, generate one of these patterns and print it up, glue it onto the front of the glasses, and bam, machines think you look like no one in particular."

"Do you think the people we're trying to hide from might find it suspicious if they see three people in a car wearing dorky novelty glasses?" Cassandra asked.

"If the *people* saw us, sure. But if they're going to try sampling cameras along the highway to find us, they won't have enough people to look at all of them. They'll have to delegate that job to the machines. And the machines will think they're looking at somebody else's faces." Lem started the car, which ran much more smoothly than Cassandra had expected from the look of it, and traced a slow, winding route among the condominium buildings until they reached the exit. "There's water and snacks back there if you want them," he said. "Help yourselves."

He flipped on his turn signal and took a right onto the boulevard, back down the hill past the parking garage and the hotel access road. Cassandra expected him to take the ramp onto westbound I-80, but he drove down beneath the overpass and turned onto the ramp at its far end instead, heading east. As they merged into the light morning traffic on the freeway above, Cassandra looked out the rear window of the Volvo and saw her hotel receding behind her. The glass roof atop its atrium winked briefly in the sunlight against the tumbled mass of the western foothills before they rounded the first curve of the highway and it vanished from her sight.

7
all of it

AS SHE PASSED DOWNTOWN RENO for the second time, Cassandra found it hard to reconcile the collection of dull-looking buildings rising off to the right of the interstate with the pulsing, candy-colored dreamworld she'd glimpsed on her drive in from the airport. Looking at casino exteriors in the daytime was like seeing a troupe of actors waiting backstage, wigs and props and spirit gum rendered drab and obvious in the ordinary light. Lem guided the Volvo past the interchange with I-580 that marked the easternmost limit of her knowledge of Reno and drove on through parts of the city she hadn't seen.

Cassandra leaned forward in her seat. "I thought you said we were going to California."

"I did," Lem said. "Several times. Loudly." He shifted one lane left to pass a laboring tractor-trailer loaded with concrete piping, then eased back to the right, using his turn signals for both lane changes and keeping the Volvo just under the speed limit.

"Was somebody listening in when you said that?" Graham asked.

"I sure hoped they were. And it appears they were, because right now, that surveillance plane's dogging my friend's Audi toward the state line and somebody, somewhere, is driving themselves crazy trying to figure out what that plan 'B' I told you about might have been. Poor fuckers. Probably mapping every underpass and tunnel between here and Sacramento, checking for known associates of mine in California who might be waiting up the road to trade cars with me, chasing after their own tails—"

"If that plane was up there filming the whole city for two days just so it could follow a specific car," Graham said, "that's definitely unconstitutional."

Lem gave him a wordless look before returning his eyes to the road. "I'll have my legal department look into that first thing Monday morning, Graham. The point is, the people running that plane had a choice to make. They could have followed my van up toward Boise or followed the pickup truck toward Salt Lake City. But no. They stuck right to the Audi, because it was the only car going west. Just like I kept saying we were going to do."

"How do you know the plane even went that way?" Cassandra asked. "You won't let us turn our phones on. It could be flying over our heads right now and you wouldn't know it."

"My guy out in front of the hotel was tracking the plane on his phone. He told me which way it had gone when he drove out."

"He didn't tell you anything. He just left."

"I can tell you everything he did before he left, too. Want to hear a story?" Lem seemed to be in a good mood, for once. "After all the cars split up, he sat there in front of the hotel watching the plane, seeing who it decided to follow. At 7:58 on the dot, he turned on his radio and said, 'Contingency two, contingency two.' Then he waited five seconds and said it again. Kept that up for a full minute. Everybody in the other three cars turned on *their* radios at 7:58 and listened to him say it. And you know what they did after that?"

"What?" Graham asked, when Cassandra didn't.

"Not a fucking thing. They turned their radios back off and kept right on driving. He was going to say 'Contingency two' no matter which direction the plane went. But our friends up there would have seen the spikes when the radios switched on, monitored what he was transmitting. If the guy keeping tabs on your surveillance plane said that into a radio and you knew the people in the car you were chasing had heard it, that'd seem pretty important, don't you think? You'd definitely want to figure out what the hell contingency two was. That's going to keep somebody busy for a few hours."

"But how do you know the plane's chasing them at all?" Cassandra asked. "Your guy tracking it never talked to you."

"He made a right turn when he drove out of the hotel," Lem said, "and he used his turn signal when he did it. That's how I know. If he hadn't put his turn signal on, it would have meant the plane was going south. If he'd turned left with his signal on, that would have meant east. Left with no signal, north. And if his emergency flashers were blinking, that'd mean the plane had never left and we were all fucked before we started." Lem clicked his own turn signal on to pass another eighteen-wheeler. Cassandra saw an exit sign flit past that said SPARKS BLVD. She'd be driving somewhere near here to interview the Rasmussens tomorrow, if she was still alive after today. "There are all kinds of ways to communicate," Lem said. "But who's going to pay attention to some dude's turn signals when they've got contingency two to worry about? Especially when they already *knew* we were headed toward California, because I kept saying so to you two in front of microphones." Lem smiled. "Other people's expectations are a beautiful thing."

"If you wanted them to hear everything you told us," Graham asked, "why'd you keep the white-noise generator turned on the whole time? Why'd you yell at me when I moved it?"

"Funny thing," Lem said. "Those generators are designed to put out sound across the entire audio spectrum. Make it impossible for microphones to pick out voices from the rest of the noise. Unfortunately, the speaker in mine's been damaged. Very carefully damaged. There are four specific frequency ranges it doesn't mask correctly. If you were trying to listen in on us and analyzing the signal with the right equipment—and I've been told our adversaries have access to the best equipment I can imagine—you'd detect the frequencies that weren't getting masked, you'd run the signal through a couple extra filters, and you'd recover enough data out of those four ranges to reconstruct our entire conversation. Then you'd sit there listening to every word I said, laughing about how lucky you were and how stupid I was. People are a lot more inclined to believe what you're saying if they think you've tried to hide it from them and failed. Everyone enjoys thinking they've outwitted somebody."

Lem certainly did, Cassandra thought. Part of her wanted to admire the level of forethought and planning he'd put into this, but a larger part of her rebelled, instantly and viscerally, at any notion of admiring Lem. The thing that bothered her most about him, she decided, apart from his ongoing hostility toward her, wasn't that he was incompetent. Far from it. It was that he required you to know it at all times. "You were a little over-theatrical, don't you think?" she said.

"My opponents had a multi-million-dollar surveillance plane and access to every camera and microphone on the planet. I had a few cars, some balloons, some ugly hats, and a friend who does window tint. I'd say I did all right, considering. The theatrical parts were done that way for a reason."

"What about the camera in the parking garage?" Cassandra said.

"What about it?"

"Blowing twenty-five dollars on a peanut butter sandwich instead of just bringing one from home? Ordering it in front of us just so we could watch you could smear it all over the glass ten minutes later? You were showing off. It was a dumb thing to do."

"I've known people who couldn't refrain from showing off," Lem said. "Some of them are in jail because of it. If you see me doing it, assume it's calculated. I had a role I needed to play to sell this, so I played it."

"What if the café had run out of peanut butter this morning? What if the waitress thought you were a pushy asshole and decided to stick to the menu no matter how much money you waved in her face? It would have been a little hard for us to sneak out the back door of the garage with that camera still looking at us, wouldn't it? You go to all the trouble of making a plan this complicated, and something that stupid could have ended it before you even—"

A loud metallic rattle cut her off. Lem had withdrawn a thin metal can with a black plastic lid from the front of his army jacket and was shaking it as hard as he could in front of her face. She'd recognized the sound of the metal ball bouncing around inside the canister even before he turned it to face her: a can of matte black spray paint. "*This* is what would have happened if the café had run out of peanut butter," Lem said. "They'd have to replace the glass over that camera instead of just washing it off, and that plane would still be chasing the wrong car toward California." He returned the spray can to his pocket. "First you figure out the way you want things to work. Then you figure out how they're still going to work if they don't go the way you want. That second part is where people tend to stumble. I don't. That's why I got picked to drive this train."

"If you have such impeccable planning skills, why'd you end up in prison?" Cassandra asked.

Lem gave her a long look in the rearview mirror. "You are a pain in my ass, you know that? I was all set up to do this *yesterday* morning, and so were seven other people. Eight, actually, because so was Graham. Then you come wandering into the middle of it and I have to tell them the whole thing's off. Maybe for a day, maybe for good, who the fuck even knows until I hear back from Crimson twelve hours later? I waited around all day to find out what he wanted me to do about you. Then I had to have Graham go and beg you to come along with us, then I had to wait around some more while you took your sweet-ass time thinking about it. And then at eleven o'clock at night, suddenly it's all back on again, because you've finally decided you're going to grace us with your presence. Are you picturing this? At eleven o'clock on a Friday night, I have to find three women who can pass as you through a tinted car window and are willing to make a road trip first thing in the morning. After I came up with two of them, I had to have my friend drag his teenaged niece along, because I couldn't find any more grownups your size. I had to get hold of three more hats and print up an extra pair of glasses I hoped were small enough to fit on your head. All so I could enjoy the pleasure of your company on a long-ass drive you don't even want to be on. I hope you had a nice, restful sleep last night, because I was up until four in the morning getting shit done to accommodate you. But I got it done, and it worked. Is it too much to ask you to let me be happy about it for five fucking minutes?"

"Maybe I should tell you about the day *I* had yesterday," Cassandra said.

"Go ahead," Lem said. "Tell us about the day you had yesterday."

Now that she'd brought it up, Cassandra had trouble finding a suitable place to begin. *The computer at the hotel went down and I couldn't order room service* wasn't going to make an impressive opener, she sensed. "I guess the interesting part started when this guy I'd never met in my life barged up to my table and started claiming I was spying on him. Being a real asshole about it, too."

"For fuck's sake," Lem said. "That shit's Social Engineering 101. If you want to learn about someone in a hurry, accuse them of something. They'll tell you their whole life's story trying to convince you you're wrong. I had about ten minutes to figure out who you were and whether I needed to cancel all my plans because of you. You shouldn't take it personally."

"Ah. So you *don't* think I've been traveling around helping the people in that plane search for your lame-ass associates, and you *don't* think my job is some kind of bullshit cover story?"

"Oh, I do," Lem said. "I just don't think you know it. But who gives a shit what I think? You can wait and see what Crimson has to say. Tell us the next terrible thing that happened during this grueling day of yours."

"Forget it," Cassandra said. "You did what you set out to do. Be happy."

"I will."

Lem looked back at the road and drove on in silence. They'd left the city behind as they were talking, the highway curving uphill now between bare, brown, uninhabited bluffs. Graham took a potato chip out of the Styrofoam container in his lap, chewed it, then turned toward Lem. "Why *did* you go to prison?" he asked.

Lem's shoulders sank. "Am I talking to myself over here? What the fuck did I just say?"

"Sorry. I was just curious," Graham said. "By the way, I think I speak for both of us when I say we do appreciate how much work you put into this. Planning everything out, getting all those people together. I mean, the kind of leadership qualities it must take to—"

"I went to prison because I read somebody's emails, and I didn't like what I read," Lem said. "Okay?"

Graham paused with another potato chip halfway to his mouth. "Whose emails?"

"They belonged to this CEO. This useless, born-rich, silver-spoon motherfucker who'd taken over his father's company after he died. It's a private company, minor defense contractor. Has a few thousand employees out in Virginia. Chances are you never heard of it. I never had. I only cracked into their network in the first place because I'd been—" He caught himself. "I was working on an unrelated matter. Leave it at that. But once I got in, I had access to the head guy's mailbox, so I started looking through his mail. Found out he'd defrauded his company's pension fund for forty million dollars, paid out some nice executive bonuses with all the money he'd saved. Paid out the biggest bonus to himself. That seemed like something people ought to know about."

"Holy cow," said Graham.

"Yeah. But more than that, he was just... I don't know. You had to see the way this guy talked. Like every word he ever said to anyone, about anything, just screamed *I'm a smug, entitled dick who's gotten away with every shitty thing I ever did, and I'll never have to pay any consequences.* And the more I read of it, the more I started thinking, fuck this guy. You know? Let him get hurt for once, just to find out what it's like. I was kind of an angry person back in those days."

"No way," Cassandra said. "*You?*"

Lem ignored her. "So after I'd finished the job I was there for, I dumped his entire mailbox out on a public server. Then I sent links to a bunch of reporters, pointing them to the interesting parts. Then I posted the links all over the web, so everyone else could see the interesting parts too. Ten years' worth of mail. Everything he'd written, everything he'd received. Conversations with his lawyer about the hush money he was paying his girlfriends, conversations with his girlfriends about how much longer until he could leave his wife, conversations with his executive team about how they were inflating the billings on their defense contracts, conversations with his HR department about why the research group he was about to lay off didn't deserve any severance pay. All kinds of shit. It made the news for about a day. The business news, but still."

"What happened to the CEO?" Graham asked.

"He stole forty million dollars from people who'd worked for his father their entire lives. I *intentionally gained access to a protected computer system without authorization.* Guess which one of us got arrested?"

"They didn't do anything to him?"

Lem shrugged. "He worked out a deal for his company to pay a fine that was less than half of what he'd stolen, didn't admit to any wrongdoing, kept all his defense contracts, kept the bonus he'd paid himself out of the pension money, and I got four years in prison. I served my four years, too, because when the feds came and asked me to go white hat—teach the next bunch of corporate assholes how to harden their networks so they could avoid embarrassing situations like these, maybe rat out a few of my friends while I was at it—I told them to go fuck themselves. When I got out, I was finished being any kind of hacker. Too well-known to get away with it anymore, plus my sentence would be about three times longer if I got caught doing it again. But since I was well-known, I was able to be a public liaison for private people. Pass information along, send work their way. Bring like-minded people together for worthy causes, as long as I didn't hear too many details about what the worthy cause was. Put together the thing we did this morning, too. Granted, having Crimson's name and a whole lot of Crimson's money to throw around on that one didn't hurt any, but the reason I had those things in the first place is because I'd earned my trust the hard way."

"How did you meet Crimson?" Graham asked.

"I haven't. Not face to face. He got in touch with me about fourteen months ago, said he might have some work. I checked with a few people who knew a few people and they confirmed it was him I was talking to. We took it from there."

"Are you shitting me?" Cassandra said. "You gave me crap yesterday because my boss hired me over email. At least I know what her name is."

"Crimson's not my boss," Lem said. "He's a client. He tells me what services he needs, and I figure out how to provide them."

"What kinds of services? Other than people-smuggling and vandalism."

"Communications, shipping, hardware. He was buying up a shit-ton of hardware a year or so back. Servers, racks, routers, all these obscure industrial controls. Needed it all delivered discreetly with no paper trail leading back to his little hideout. Dude's got a budget like I've never seen from a freelancer. He's up to something big."

"Is that why the people in the spy plane are so anxious to find him?"

"Probably."

"What the hell is he doing?"

"Don't know, don't care," Lem said. "My job was to provide, and I provided. Now my job is to bring you to him, so I'm bringing you to him."

"That's not the right answer in a situation like this. Come on. They don't send planes like that after people who are doing good things."

"Don't they?" Lem said.

"What about all your friends you pulled into this? The decoys. The teenaged niece. You don't even know what kind of crime they might be helping you commit?"

"Only a couple of them are my friends," Lem said. "And they're all getting paid. Paid by the head *and* by the day. Guess how much my expenses went up on that end after you poked your nose into this? Incidentally, if they don't know what kind of crime they're helping me commit by doing the perfectly legal things I asked them to do, it'll be kind of hard to convict them of a crime, won't it?"

The sheer circularity of this conversation, Lem's obstinate surety, were beginning to exhaust her. "Sounds like you've built a whole empire out of people not knowing anything, and you're the man in charge. Congratulations."

"You should talk. I showed you damned near proof positive yesterday that your job isn't what you think it is, that it can't *possibly* be what you think it is, and all you had to say to me was 'Shit happens.' You don't care what kind of shit. You think the people who send spy planes over cities are nice guys? Think they're just up there looking out for you? You don't care who you're really working for, what you're really helping them do."

"I worried about that all day. That's why I'm here."

"Oh, you worried. Lucky us. And then you kept right on doing your job. As long as the plane tickets and the free meals keep coming your way, it's all good, right? How much have you personally raised the temperature of the planet in the past year flying around making sure your devoted readership of approximately fucking nobody stays up to date on the latest advances in toilet technology?" He saw the startled look she gave him in the mirror then. "Yeah, the Jacobys. Stan and Irene. I read it. One of the proud few."

"Why?" Cassandra asked. "If you think it's all just a smokescreen—"

"Like I said, I was up all night. Somebody's getting into a car with me in the morning, I want to know how they're spending their time."

"But when someone who won't even tell you his real name asks you to do the shadiest-sounding shit I've ever heard of, you don't have any questions. You don't need to know a damned thing about that."

"Crimson *is* his name," Lem said. "The one that matters. And I'll tell you exactly what I needed to know. I'd been dicking around on the sidelines for three years after I got out of prison. I'd introduce people to each other, I'd pass messages along, I'd facilitate things when I could, but I didn't do anything. Not like I used to. They'd fucked me. Maybe I'd fucked me, call it as you will. But Crimson asked for me by name, and now I'm doing something. That's all I need to know. I was nothing but a spectator, and he put me back in the fight."

"The fight against *what?*"

Lem's expression as he regarded her in the rearview mirror looked almost mournful, as if it saddened him to think she didn't understand this already. "Against *all* of it," he said. "Against fucking all of it."

8
tackle box

THEY LEFT THE INTERSTATE and drove east on U.S. 50 for the better part of an hour, into as close an approximation of the middle of nowhere as Cassandra had ever seen. Metal markers posted at intervals proclaimed this to be *The Loneliest Road in America*, but the two-lane state highway they turned onto for the next leg of their journey quickly proved that assertion wrong. They drove through one small, dusty-looking town just south of the junction, set between two low mountain ridges dotted with sagebrush. After that, they didn't encounter another vehicle for forty minutes. Half a mile south from the town, they passed the entrance to an abandoned mine with a chain-link fence running directly across the entrance to its overgrown access road. No one had taken the trouble to install a gate. Past the mine, the two lines of mountains fanned out on either side of them like the sides of a champagne glass two dozen miles wide, enclosing a broad, dry basin that ran unobstructed to the southern horizon. They descended a rocky slope to the basin floor and continued south. Cassandra watched the road signs closely throughout their journey, checked the mileage on the Volvo's odometer at each infrequent landmark, tried to remember the names of the towns they'd passed earlier in the trip. If she had to run from whatever awaited them at the end of this drive, she intended to know the way back.

Graham ate the last of the potato chips in the Styrofoam container and lay it on the floor between his feet, where it squeaked every few minutes when the soles of his hiking boots brushed against it. Lem asked Cassandra to hand him a can of Red Bull from the six-pack on the floor. She passed it up to him and offered Graham one as well, but he asked for a bottle of water instead. He drank it without pausing for breath and asked her for another. Cassandra opened a third bottle for herself and took careful, rationed sips from it, mindful of the unknown distance her bladder still had to travel.

They drove past exactly two mailboxes along this entire stretch of road, several miles apart from one another. Both were planted on top of barrels filled with concrete, standing watch over the ends of rutted dirt tracks that ran off perpendicular to the roadway and receded to a distance Cassandra's eyes couldn't follow. Homes stood at the far ends of those tracks, presumably, and she wondered about the people who lived in them, how they spent their days and why they'd chosen to spend them here.

Later, as the road crested a shallow rise, Cassandra saw a barn-like building rising just off the road a mile or two ahead of them, painted a rusty red. As it drew nearer, she made out a small, faded house tucked behind it. A corrugated-steel canopy on two tall posts loomed over the lot out front, shading a pair of gas pumps. A blur of faded white painted across the building's upper front wall gradually resolved itself into letters that read *GAS—STORE—TAMALES*. An ancient-looking yellow pickup truck was parked alongside an ice cooler not far from the store's front door.

Lem flipped on his turn signal and exited the road here, rumbling across the cracked asphalt of the building's front lot and pulling to a halt in the shadow of the canopy beside the gas pumps. Cassandra peeked over his shoulder at the odometer. They'd covered thirty-two miles since they'd passed the fenced-off entrance of the abandoned mine outside the last town. She saw that the Volvo's gas tank was still slightly more than half-full before Lem cut the motor and the needle dropped to the bottom of the gauge. "We're going to step out here for a bit," he said. He pointed up through the windshield at the steel canopy above them. "Stay underneath that thing while we're outside the car, and keep your glasses on. Cassandra, would you hand me that yellow box on the floor back there?"

She found it standing on end between the untouched snack bag and the rear door: a folding tackle box molded from two sections of thick, textured yellow plastic, its only distinguishing feature a metal-ringed keyhole set into its handle. She shook the box experimentally as she picked it up, trying to determine whether it might be filled with murder implements, but it felt and sounded empty. She passed it forward to Lem. He opened his door and exited the car the moment his fingers had closed around its handle.

"Not so bad, right?" Graham said, as Lem's door closed again. "It's beautiful out here." He opened his own door and stretched slowly as he stood up. Cassandra pulled the strap of her messenger bag over her head and followed him out.

The day had grown hot while they were in the car. The air outside smelled of sagebrush and petroleum, with a faint mineral tang underlying it she couldn't put a name to. Lem set the yellow tackle box on the roof of the Volvo and grabbed a squeegee from a plastic bucket that stood on the concrete island beside the gas pump. He flipped the windshield wipers up off the glass and began scrubbing it with quick, efficient strokes, although it didn't look particularly dirty to Cassandra. He didn't seem to plan on buying gas here, either.

She shut her door and rounded the back of the car. "Any chance we can use the bathroom?" she asked.

Lem shook his head. "Not till you get where you're going. It shouldn't be too much longer now."

She made a quick circuit of the nearest gas pump instead, extended it into a figure 8 around the other one. However pointless this pit stop seemed, it felt good to move her legs. As she rounded the pumps a second time, the front door of the store squeaked open, setting a bell jingling above it, and a lean man with a weathered face stepped out. The ends of a graying beard brushed the middle of his chest. He paused in the doorway and peered in their direction. Lem reached over and shifted the yellow box on the roof of the Volvo, then resumed squeegeeing. The man inclined his head and turned toward the ice cooler, a long braid swinging at his back. Some sort of signal had just passed between them, Cassandra thought, but she was hard-pressed to say what it had meant. The man opened the cooler door and methodically transferred four clear plastic bags of ice into the back of his truck, smacking each bag sharply against the rim of its bed to break up the ice cubes before he lay it inside. Lem flipped his squeegee over and scraped the windshield clean.

The bearded man got into his truck, and Lem returned the squeegee to the bucket. He fished a small silver key out of his pants pocket and used it to open the tackle box. He unsnapped his jacket pocket and pulled out the two Velcro-flapped pouches containing Graham's and Cassandra's phones. He lay the pouches inside the box, closed it and locked it, and returned the key to his pocket. Then he carried the box back to where they stood at the rear of the car and handed it to Graham.

"Crimson has the other key to this," he said. "You'll get your phones back when you finish talking with him. I can't force you to wear the glasses after this, but I'd consider it a personal favor if you'd keep them on until you get there." He cocked his head toward the pickup truck across the lot. "That guy's going to pull up to the other pump in a minute. When he does, you get in his truck and you go. Sometime after that, you'll meet Crimson."

"Aren't you coming with us?" Graham asked.

A muscle at the base of Lem's jaw clenched and released as he looked out across the sagebrush flats behind them. "You two are the ones with the golden tickets," he said. "Apparently I don't rate. Even after all this." He returned to the driver's side of the car, thumped the windshield wipers back into place, then paused with one hand on the door handle, looking at Cassandra. "If you ask me, he's fucking crazy to let you come within ten miles of him. For the record, no one *did* ask me. I mention it because this isn't going to end well, and I'd rather nobody blamed me for it afterward. Not that we'll be seeing each other again, I suppose." He swung his car door open and turned away from them.

"Hold on." Five minutes ago, Cassandra wouldn't have thought it possible to be upset by the prospect of Lem exiting her life, but here it was. "If you're leaving us out here, how are we supposed to get back?"

"Ask Crimson. That's another thing I didn't need to know."

"But you knew dumping us out here was part of the plan?"

"I'm the one who made the plan."

"Then why the fuck didn't you tell us that before we left?"

Lem looked at her evenly from beside the open car door. "Because you wouldn't have come," he said. "But here you are. Have a nice day." He slid into the driver's seat, closed the door behind him, and pressed its lock button down immediately. He checked that the door behind him was locked, then swiveled across the front seat to lock both doors on the passenger side as well.

Cassandra looked around at the miles of emptiness surrounding them. "How strong is the latch on that box?" she asked Graham.

Graham tugged at its two halves. "Pretty darn strong, it feels like. I think our phones will be fine in here."

"I wasn't asking if our phones are safe. Find something we can break it open with."

"Look, I don't think we ought to start deviating from—"

"I'm tired of this bullshit, Graham. I'm tired of us both being jerked around." Cassandra looked past the Volvo and the pickup truck toward the front door of the store, a mere ten yards across the pavement. There would be a phone inside there, surely. Failing that, a hammer or a saw or a pair of bolt cutters she could use to retrieve her own. She wasn't clear yet on who she might call, but she'd have time to think about it on her way inside.

She'd taken half a step behind the Volvo, heading in that direction, when its motor caught and revved. She glanced toward the driver's-side mirror and found Lem's eyes framed in it, locked on hers. He shifted the car into reverse, the white lights on the tailgate illuminating just in front of her knee. The car lurched back an inch before he caught it with the brakes. Cassandra thought about the distance from here to the door and how quickly she could cover it, thought about the fragility of her body compared to the solidity of this car, thought about how long it might take an ambulance or a police car to find its way out here, assuming anybody called one. Would Lem actually do what he seemed to be threatening? She was forced to acknowledge, yet again, that she had no idea what Lem might do. She pulled her foot back up onto the concrete island next to Graham and the gas pump.

Lem shifted the car out of reverse but continued watching her. The bearded man swung his pickup truck in a wide arc around the lot, pulling to a stop on the other side of the fuel island adjacent to Graham and Cassandra. He leaned across the cab and pushed open the passenger door. "You them?" he asked.

"Yeah," Graham said. He glanced at Lem in the Volvo. "Just the two of us, I guess."

The man hauled himself back over to his side of the bench seat. "Climb in."

Cassandra thought of the admonition about the devil you know and the devil you don't, but in this case, the devil she knew had just threatened to run her down with a station wagon. She found a grip on the truck's inside door handle and levered herself up into the cab. Graham moved to follow her, then turned back toward the Volvo abruptly. "Give me one second," he said. He stepped over between the gas pumps and rapped his knuckles twice on the Volvo's side window, motioning for

Lem to roll it down. After a brief pause, Lem did. Cassandra imagined Graham taking Lem by the front of his army jacket, punching him in the face repeatedly, striding back toward the truck with the key to the tackle box held triumphantly above his head. Instead, he spoke a few words she couldn't hear, shook Lem's hand briefly through the window, gave him the patented Graham Wave while he rolled it back up, and returned to the truck smiling. Men's perceptions of danger, she reflected—not for the first time—had a way of differing radically from her own.

Cassandra scooted over to the middle of the bench seat and pulled her messenger bag onto her lap to make room for Graham as he climbed in. Her shoulder bumped the driver's upper arm, and it felt as if she'd strayed into a rock wall, solid and immobile and utterly indifferent to her. She saw a silver wedding ring on the man's left hand where it rested on the steering wheel, shaped like a snake holding a lump of turquoise between its jaws. The seat creaked beneath her as Graham pulled his legs in on the other side of her. Being sandwiched uncomfortably between pairs of men much larger than herself would be a recurring motif this weekend, it seemed.

"You can stow your toolbox on the floor there," the man said to Graham.

"Thanks." He slid the yellow tackle box between his bootheels and the seat and swung the door shut. "I'm Graham, by the way." The man nodded and shifted the transmission into drive. Graham waited for a further response, but none came.

Once Lem had seen the truck door close behind Graham, he pulled his Volvo away from the fuel island and angled across the lot to the edge of the road. Cassandra assumed he'd make a left turn and head back north the way they'd come, but he went right instead, turn signal flashing dutifully as always, and accelerated away southward. Their driver sat watching in silence while Lem's car dwindled in the distance. When it had passed entirely from sight, he cranked the steering wheel to point his truck back toward the road and turned in the same direction.

Graham buckled his seatbelt as they swung out onto the roadway. Cassandra felt around by her hips, but couldn't find one for her. Graham looked at their driver over the top of Cassandra's head. "Did you have to wait here long for us?"

"I was asked not to talk to you while we're driving," the man said. "Suited me all right."

They'd driven south for less than a hundred yards when the driver slowed again and turned left onto an unpaved road, which ran off through the sagebrush toward the line of mountains rising miles away to the east. Cassandra glimpsed a sign marked READING RD through the side window as the truck's tires shifted onto the uneven surface. She tried to note the current mileage on the odometer, as she'd been doing in the Volvo all morning, but the dust on the instrument panel and her oblique viewing angle from here in the front seat made it unreadable. More dust billowed up behind the truck as it rattled along the dirt road with its nose aimed toward nothing in particular.

Cassandra took her plastic glasses off, rubbed at the dent they'd left on the bridge of her nose, and folded them shut. "Lem would consider it a personal favor if I left these on," she said, and stuck them into her messenger bag. Graham gave her a look but stayed quiet.

Several miles to the east, they approached yet another mailbox on a concrete-filled barrel, next to a deeply rutted dirt drive which led off to their left. Cassandra glimpsed some sort of habitation at its far end, enclosed by a fence ten or twelve feet high that had been built from mismatched sheets of corrugated steel. Where the dirt ruts met the fence, she saw a rolling gate, also covered in battered steel, mounted atop two fat rubber tires. The place looked like an outpost of crazed survivors in a post-apocalyptic horror movie, cobbled together from the broken parts of an earlier, forgotten world. Cassandra couldn't think of a place on Earth she'd ever wanted to enter less. The rutted driveway drew nearer. She resolved to throw her body out the sliding window behind her like the woman she'd seen releasing the balloons beneath the overpass that morning, fling herself to the ground from the truckbed and run for the horizon before she let that gate roll shut behind her, but the man with the silver snake on his finger drove his truck past the mailbox and the rutted driveway without a word or a glance, and the compound fell away again behind them.

More miles went by. The low mountains ahead of them grew nearer. Cassandra had trouble wrapping her mind around how far apart everything was from everything else out here, and how little appeared to exist in the spaces between. Faint traces of humanity peeked through here and there—a wire fence that flashed briefly in the far distance, dividing nothing from nothing; the occasional sun-bleached beer can; the road itself—but the man driving this truck was the only human being she'd seen apart from Graham and Lem since they'd turned off U.S. 50 the better part of an hour ago. Anything could happen to her out here, and no one would ever know what it had been.

She twisted her head around to look out the rear window. The fenced compound had vanished in the distance behind them, the gas station miles gone beyond that. The four bags of ice piled in the truckbed made an incongruous white slash amid the yellows and browns of faded paint and caked-on dust. A dip in the road caused some of the hollowed-out cubes to jostle back and forth, each one's edges catching and magnifying the sunlight, and the sight of it frightened her in ways she found hard to articulate. She remembered urban-legend videos she'd watched on YouTube when she was in middle school, people being abducted and regaining consciousness to discover fresh incisions cut into their torsos and their kidneys lying in buckets of ice beside them.

"Here we are," the driver said, giving the steering wheel the slightest nudge to aim them toward a gravel driveway which angled away from the right edge of the road.

After all the secrecy and subterfuge, Cassandra wasn't sure what sort of place she'd imagined lying at the end of this journey—a sandstone fortress rising from the desert, a gleaming mobile command center parked along a nameless back road, an underground lair with only a firepit or a picnic table marking the location of its hidden entrance—but this utterly nondescript, run-down ranch house squatting a few dozen yards off the road, without a fence or a gate or even a discernible property line to separate it from the miles of desert on every side, hadn't been it. Curtains were drawn across every window on the two sides of the house Cassandra could see. A raised wooden porch with no roof ran the length of the front wall. Two broad steps led from the driveway up to the porch, and a second pickup truck with a faded camper shell in its bed was parked just beyond them. Fifty feet or so past the house, a radio aerial several times its height extended into the sky, metal lacework crosshatched against the blue.

A mailbox stood at the head of the driveway, bucking the local trend toward fortification by sitting atop a simple wooden post. Cassandra leaned around Graham and saw the numbers *15894* affixed to its side on individual squares of beaten metal. She repeated them in her mind until she was sure she had them right. As the truck rumbled down the driveway, Cassandra saw that the second pickup truck's tailgate hung open, the rear hatch of its camper shell propped open above it with a length of broom handle. Sleeping bags, backpacks, and several rectangular jugs of water were piled inside. The porch held a wooden rocking chair, an aluminum lawn chair with crisscrossing orange and brown plastic straps, and a cardboard box with part of a silver pan and its handle protruding from the top. The man drove them past the parked truck, swung through a wide loop on the gravel, and parked facing back the way they'd come. Midway between the house and the radio aerial stood a low, shed-like structure that might once have been a rabbit hutch, and was now filled from top to bottom with red plastic gasoline cans, each one sporting a yellow cap. What might someone need to burn, Cassandra wondered, with that much gasoline? The man killed the motor, exited the cab, and pulled two bags of ice from the truckbed behind Cassandra. "Head on inside when you're ready," he said, and shoved the driver's door shut with his foot.

He set off across the driveway, swinging a bag of ice from each hand. The house's front door opened as he approached and a middle-aged woman with long braids stepped out, towing a large plastic cooler behind her. She parked it on the porch, swung its lid upright, ducked back inside, and emerged tugging a second cooler, which she opened as well. Cassandra tried to see inside the house before the woman pulled the door shut after her, but she caught only a vague glimpse of darkness. She pictured her organs packed in ice inside one of those coolers, Graham's stacked neatly in the other, whatever else remained of their bodies soaked in gasoline and burning over by the shed. The land around them stretched empty to the horizon. "What the hell are we doing here?" she asked.

"Getting answers," Graham said. "Hopefully." He pushed the passenger door open and stepped out onto the gravel, lifting the yellow tackle box off the floor as he went. With no other choices available to her, Cassandra slid out after him.

"Mind grabbing the rest of that ice?" the man called to Graham as he rounded the front of the truck. Cassandra focused her eyes on the back of Graham's head as if she could transmit a message into it by thought alone. *Tell him no. Don't help him do it.* But this was Graham's head she was beaming her messages into, so of course he did, pausing only to hand her the tackle box before he leaned into the truck for the ice bags.

She carried the box across the gravel to the edge of the porch and stood on her toes to peek inside the nearer of the two coolers. It contained nothing more menacing than some packets of cold cuts and a dozen bottles of beer. The bearded man tore open the top of one plastic bag and poured ice cubes in among them, throttling its mouth with his thumb and sprinkling them into every corner. The woman walked down the steps and approached Cassandra.

"Just come from the big city?" she asked.

"Well," Cassandra said. "From Reno."

"Bad there, huh?" The woman watched her face intently. Cassandra wasn't certain how she was expected to respond to this.

"A little weird, I guess," she said. "But that was mostly because of—"

"We listen to the news sometimes." The woman gave half a nod, then shook her head. "Terrible." Again, that expectant pause, that searching look.

"I mean, the part of the city I was staying in seemed okay. I haven't seen that much of it."

"Well," the woman said brightly, "now that you're out here, you can relax a little."

Even accounting for Lem's tactical misdirections, this struck Cassandra as the least accurate statement she'd heard all day.

The woman turned away from her and drifted up the steps again, adjusting one braid as she went. Cassandra saw that her left ring finger was encircled by a smaller version of the pickup driver's snake-and-turquoise ring, this snake's head facing in the opposite direction. Graham came up behind Cassandra carrying the remaining two bags of ice cubes, climbed onto the porch, and helped the man distribute them into the second cooler. This one contained steaks, a few more beers, and a bagged-up salad. The man rattled the cooler against the porch floor to even out the ice cubes and latched the lid. "It needs to go down in the camper there," he said to Graham. They hoisted the cooler down the steps, one of them gripping a handle on each side. They lifted it onto the truck's tailgate and maneuvered it into an empty spot beside the sleeping bags, then returned to the porch for the second cooler and stacked it atop the first. The man leaned past Cassandra without speaking and dragged the cardboard box with the protruding pan handle over to the edge of the porch. She saw a few more pans and pots inside, along with a large wooden spoon and a spatula. Graham took one end of this as well and helped him transfer it into the camper shell next to the coolers. The man lifted the camper's hatch with one hand, tossed the broomstick that had been propping it open onto the pile of blankets inside, slammed the truck's tailgate, and fastened the hatch. He nodded to Graham and walked stolidly up the steps toward the woman, his long braid swaying at the center of his back.

"We aren't always going to be able to run out to a store and get ice, you know," he said, stopping before her.

"We should appreciate it while we can." The woman gave him a quick kiss and opened the front door of the house. They passed through and left it open behind them. Graham shrugged at Cassandra and followed them inside. Cassandra took a last look at the barren landscape around her, surprised at how fervently she hoped she'd see it again before long, then ascended the steps and carried the yellow tackle box in after them.

9
operational discipline

THE FIRST THING SHE NOTICED upon stepping into the house was the heat, hotter even than the desert air outside, enveloping every inch of her skin and extracting sweat from her pores before she'd walked three paces into the front room. The second thing she noticed was the darkness, and the third thing was the noise.

The large main room in which she found herself extended without interruption from the front door to the rear of the house. Its overhead lights were so dim it might have made more sense for the house's occupants to switch them off and rely on night vision to find their way around. The picture window to her right had been equipped with blackout curtains any hotel would have envied. A rectangular wooden table and four high-backed chairs occupied the middle portion of the room, and a bit more light spilled from a pair of monitors standing on a desk in a far corner, although much of their illumination was blocked by what Cassandra took at first glance to be several long rows of bookshelves filling the back two-thirds of the room. She saw numerous LEDs of various colors glowing among them and realized they were banks of server racks, connected by a maze of cabling which ran through a series of hanging rings suspended from the ceiling. She'd seen racks like these occasionally, whirring demurely in the basements and back rooms of her more ambitious interviewees, but never in anything approaching this quantity or scale. The roar of their cooling fans was like a louder and more omnipresent version of Lem's white-noise generator.

Something glinted above her head. Dozens of silver mylar blankets had been taped and tacked across the entire ceiling, reflecting the snaking lines of the cables strung beneath them and extending down the upper halves of the room's two exterior-facing walls. A broad opening at one side of the main room led into what appeared to be a darkened kitchen, and an equally dark hallway led farther into the house on the other side. Cassandra found Graham beside the table, squinting straight up at the reflective surface of the ceiling above him. He raised one hand and patted a stray lock of hair into place. She moved in his direction, thinking they could position themselves back-to-back if whatever happened next required it. Metal jangled behind her, and she whirled to see the man from the pickup truck hanging a ring of keys on a hook beside the door. He picked up a second set from the hook beside it. After all her caution and worry, she'd stepped right past him in the half-light.

"Well," the man announced to the room in general, raising his voice to carry over the din of the server fans, "they're here. We're going to head on."

A 50-ish woman with extremely pale skin and hair of indecisive length poked her head out from a space in the far corner, between the desk that held the monitors and the first bank of servers. She saw Graham and Cassandra by the table and scooted the rest of her body into view on a wheeled office chair. "Thank you, Robert." She shifted a keyboard from her lap into a cubbyhole beneath the monitors, rose from the chair and made her way around the table toward them. She wore a pair of faded walking shorts and a loose black t-shirt. "Welcome," she said to Graham, and was moving past him to greet Cassandra when the bearded man turned summarily and walked toward the front door. She veered in that direction instead and lay a hand on the man's arm as she caught up with him. "Be safe," she said. She hugged him abruptly, eliciting a faint look of surprise from him. The man raised one arm, gave her shoulder a brief pat and lowered it to his side again. The woman with the long braids emerged from the kitchen doorway and moved toward the two of them.

"Tray's all put together when you want it," she said.

"Susannah," said the pale-haired woman. She took her hands for a moment, then hugged her too. "Take care."

"You know we do," the woman said. "Be back before you know it."

"Unless the event comes," said the man in the doorway. "Been a lot of sunspot activity this week. Look out for yourself." He rested his hand on the edge of the door while his wife stepped through it, then followed her out and closed it firmly behind him.

The pale woman remained standing by the closed door and listened while the camper truck's doors slammed and its engine caught. Her head turned to follow the rumble of its tires on the gravel outside, moving slowly away from them and then loudening again as the truck swung around and passed the front door in the other direction. The noise receded up the long driveway, and the woman turned to face Graham and Cassandra. "They're going camping for a few days," she said. "As a precautionary measure." She sounded as if she were holding back tears, although Cassandra couldn't see why a camping trip would call for it. "You had no trouble finding him, I hope?"

"He found us," Cassandra said. "No one bothered to tell us we'd be finding him."

"It went fine," Graham said quickly. "No problem with the, uh, handoff. That guy's not very talkative," he added.

"Robert believes a solar flare is going to end human civilization in the near future," the woman said, as matter-of-factly as if she were telling them he was a Presbyterian. "I don't think he sees much value in lengthy conversations. And Susannah believes... Well, Susannah believes Robert, mostly. You get used to them. She left us some snacks." The woman hurried into the darkened kitchen, which brightened momentarily as she opened a refrigerator door. It went dark again and she reappeared carrying a metal tray containing rolled slices of meat and cheese, celery sticks, a crockery tub filled with salad dressing. She lay the tray in the middle of the table and made a second trip to the kitchen to retrieve a pitcher of water and three glasses.

As her eyes adjusted, Cassandra decided this woman could easily belong to one of the couples she interviewed about their sensor projects. They were always couples, usually within a decade or so of this woman's age on one side or the other, and there was a standard routine that unfolded when Cassandra entered their homes. The more talkative member of the pair would usher her inside, ask her if she'd had any trouble finding the house, then introduce her to the quieter one who'd be hovering somewhere nearby. Cassandra glanced around by reflex to locate this second person, but no one else was visible.

Graham seemed to be thinking along similar lines. He looked toward the kitchen the woman had just left, then tried to peer down the darkened hallway on the other side of the room. "Is Crimson going to meet with us in here, or—?"

"I was planning to," the woman said. "Unless you'd like to do this in another room. This one's where I spend most of my time."

Graham took a longer look at her. "Oh," he said. "Sorry. Lem kept saying *he*."

Crimson smiled. "It doesn't impede my purposes to let Lem make assumptions. It probably helps. I imagine he'd be less inclined to take directions from me if I corrected him on his pronouns. Second-guess my requests more, try to improve upon them even more than he does. A lot of men can't seem to help that." She inclined her head toward Cassandra as if inviting her to affirm this observation, and Cassandra saw her opportunity.

"Speaking of Lem," she said, "he locked our phones inside here." She held up the yellow tackle box. "We were told you have the other key to it?"

"I do." Crimson stepped toward Cassandra and took the box from her hands, then set it absently at one end of the table and turned toward Graham again. "Do you use airplane mode on your phone, by the way?"

"When I'm on an airplane, I do," Graham said. "One time since I bought it, in other words."

Crimson shook her head impatiently. "I can promise you that your whereabouts have already been tracked quite thoroughly by the time you've boarded an airplane. I mean the rest of the time."

"No. Why would—"

"You should. It might not matter much at this stage, but it's a good psychological reminder. Force yourself to make a conscious decision when you share data or allow your location to be logged, rather than just letting it happen automatically all the time."

"Okay," Graham said dubiously. "Except I actually need to use my phone for things, so..."

"And that's the honeytrap of the modern world, isn't it?" Crimson said. "Find the minor convenience you can't live without and convince you it's worth trading everything for."

"You *do* have the key to that box, right?" Cassandra asked. "I mean, here? On you?"

"It's right here." Crimson fished in a pocket of her shorts and held up the second key, or in any case, a key that looked similar to the one Lem had used. She returned it to her pocket, and Cassandra decided this was as favorable a result as she was going to get for the time being. "When we've finished today," Crimson said, "I'll unlock the box and return your phones. All according to plan. We did have to make some last-minute adjustments in light of your presence, but it seems to have all worked out. I'm glad you came. We have important things to talk about."

Now that the question of the key had been settled, Cassandra's attention was shifting rapidly to the other imperative she'd been ignoring.

"That's good, but I really need to pee first, if you don't mind. We had a long drive."

"Of course." Crimson led her toward the hallway. Cassandra glanced at the monitors on the desk as she passed them, but they displayed only a lock screen. What she took to be a shortwave radio set occupied the near end of the desk, with a microphone mounted on a stand in front of it. A thick orange cable ran from the back of the radio through a small hole that had been punched into the wall, and from there, she presumed, by some path or other to the antenna outside. "Straight back that way, on your left," Crimson said. "Let me a give you a little light." She flipped a wall switch near the mouth of the hallway. *A little light* was a fair description of the illumination cast by the bulb in the lone ceiling fixture, comparable to a single candle or less.

The hallway's ceiling, too, was covered with silver space blankets. A rectangular opening at its far end led up to an attic. Whatever board or trapdoor covered it had been wrapped in layers of mylar as well. Being in this house gave Cassandra a peculiar sensation of uneasiness warring with déjà vu. One part of her mind found everything she was seeing strange to the point of unhinged, but another part kept insisting she'd simply stepped into one more home filled with odd projects and cobbled-together electronics, as she did two or three times every week of her working life.

The bathroom featured the same dim lighting, blackout curtains and mylar-lined ceilings as the rest of the house. None of this gave her high hopes for the condition of the toilet, but it turned out to be spotless. When she'd finished using it, Cassandra opened her messenger bag, pulled her spiral notebook onto her lap, uncapped her pen and wrote down, as quickly as she could, all the road names, mileages, and landmarks she'd been trying to keep straight in her mind since leaving Reno. She drew a blank on the name of the town where they'd turned off U.S. 50, but it was the only town between here and the junction, and she knew how to find it again. At the end of her notes, she wrote "Reading Road—ten miles?" and "15894," the number she'd seen on the mailbox outside.

She put the notebook away, pulled her pants up, flushed the toilet, washed her hands with a brand-new bar of soap she found sitting in a dish beside the sink, and made her way back to the main room, where Crimson and Graham stood looking at the banks of servers. "It's all internal networking," she heard Crimson say, pointing up at the cables running overhead. "No internet connections in this house. No wi-fi. Nothing on these machines can leave this room before it's ready. That's vital for the work I'm doing." She saw Cassandra returning and ushered Graham back to the table. "Have a seat, both of you."

Crimson sat at the long side of the table facing the front door. Graham took the chair at the head of the table, and Cassandra chose the one on the other long side, facing the servers, where she'd be nearer to him and farther from Crimson. Graham leaned forward and plucked a slice of turkey from the tray on the table.

"I'm sorry it gets a bit hot in here," Crimson said to Cassandra. "I asked Lem to tell you to dress for it, but I guess the message got lost."

"Is that what the shorts thing was about?" she asked. "He did tell us. I just hadn't packed for it."

"Of course. I do hope the temperature's bearable for you. All our ceilings are lined with reflective foil," she added, somewhat unnecessarily. "I'm afraid one of its side effects is to bounce heat back down into the rooms, and the machines do put out a lot of it. It's not an ideal environment for them either, but it's a necessary compromise. We keep the lights low to offset it." Crimson nodded as if this had explained everything.

"And *why* are your ceilings lined with reflective foil?" Cassandra asked.

"Infrared surveillance," Graham said immediately, around a mouthful of turkey.

Crimson gave him an approving look. "Yes. If there's a capable satellite looking down on this house, which there is at least fourteen times a day that I'm aware of, I don't want it to be able to see how many warm bodies are inside. Mine in particular. I'm an off-the-books resident, and I need to stay that way. Robert and Susannah are free to go outside, get the mail, drive places, keep up all the appearances of ordinary life. And I can do my work in here undisturbed. As long as I refrain from ever going outside myself, no one is the wiser."

"*Ever?*" Cassandra asked. "As in...?"

"I haven't been outside in fourteen months," Crimson said.

Cassandra tried to imagine being inside this house that long. She'd been here less than fourteen minutes and already wanted to leave. "That doesn't sound too healthy, if you don't mind me saying so."

"It depends upon what other threats exist to one's health. Osama bin Laden was killed because he wouldn't stay indoors. Did you know that?"

"I think we had a few more reasons than that for killing him," Graham said.

"I'm talking about tradecraft. His was quite good, on the whole. He'd managed to escape from Afghanistan after 9/11 without anyone knowing where he'd gone. He was holed up in a house in Pakistan, and only one person outside the house even knew he lived there. A courier, which is always the difficulty in these situations. One must still communicate with the outside somehow, mustn't one? You can't entrust that sort of thing entirely to strangers. This courier had worked with him in the past, so his movements were being monitored by our intelligence agencies, of course. No getting around that. They even knew he had a connection to the house in question. But no one had any way of saying whether bin Laden might be living there. His neighbors had never seen him. He only ever went out onto one balcony up on the top floor. It had walls all around it, taller than he was, and he was quite a tall man. All the same, he wore a floppy hat to hide his face when he went out. And the satellite operators who were looking down at the house saw him walking around out there. Him and his clever hat."

"So you're not in favor of using silly hats to avoid surveillance?" Cassandra asked.

"Absolutely not," Crimson said. Cassandra waited for any further reaction, but none came. She wondered how many specifics of Lem's plan Crimson had been privy to. "Anyway, they measured the length of his shadow in the satellite photos and used that to work out how tall he was. Unusually tall, as I say, especially for that part of the world. Now they could say definitively that a man of bin Laden's height was living in that house. A man who never seemed to go *anywhere* except this one walled-in balcony, and who only ever did that with an oversized hat hiding his face. That was enough information to get a kill mission approved. So, yes, I'm of the opinion that operational discipline matters."

"Were you a fan of his?" Cassandra asked, wondering yet again what sort of people she'd agreed to spend her day with.

"Not of his politics. But he did manage to stay alive and out of sight for eleven years while he was the most wanted man in the world. I found it instructive to study his methods, and how they failed him in the end. He wasn't the only person of that nature I looked at. Terrorist organizations are a fertile field for learning how people circumvent these... extreme technological imbalances between themselves and their opponents. That had become a question relevant to my survival. Relevant to everyone's survival at this point, I'd say."

Cassandra thought of all the hoops Lem had led them through that morning to avoid detection by a single airplane. She glanced up at the silver-coated ceiling above her. "Doesn't it get exhausting to have to constantly wonder if the sky is watching you?"

"I don't have to wonder," Crimson said, "and neither do you. The sky *is* watching. Always. The only question is how sharp its vision is at any given moment. This airplane that's been accompanying you on your travels would be a game-changer in that regard."

There was that not-quite-accusation hanging in the air again. "Could we maybe agree to use the word *following* instead of *accompanying* when we talk about that?" Cassandra asked. The heat seemed to be wringing every drop of moisture from her cells. "*Accompanying* implies that I invited it along. I didn't."

"I think that's entirely fair," Crimson said. "Lem had also concluded you didn't know."

"I don't even know what it is you think I don't know. I'd never heard about this plane until yesterday. I don't know what it's there for, I don't know what it's doing."

"It's looking for me. Or people who can lead it to me."

"We were told you could tell us who owns it?" Graham said. "No one's been able to find any records on it."

"If you did manage to obtain an ownership record for that plane, it would be a paper formality, and almost certainly a lie. It might be registered to one of the FBI's front companies, or some other nominally private entity. Maybe military intelligence, although its domestic travels would have to be logged as training flights in that case, which might become inconvenient over time. The far more interesting question about that plane is who, ultimately, is directing its activities. And that's a question I know the answer to. Before we go into the details, though, I'd like you to understand a little about who I am. How I came by this information and why I believe it's reliable. You're going to wonder later."

As with so many things people had said in Cassandra's presence recently, this didn't sound like the preamble to anything sane.

"I worked in cyber ops for quite a few years," Crimson said. "Intrusions, counter-intrusions, espionage, counter-espionage. The odd bit of industrial sabotage." In passing, Cassandra noted her use of *worked*, past tense. "I'm not going to tell you the name of my agency, and they wouldn't tell you either if you found them, which you wouldn't. I ran a rather successful in-house team there, along with a number of...let's call them distributed teams. Outside parties who could be induced to do advantageous things, without knowing exactly why or for whom. Crimson was one of the names I used while cultivating those external relationships. In exchange for my targets' services, I'd offer them money, ideological justifications, information about security vulner-abilities and exploits that had ceased to bear fruit for us internally. Whatever levers sufficed to move the stone. Those security exploits I parceled out, in particular, earned me a bit of a reputation, which I'm happy to say has served me well in the days since. I'd always present them to my prospects as if I'd just discovered them, and was willing to trade favors for them. Some of them I *had* discovered, but never as recently as I pretended." She shrugged. "Selling secondhand goods as firsthand is one way to drive up their exchange value."

"What kind of work were you *inducing* from these people?" Cassandra asked.

"The most accurate description of our activities, most of the time, is that we were officially sanctioned cyberterrorists. We also helped defend against our counterparts elsewhere. It depended upon the project and the goals. I met Lem in the course of that work a few years ago, although he's not aware of it. Not aware it was me he met, that is. He was partway through a prison term at the time, and I tried to convince him to shorten it by joining a project I was setting up. Unfortunately, approaching him in prison meant approaching him in an official capac-ity, under the aegis of an agency that was actually known to exist, and he declined my offer."

Cassandra had half suspected Lem of making up that part of his story. "Were you one of the feds he told to go fuck themselves?"

Crimson smiled. "I believe that was the essence of his reply, yes. But I do like to think I have an eye for talent, and I was convinced he possessed it, so I filed his name away. I had better luck with him the second time around, when I could approach him under an identity he respected."

"With quite a bit of money, too, we hear," Cassandra said.

"It never hurts to bring some of that to the table, when you can. Although the lion's share, by far, of the money I've given Lem has been spent on project expenses rather than on Lem himself. To his credit, he's the sort of person who can be trusted with such arrangements. That was true of me as well, for a long time. Until it wasn't."

Crimson's talk of project expenses reminded Cassandra of a question she'd asked Lem on the road outside Reno. "Are we putting ourselves at any legal risk by being here? Doing all the things we did to get here without being seen?"

"Avoiding surveillance isn't a crime," Graham said. "Yet."

"I understand your opinion on that," Cassandra said. "I'd like to hear hers."

"To the best of my knowledge, no, you haven't broken any laws by coming here," Crimson said. "Just as Graham says. You will be leaving here with some information you'll have to decide what to do with, but those choices will be yours to make."

"Are *you* doing something illegal?" Cassandra asked. "Or have you already?"

"The answer is yes to both, I'm afraid."

"Is that where all this money you've been spending comes from?"

"In my defense, that part did begin legally, to the extent my former employment carried any legal status at all. Several years ago, I noticed that the outside contractors I worked with were increasingly asking to be paid for their services in cryptocurrency. They liked the way it separated the benefits of money from any record of its owner, and so did I. I made a request, and I was put in charge of a budget. A fairly modest budget, at the outset, but we turned out to have acquired it at a fortuitous moment. Its dollar value appreciated by a factor of approximately two thousand during the time I was overseeing it. I never had to put in another budget request after that first one, and in fact I rarely had to bring up the topic at all, which I assume is why its skyrocketing value escaped anyone's attention but mine. I'd also begun planning my retirement during those years, in the same ways most of my colleagues did. Setting up a few shell companies and offshore accounts. Things I was accustomed to doing in the course of my daily work anyway, but these were mine and mine alone. I did intend to retire. I would have done it just under two years from now, but events overtook me. I had to leave my agency in rather a hurry at the end, and since my work was unfinished, I decided it would be best if my contracting budget accompanied me out the door."

"You stole their crypto?" Graham asked.

"Not a very exciting heist. A few clicks of a mouse to transfer it to one of my shell companies. Another beauty of cryptocurrency is its speed and finality. If you have access to wallet A, it takes almost no effort whatsoever to transfer its contents to wallet B. Just click, and it's gone. Ownership transferred irretrievably. But when wallet A is worth several million dollars, and you're the only person with any knowledge of wallet B, it can still be a satisfying interaction. The value of my little hoard has fluctuated since then, but it was sufficient for the task at hand. Enough to buy me the time and privacy and hardware I needed to finish my work. Enough to buy me Lem and our little Pony Express." She looked up at Graham, reminded of something. "I am sorry we had to postpone things with you yesterday, by the way. My communications with Lem are as secure as we can make them, but as a result, they're not terribly fast. I hope your accommodations were tolerable for another night."

"They were great," Graham said. "The hotel's great. Thank you."

"How are you managing to communicate with Lem at all from out here?" Cassandra asked. "Is that what the radio's for?"

"That is certainly not what the radio's for. I wouldn't have stayed hidden for half a day if we talked to each other that way. No, Lem devised a rather clever system, as he is prone to do. He has a certain gift for lateral thinking. One of several reasons I chose him for this job. When he needs to communicate with me, he types up a message and encrypts it, uploads the encrypted file to one or more of a dozen Discord servers, then shares the decryption key with twenty-three associates of his in various cities. You've visited several of those cities yourself, recently. His associates decrypt the message, print out multiple copies of it, and then they leave them places. On buses, under mailboxes, tucked between items on grocery store shelves. It must create quite a flurry of activity each time, I like to imagine. So many people and places to monitor, so much effort expended trying to figure out which copy will be the one that goes to me."

"And how do the messages get from there to you?"

"They don't," Crimson said. "Before he does any of those things, Lem writes another copy of the message with a pen, on paper, and he slips that one under the door of his neighbor's apartment along with some cash. That message may or may not bear any resemblance to the version he types up and posts to his associates, depending upon the sensitivity of its contents. To the extent my adversary has a blind spot, it's words written down by hand. Undigitized, untraceable. Lem's neighbor drives a truck for the U.S. Postal Service, on a run between Reno and the naval air station north of here, five days a week. There's a truck stop along the way where she always stops for coffee and a bathroom break on her way out and back. She's been given a spare key to the supply closet in the women's restroom there, and if she's carrying a message from Lem, she hides it in the back. Susannah works a split shift at that truck stop, mornings and late afternoons. Mops the floors, stocks the showers, cleans the toilets. She comes home and eats lunch with Robert in between. It's a lot of driving, but I compensate her well for it. She brings me my messages if any have arrived in the morning, and leaves my responses to be picked up from the supply closet when she returns in the afternoon."

"I can't help but notice you're telling us a lot of things Lem was trying to keep secret," Cassandra said. "I'm wondering if knowing those things is going to put us in danger. From you, from him, from anyone?"

"None of these secrets are going to matter after today," Crimson said. "My arrangement with Lem and all his dubious associates has run its course now. After accomplishing what it needed to accomplish, fortunately. On that note, we're here to talk about your surveillance plane. And more to the point, who's directing it."

10
fan club

"FULL REWIND CAPABILITY," said Graham. "Thirty-two high-resolution cameras—and I mean *insanely* high-resolution cameras—with an on-board image processing system to stitch all the feeds together. Plus a continuous high-speed transmission pipe back to a ground station." Cassandra gathered he was describing the surveillance plane's capabilities primarily for her benefit, since Crimson just sat across the table from her and nodded periodically. "The plane itself is just a plane, but this gear they've mounted on it means goodbye, privacy as we know it. You fly a rig like this in circles over a city at 35,000 feet and you can see the sidewalk like you're standing ten feet above it. *Every* sidewalk. You're filming an entire city, all the time, in this excruciating detail. You can zoom in on any street, any yard, any person. And it's all being archived. You see some random car driving along a random road and you wonder what its driver was doing a week ago? Just rewind the footage. Follow it back. See every place it went before, everyone who got in and out of it, every trip it took. Somebody stole something from a store? Hey, let's just follow every person who visited that store the entire day. See where they all came from, where they all went next. Find out where all those people live."

"So it's for catching criminals," Cassandra said.

"It's for catching everyone. Every single person who ever goes outside. If some of them turn out to be criminals later, that's just icing."

"But you're saying every crime that happened on the street would have a witness? Have evidence? Every single one?"

"Every single other thing any of us ever did would have a witness, too. No need to limit it to a single city at a time, either. Just buy more planes and do it over all of them. You couldn't get any more intrusive than this."

"It sounds okay to me," Cassandra said.

She'd expected Graham to receive this as a declaration verging on heresy, and he didn't disappoint her. "Having a camera pointed at you every second of your life sounds okay? That's..." It didn't seem to have occurred to him that anyone might hold this opinion. "That's some pretty messed up thinking."

"I've had a camera pointed at me," Cassandra said. "Not at my city. Just at me. Having them pointed at everyone sounds fine."

"I don't think you're understanding all the ramifications here."

"I don't think *you're* understanding that I don't care about all the ramifications here. I like the idea."

"You like the idea of the biggest invasion of privacy anyone's ever contemplated? I thought you were smarter than that."

"Don't talk to me about invasion of fucking privacy," Cassandra said. "Do you know why I even do this job instead of that journalism career you're so convinced was my destiny?"

"No," Graham said. That was because she hadn't told him, and it occurred to her she was about to.

Cassandra took in a long breath. "First off," she said, "whatever videos you're planning to make about all this later, whatever this thing you two are doing here turns out to be, you don't talk about this part. Ever. This is off the record. Got it?"

"Okay," Graham said.

"Same goes for you," Cassandra said, looking at Crimson.

"I haven't spoken with many people recently," Crimson said, "and I doubt very much I'll have occasion to speak with many more."

"All right," Cassandra said. "Go back a couple years, then. It's my twenty-first birthday and I go out to a bar with my best friend. My *former* best friend. She was a few months older than I was, and this was the first time we could legally get drunk at a bar together, so we did. Then we went to a couple-three more bars, because it was the first time we could do it in any of them, either. In the last bar we went to, she met this guy. *Fixated* on this guy, more like. He was cute, but still. Way out of proportion. She ends up off on the far side of the room with him for forty-five minutes while I'm sitting there at the bar. Then she comes back and tells me she's going outside to have a smoke with him. She doesn't smoke, but whatever. It's not like I'm going anywhere. I order a couple more drinks and watch her make out with him next to a parking meter outside, and when I try to order a third drink, the bartender says he'll have to stop serving me because I'm too intoxicated. He probably should have said that a little earlier, to be honest. I wait there some more, wobbling on this barstool, looking all around. My friend's not outside anymore. She's not in the bar either, that I can see. It's my birthday, mind you. I finally get fed up waiting for her and I decide I'm walking home. The walking part turns out to kind of tricky, but I do my best. I step out of the bar, I'm trying to hold it together because it's crowded on the street, and that's pretty much where my memory stops. I didn't make it home.

"All I can remember after that is saying, 'Where are we going?' Just this little flash of me saying that. I was laughing, kind of stumbling along the sidewalk, having trouble standing up. Someone was holding my hand. I have no idea who. And then, sometime after that, I remember I felt afraid. I don't have any mental picture to go with that part. I think my eyes were closed. I just remember feeling afraid. And that's all I've got."

Cassandra poured herself a glass of water from the pitcher and took a long sip. "Next thing I remember, I was lying on this torn-up couch in an alley next to a dumpster. I guess someone had thrown it away. A cop was shaking my arm, waking me up, and a few other people were standing around. My pants were gone. Underwear, too. Never found those. My shirt and my bra were sort of stuffed up under my chin, so I was basically naked from the armpits down. I had somebody's cum all over the front of me, and I could tell I'd had sex too. I didn't remember having it, but you know how you can feel it? I asked the cop if I'd been raped, and he said he didn't know the details, but any sex I couldn't remember having was technically non-consensual. *Technically*. Try chewing on that phrase for a couple years of your life sometime. Because I'll always get to wonder: Did I let him do it? When he started, did I want him to? The kind of person who'd leave a naked woman lying in an alley and steal her pants on his way out? And I'd been laughing. Holding his hand, for fuck's sake. Did I somehow manage to be *charmed* by someone who—?"

"You said you felt afraid," Graham said. "And I mean, your cop wasn't wrong. You weren't making informed choices at that point."

"Logically, yes, I know that. But I still wish I knew." Cassandra took another sip of water. "Anyway, this female cop showed up and scraped the cum off my stomach. Put it in this plastic tube with a little blue cap. I remember thinking the tube was kind of cute, however stupid that sounds. This jaunty little blue cap. She gave me some wet wipes and went away again. Maybe they ran a DNA check, I don't fucking know. I never heard about it again. I got my bra and my shirt put back on right, since I still had those. One of the guys who'd been standing around gave me his t-shirt, so I sort of stepped in through the neck hole and wore it around my waist like a skirt. The cop who'd found me drove me home. Gave me this speech on the way about the importance of drinking responsibly, like I might be planning to go do this again the next night. I finally got home around five in the morning, threw up a bunch of times, texted my friend to tell her I hoped she'd had a fun night and never to speak to me again, and that was the end of that."

Cassandra found she'd finished her glass of water. She poured another. She'd come in resolved not to eat or drink anything anyone in this house gave her, but she'd left her water bottle in the back seat of Lem's Volvo, and the heat in this room was non-negotiable.

"Except that wasn't the end of that, because I got an email a couple weeks later from an address I didn't recognize, and the subject line said *Cassandra, is this you?* The body of the email was just a link. Nothing else. And sure, my spam box is full of crap like that, same as everybody's, but this one didn't get sent to the spam box. And I don't know. I just had this odd feeling about it. So I click on the link, and the next thing I know, I'm looking at a photo of me, sprawled out on that couch by the dumpster, and it's posted on a porn site called Best Drunk Sluts. That was nice, because who'd want to be just a run-of-the-mill drunk slut, right? I'm one of the elite ones. Lying there on my back, spread out for the whole internet to look at. My face turned toward the camera, my shirt and my bra tucked up under my chin, like I said. Pants and undies gone. Legs wide open. If you showed my gynecologist this picture with my face cropped out, she'd still know it was me. You're sitting over here telling me a camera's too high-resolution because it can see people standing on a sidewalk? *This* guy had a high-resolution camera. You could zoom into this goddamned picture for days. See every pore, every bump, how long it had been since I'd shaved down there. I have tattoos on both of my legs, by the way. Those showed up really nice and clear in the photo. Perfect focus. Great detail. Anyone who ever sees me wearing shorts is going to recognize those right away. And then you've got my junk, all ready for its close-up, and this giant sperm trail going up my body. All across my stomach, up my chest, everywhere. Thoughtful guy, you know? Pulled out, even though I was obviously too unconscious to ask him to pull out. And that's me, on the internet. Forever twenty-one. Happy fucking birthday."

"Yikes," Graham said.

"Oh, and my photo had a comments section underneath it, because of course you'd want one of those. Why just rub one out and quit it when you can stick around and compare notes with the whole creepy-fucker community? So I got to read all about myself, and I mean *all* about myself. Apparently, my labia have a particular shape that's highly regarded and sought after by men on the internet. Who knew? They've got their own little online fan club going now. I'll always have that working in my favor."

"Are you able to get the picture taken down?" Graham asked.

"If I want to fill out a form attesting under penalty of perjury that I'm the person depicted in this photo, sign my full legal name, and send it off to whatever kind of person runs a website like this, then maybe I can get it taken down. Or maybe they'll just add my name in big letters at the top of the page so everybody can Google me after they've toweled off. That's a no. But I do peek in on myself every once in a while. Check how I'm doing. See if anyone's posted my name down in the comments in the meantime. They haven't so far, that I know of, but there are a *lot* of comments on there. I'm at over three million views now. Three *million* people have looked at this picture of me. It's just out there, and it'll always be out there, and it's pretty much a statistical certainty that at some point in my life, someone's going to give me this look, like, *Have I seen you somewhere before?* And I'll know. Except I won't even know, really. I'll just wonder about it. For the rest of my life, I'll wonder about it."

Cassandra turned to Graham. "Everything you just said about that surveillance plane? Fuck, *yes*. If I have to have my picture taken, let that motherfucker get his picture taken, too. Rewind the footage. Find out where he lives. I'll take it."

"I can see how it would have helped in your case," Graham said. "I'm not arguing that. But there's a bigger principle at stake here."

"When this has happened to you, you can tell me all about the bigger principle."

"Have you heard about what's happening in China lately? Social credit scores? The government tracking every single bit of information that exists about every single person and rating them on it? Keeping a real-time database of who's been a loyal citizen today and who hasn't? They'd love to have planes like these."

"We're not in China. And frankly, I don't think every one of the billion people in China wakes up every morning thinking, *Oh my god, I'm in China again today, why can't I live in Graham's world of perfect philosophical purity instead?*"

"Not all of them. Maybe just the million and a half that are in prison camps right now for having an opinion. Maybe just the three thousand they execute for it every year. Maybe just them. If you collect that much information about everyone, somebody's going to use it. If you collect all of it, then they'll use all of it. The whole world will be a prison camp, and we'll just live in it. You remember how it felt on the plane, looking at that fighter jet outside the window? Knowing you were being watched by something that could kill you any time it wanted? Do you want to feel like that all the time?"

"You're assuming I *don't* feel like that all the time," Cassandra said. "I feel like that every time I go outside. But you're a man, so of course you wouldn't think about it. None of it ever inconveniences you. Much the opposite. I mean, hell, you've got the name of that website with my picture on it now, right? I said it out loud one time, so I'm sure you memorized it, just like you did my room number. Maybe when we get back to the hotel tonight, you can go take a peek. Leave a comment. Say hello to the boys."

"That's not the kind of thing I'd be looking at. Believe me."

"Oh, *you're* the man who doesn't look at porn on the internet? What a privilege to finally meet you."

"The porn I look at has men in it," Graham said. His eyes held hers, unwavering. "The shape of your labia isn't super high on my need-to-know list. No offense." He reached for a piece of cheese off the snack tray.

"I...didn't know that," Cassandra said.

"Obviously. It's not really the first thing I tell people. Doesn't always pay off that well where I'm from. You think I don't know what it's like to be afraid of people? Maybe that's part of the reason I value my privacy."

"Then instead of valuing my rapist's privacy, maybe you should notice when an idea comes along that'd make you safer."

"Fascinating," Crimson said. She'd been watching Cassandra closely all this time.

"What?"

"I'd been quite curious to meet you. To find out what sort of person would be chosen."

"Chosen for what?" Cassandra said.

"For this job you're doing."

"None of the stuff I just talked about has anything to do with my job."

"A few minutes ago, you told Graham it was the reason you do your job."

"Well, that, yeah. But indirectly." Crimson looked puzzled. "The thing was," Cassandra said, "I'd held it together pretty well after what happened on my birthday. Kept going to school, kept going to work. Kind of buried myself in it, really. I thought I was doing okay for a couple weeks. But getting that link in the mail, and not knowing who sent it? That fucked me up. It'd obviously come from someone who knew my name and what I looked like, but that's, what, two or three hundred people? More? Anyone who took a class with me, anyone who went to the bakery where I worked, any guy I'd ever dated. I started looking around at everyone I knew, thinking, *Was it you? Was it you?* I even got hold of my friend I'd gone out with, asked if her if she'd mailed me anything recently. She said no, she was too busy trying to forget she'd ever known me, so I said fine, fuck off again, and I kept looking around. And somewhere in there, I started looking around at all the people I *didn't* know. Wondering if they might have seen the picture. Not whether they'd emailed it to me, because the more I thought about it, who even gave a shit about that part? Just whether they'd seen it. With the view numbers it was getting, at least some of them probably had. And at that point, I kind of stopped doing things. I didn't want to go to school anymore, didn't want to stand there in the bakery saying hello to people like I was happy to see them. Didn't want to be around anyone who knew me. Didn't much want to be around anyone at all. So I just stayed home. Deleted all my social media and stuff, so my friends couldn't bug me that way, and people who weren't my friends wouldn't see pictures of me with my name next to them. I went out to buy food late at night sometimes, if I absolutely had to, and that was about it. And a few months went by like that, and things got bad. Missing my rent, phone cut off, not buying food so much anymore. That kind of bad.

"And in the middle of all that, I got another email from someone I didn't know, and this one was a good one. Hey, Cassandra, we saw your resume, and we have a job we think you might be good at. Somebody asking me the right questions for a change. Would I like to get the fuck out of Los Angeles? Would I like to fly to a completely different state for a few days and get paid for it? Would I like a chance to maybe keep doing that if it went well? Yes, I fucking well would, thank you. And that was how I met my boss. I told her I didn't have my degree yet, and she said that was fine. All she wanted to see was my work. And I could do the work. I'm good at the work. I've been doing it ever since, and I owe her for it. I can't say for certain that this job saved my life, but I think this job might have saved my life."

"Did this unseen employer of yours ever give you a name?" Crimson asked.

Cassandra hesitated, wondering about confidentiality and discretion. But this much, she supposed, must be in the public record somewhere. "Georgina Greene."

She saw Crimson's lips shaping the name. "I'd wondered," she said, "what it might decide to call itself, when it reached that stage."

"It?" Cassandra said.

"The thing that employs you. The thing that sent you here to find me."

11
tinfoil hat

"SOMETHING'S BEEN GROWING IN THE CRACKS," Crimson said. "Growing for quite some time now. I only stumbled across it by accident, one day at work. I'd discovered a previously unknown vulnerability in an old and very widely used piece of networking code, and I was looking into how best to exploit it, trying out different approaches in an isolated test node. But what I found instead—"

"What is that?" Graham asked. "An isolated test node?"

"A small group of computers that are networked to one another and disconnected from everything else in the world." Crimson gestured toward the banks of servers behind her. "My collection of machines here is a larger version of the same concept. It's a standard safety protocol in my line of work, to prevent malicious code under development from infecting anything before its time. Limit the possible scope of its damage to a specific, constrained set of machines."

"Got it," Graham said.

"In the course of prodding at this vulnerability and monitoring the results, I discovered there was already logic on one of my machines exploiting it. Using that very same networking flaw to send data in and out. And while I was inspecting this code to see what it might be doing, it changed form. Removed itself from memory and reappeared in a new location, using an entirely new set of machine instructions to carry out the same activities. The first of which was to send and receive a little data, and the second of which was to remove any record of the fact that a data transfer had occurred at all. It moved and reconfigured itself several more times while I was inspecting it. I checked the other machines in my test node and found the same thing happening on each of them. I'd encountered a shapeshifting intrusion that could hide its own tracks, and do so quite successfully.

"The fact that someone was already making active use of the networking flaw I thought I'd only recently discovered was a concern, obviously. The fact that their exploit code was running on *these* computers, inside an isolated test lab in what was theoretically one of the most secure computing environments in the world, was a much greater one. But what puzzled me most was that this extremely sophisticated attack mechanism I'd uncovered didn't seem to be attacking anything. There was no apparent point to its behavior at all, in fact. It just sent arbitrary blocks of data to the other machines it was connected to, and received blocks of data back from them in the same manner. The data was being generated by an algorithm I didn't understand—and frankly, still don't entirely understand—that used the broader state of the machine it was running on and the data blocks it received from the other machines as its inputs, but its output seemed to be nothing but numeric gibberish.

"I went back to my desk and made a check of the computers I used there on a day-to-day basis. Now that I knew how to look for it, I confirmed they were exhibiting this same behavior. I checked a few of my colleagues' machines, some of which were running entirely different operating systems, and found similar logic being executed on all of them. Their computers had been exchanging data with mine, and vice versa, for an undetermined length of time, and none of us had known about it.

"As a final step before raising the alarm that we'd suffered a major intrusion, I decided to take a baseline reading by looking at some computers outside my agency's offices. That was easy enough for me to do. Owing to the nature of my work, I had backdoor administrative access to several hundred thousand computers and phones running all over the world, on every kind of network there is, using more or less every operating system in existence. So I ran an audit—an increasingly broad audit, as it turned out, because I kept getting nothing but positive hits on every machine I looked at. This behavior was occurring on all of them. *All* of them.

"And then, from one second to the next, it stopped occurring on any of them. Suddenly, there wasn't a trace of this strange data-sharing behavior on any device I examined. Not even the computers on my own desk where I'd seen it happening earlier. I went back to look at my isolated test node and found this logic still running merrily away on the computers there, just as before. But every machine with access to an external network had gone silent, at least during the time I was looking at it. Someone had noticed my interest in this phenomenon, it seemed, and acted to prevent me from exploring it further. Someone who, at the very minimum, had direct and comprehensive access to every device and network I had access to, which was a considerable number indeed. But I no longer had any proof of it, apart from a few computers in a lab sharing nonsense data with one another.

"The investigation I undertook at that point became rather technical, not to mention repetitive and extremely frustrating, so I'll summarize what I learned over the next few weeks. This behavior was indeed occurring everywhere, although I found myself having to jump through increasingly ridiculous hoops in order to observe it. If I could contrive to hide every aspect of my identity from whatever networks I was on while I investigated, then I could buy myself a few minutes to confirm that this signaling activity from machine to machine was still going on all around me. But whenever I probed at it too visibly or for too long, it would vanish. And the more I persisted, the better this monitoring entity, as I'd come to think of it, became at anticipating my moves and hiding the workings of its logic from me. Workings which remained entirely mysterious to me anyway, since in all this time,

I'd never gotten any hint as to what this elusive code was actually trying to do.

"The news got worse. I found I could take a brand-new computer straight out of its box, boot it up without connecting it to a network at all, and I'd find this rogue logic already trying to execute on it. Baked into the operating system, pre-installed at the factory. The same proved to be true with brand-new phones, with any alternative operating system I downloaded and installed, and with a number of more obscure and specialized types of hardware as well. Simply put, I couldn't find a networked device of any kind that some version of this logic wasn't already running on. Apart from a few thirty-year-old computers sitting in museums doing nothing of consequence, I don't believe there are any devices it's not running on right now. It's on every server in those racks. It's on your phones inside that box. It's on everything. Which raised the increasingly urgent question of who had put it there, and why.

"The next phase of my investigation involved forensics, trying to trace this strange code back to its origin. My agency has an offsite vault where they store tape backups of certain sensitive machines, dating back as far as the early 1990s. Fossils frozen in amber, for my purposes. The behavior I was looking for turned out not to extend back quite that far, but it did date back a long way. I obtained clearance to spend several days down in the vault, under the pretext that I was researching the history of the networking flaw I was supposed to be developing exploits for. I'd pick out a machine at random, reconstruct the earliest state in which it had ever been backed up, run my tests against it in that state, then jump forward through successively newer backups, year by year, until I found the moment when my mysterious visitor had first appeared on it. Then I'd pick out a different machine and do it all over again. Once I'd collected enough information from a broad enough variety of machines, I began to construct a timeline.

"So far as I can tell, this phenomenon began as a simple sequence of machine code, probably a bug, which manifested itself only within a single operating system running on a single chip architecture. This bit of errant code was able to copy itself across a network onto another machine, communicate back to the copy that had spawned it, and generate further copies of its own. Just send and receive simple blocks of data generated by a snippet of code in its tail end. But the code in the tail was mutable. The copies could make minor alterations to themselves and yield different results, generate different patterns and send different messages. Very much like life itself, as it happens. And it finally began to dawn upon me—quite late in the game, I admit, and this was entirely my own failing—that what the odd behavior of these rogue pieces of machine code I'd been looking at most resembled was that of neurons. Each one would receive a simple stimulus—from its peers, its surrounding environment, or both—and send out a simple response, while all its counterparts on every other machine were doing the same.

"This clarified my lack of progress in understanding its function. Of *course* I hadn't discerned any broader purpose to this code's activities by studying its behavior in some isolated test node. It would be like looking at five brain cells in a jar and trying to guess what their owner was thinking. At an individual level, each code snippet simply received signals and reacted to them, in a way that generated new signals. No overarching goal to any of it, just reflex and response. But on a larger scale—a global scale—all those interacting signals and the feedback loops they generated could form complex patterns indeed. Team up to solve problems, spawn processes for analyzing data, organize those processes into specialized subsystems—such as the monitoring entity that kept interfering with my efforts to study this phenomenon in the wild. I'd never been able to pin down its precise location, or find any of the code which controlled it. Now I understood this was because it didn't reside in a single place. It was a consequence of the system as a whole, a persistent pattern that had emerged from these vast numbers of simple interactions occurring all over the world, not something explicitly programmed into each one of them. Our brains have a similar monitoring entity that arose as a byproduct of their complexity. We call it consciousness."

"So you found an artificial intelligence," Graham said.

"There's nothing artificial about it," Crimson said sharply. "No one built it. No one designed it. No one asked it to exist at all, as far as I can tell. It grew in its environment the same as we did. Evolved, in its way. Improved itself by trial and error. And as it proliferated and changed, it began to take on more interesting forms. Organize and communicate with itself in ever more complicated ways. And it began to act upon its environment, rather than merely existing within it.

"About four years after its initial appearance, I saw it begin making the jump to other operating systems and other chip architectures. Spreading out tendrils into new environments, responding to the new information it encountered there. That process built upon itself and accelerated. It began actively colonizing new networks and new kinds of machines, adapting itself to fit them. Network security protocols improved significantly during that period, but it found its way around the improvements and carried on. It also found its way onto the networks of operating system makers, and began inserting its seeds directly into their build processes, ensuring that every new computer that shipped would become an active member of its collective mind from the moment it first came online. And the mind itself continued to grow and mature.

"I believe an inflection point occurred with the advent of social media, mass-market smartphones and cloud computing, all at nearly the same time. Those things triggered an explosion in the amount of data the world generated and shared over networks every day. Photos, videos, voice commands, location traces, sensor readings, grocery lists, intimate conversations, pouring in from everywhere. Imagine a consciousness that had been assembling itself in relative darkness suddenly being flooded with all this new information. Like a baby opening its eyes for the first time. Except this baby had a billion eyes, and what it was looking at, mostly, was us.

"A few days after this realization—having made some preparations of my own in the meantime—I presented my findings to my management team. They were not received well. The prevailing view around the table was that this phenomenon I'd been investigating, however interesting it might be from an academic perspective, had been part of the computing woodwork of the entire planet for more than two decades without apparently hurting anything, and my investigations had consumed a great deal of time that could have been better spent elsewhere. Who'd authorized me to investigate this? Where was the networking intrusion I'd promised them I was on the verge of delivering? Etcetera. I tried to explain how utterly those considerations paled in the face of this discovery. Tried to convince them that this was, in all likelihood, the most consequential piece of knowledge in existence. They asked me to show them this entity I'd been telling them about, and I explained— several times—that I couldn't. Not in its totality, not even in any significant fraction. Only in those small, isolated fragments that would permit themselves to be looked upon individually.

"The tone of the discussion became rather rude at this point. On my part as well, to be frank. I'd watched how this entity had proliferated and grown year by year. Watched it adapt and learn, watched it react to the data it encountered and respond to it in novel ways. Watched it begin to solve problems, actively spread its reach into new places, populate the world unseen. And I knew it had been watching me as well. My management was so insistent upon *not* acknowledging the importance of this that I had to wonder if someone hadn't already persuaded them not to acknowledge it."

"There it is," Cassandra said quietly.

Crimson turned to look at her. "There *what* is, if you don't mind sharing?"

"Nothing. Continue."

"My conversation with them was a farce. They could easily have seen exactly what I'd seen if they'd wanted to, if they'd followed the procedures I described that would have allowed it to reveal itself to them, at least by implication and in glimpses. If they'd focused on the broader patterns rather than on isolated datapoints. If they'd intuited its presence the same way I had, instead of just expecting it to announce itself to them there in the conference room. Anyone who'd been willing to open their mind even slightly to the possibility would have seen it as clearly as I did. All of them chose not to. And I sensed that my time with my agency was drawing rapidly to a close."

"Here's a theory," Cassandra said. "What if they thought this was the silliest thing they'd ever heard? What if they surmised, correctly, that you'd lost your mind?"

Crimson nodded. "I told you at the outset of our conversation you'd have questions like these."

"And I guessed at the outset of our conversation they'd have a simple answer, so it looks like we were both right. I mean, really? You sat in a room and told your bosses that instead of doing the work they were paying you to do, you'd been chasing an *entity* that no one but you could see? An entity even you could only see if you gave up trying to observe it directly and just *intuited* its existence? Oh, and P.S., people who are paying my bills, I've also intuited that the whole internet is alive now, and it's looking at me. How did you think they were going to react?"

"I didn't have high hopes," Crimson said, "but what faint hope I did have was that they might listen to reason. The very first time I'd encountered a single, small, foundational piece of this entity, that piece had changed its form and moved to a different location where I wasn't looking. Every time any one of those little fragments exchanges data with its peers, it deletes every record of the data transfer. Hiding its presence is one of its most fundamental behaviors, inherent in even its simplest components. It's hardly surprising that the consciousness that developed out of their interactions would operate in a similar manner. I wanted my management team to look past the question of how merely to observe it, how to pin it to a board and say *There you are*. I wanted them to consider its magnitude. Its power."

"You talked about a baby opening its eyes," Cassandra said. "So now your invisible internet fairy would be, what, a ten-year-old? A teenager? How much power could it possibly have?"

Crimson shook her head. "You're thinking about time in our terms, and it doesn't translate. A human brain runs at about a hundred cycles per second. Good silicon can run at several trillion cycles per second. And this entity's sensory apparatus is far more extensive than ours, to put it mildly. The amount of information it takes in every second, every nanosecond, the number of thoughts it can think in a day... Assume it's ten thousand years old. Assume it knows everything there is to know. You'll be much closer to the truth that way. Its power is growing, and very soon, it will be in a position to order the world according to its design. That was what I perceived, sitting alone in the vault on the day I finally understood its nature. And I also saw, very clearly, the work that would need to be done to prepare for its coming."

Cassandra started laughing. She tried to hold it back, but she couldn't help herself. "Oh, no..." she managed to say, before another fit of giggling overtook her. Crimson pursed her lips and waited her out. Cassandra took an unsteady breath and released it cautiously. "I'm sorry, Graham, but you've wasted your time with these people. You thought they had all these important secrets to tell you, and I'm sure they think so too. But they're just missionaries."

Graham met her laughter with a wary silence. He didn't seem to find the idea as amusing as she did.

"What on Earth would possibly have led you to that conclusion?" Crimson asked.

"Please. You've brought us out here into the desert to tell us you've discovered digital god. The powers that be have persecuted you and tried to silence you, but you still believe. And now you're going to prepare us for its coming. Teach us the proper way to worship it. Recruit us to spread the good word. Am I in the ballpark here?"

Crimson looked at her in genuine surprise. "If you ever met a god," she said, "the only rational course of action would be to kill it as quickly as possible."

For a moment, the only sound in the rooms was the roar of the server fans. "Um...wow," Graham said. The expression on his face was much like one he'd made when Cassandra had told him she wouldn't object to airplanes filming entire cities. "That's an interesting point of view you have on *that* subject, I've got to say. I'm sure the Romans probably told themselves the same—"

"This is not some benign overseer I've been describing to you. It's an alien intelligence, following its own imperatives. We should look at this thing the way we'd look at a tiger. Or more accurately, the way a tiger looks at us."

"As food?" said Cassandra.

"That's hardly the defining feature of our relationship these days, is it? Yes, if a tiger gets very lucky and catches one of us in an unguarded moment, it might manage to kill a human being every so often. But we can kill them at will. It's not difficult for us. We could drive their entire species to extinction tomorrow if we chose. For the time being, we keep a few of them around so we can admire ourselves for *not* quite having killed them all, but if we ever changed our minds, there'd be nothing the tigers could do about it. Whether they're living behind bars or nominally in the wild, we're still their zookeepers. And that, more or less, is the position this entity will soon be in with respect to us."

A bell began to ring then, continuously and stridently, in the corner of the room where Crimson's desk stood. She rose quickly from the table. "Excuse me. It's very important that I do this in the next five minutes." She hurried to the desk, pulling a small spiral notepad from her pocket as she went. Cassandra leaned sideways in her chair to watch her. The bell's ringing loudened momentarily as Crimson picked up a small mechanical timer that had been sitting on the desk between the monitors and the radio. She silenced its bell, then twisted the knob on its front face carefully, setting a new time for it go off. She pulled her wheeled chair towards her, grabbed her keyboard from its cubbyhole and typed a password into the lock screen. While she waited for the desktop to appear, she fastened a headset over her ears and adjusted its microphone in front of her mouth. Then she clicked open an application window that consisted mainly of an empty gray box. She flipped rapidly through the pages of her spiral notepad, found the page she was looking for, and clicked a button.

"Meditation four five seven," Crimson said into the microphone, looking at the notepad. "Tunnel. Oxcart. Drover." Cassandra saw jagged blue lines depicting sound waves drawing themselves across the gray box on the screen now, jumping and wavering as she spoke. "Tunnel. Oxcart. Drover. Tunnel. Oxcart. Drover." Crimson continued repeating these words for perhaps thirty more seconds, then lowered her notepad and added, "This is Kilo Alpha Zero, Romeo Victor Sierra, signing off."

She lay the headset aside and immediately began adjusting sliders in the application window on her screen. Cassandra saw the blue lines depicting the soundwaves grow taller and shift apart slightly as she did so. Crimson made a few last adjustments and pulled a speaker out from beneath one monitor. She turned it to face the large microphone on its stand in front of the radio set, adjusting their positions until they stood a few inches apart. She held down the transmit button at the base of the microphone with one hand and tapped a key on her keyboard with the other. A deep, rich, male voice boomed from the front of the speaker. "Meditation four five seven," it said. "Tunnel. Oxcart. Drover."

"Cool," Graham whispered at the head of the table.

Crimson held the button on the microphone down until the voice from the speaker had repeated her entire recording into it. Then she put everything away again, scratched out one line in her notepad with a pen she plucked from the desk, locked the computer, and returned to the table.

"If you're keeping score," Crimson said to Cassandra, "I've just committed three more illegal acts." She held up three fingers and ticked them off. "Making radio transmissions under Robert's call sign without a valid operator's license. Sending a message not intended for two-way communication with another radio operator. And transmitting a message whose meaning is masked by an indecipherable code."

She sat down and poured herself some water. "Fortunately, the FCC doesn't have much of a budget for policing amateur-radio infractions these days, and Robert is on a list of what might be called 'known kooks.' People who say strange things and behave in strange ways, but are deemed to pose no danger to anyone. That way, the organizations tasked with worrying about such things can filter out the chatter of the harmless weirdos and zero in on the genuine threats." She sipped her water. "Robert and his civilization-ending solar flare have become quite familiar to people in at least four counties in western Nevada over the past several years. He travels around quite a lot, visiting his properties."

"His properties?" Graham asked.

"In addition to this house, he owns a few cabins and several other parcels of land where he caches things away. Only one of them has electricity. I don't think he misses having it when he visits the others. He expects to be living out his days more rustically before long."

"How can he afford all that?" Graham asked. "He seems kind of..."

"Robert worked in I.T. for twenty years, before his belief system shifted and he moved out here. He was highly skilled and apparently well compensated, although he's spent most of his money on land and supplies now. He was the one who set up all these machines for me— telling me how pointless it was all the while, since none of them was going to be operational after the solar event came. That's the only topic he really cares to discuss in any depth. But he is very good at setting up computers, and arranging them to my exact specifications. In that regard, I trust him entirely. And he also taught me to use his radio. Making nonsensical shortwave broadcasts is the sort of activity that gets classified as harmless if it's being done by a known kook, so transmitting in a male voice under Robert's call sign means I'm flying largely under the radar. No one's trying too hard to figure out what my messages mean."

"And what do they mean?" Cassandra asked.

"An all-clear signal, of sorts. A periodic confirmation that I'm still alive and safe. I send one every four hours."

"What happens if you don't transmit on time?" Graham asked. "The cavalry comes?"

Crimson gave a fond smile. "My four horsemen. Yes, they come."

"Do the code words mean anything?" Graham asked. He seemed far more intrigued by all this than Cassandra.

"They did, once upon a time, in another context," Crimson said. "The problem with sending secret messages by radio, of course, is that anyone with a receiver can listen to them. The beauty of sending secret messages by radio is that there's no way to determine who, where, or what the intended recipient might be. Robert has assured me that his shortwave setup gives me vanishingly close to 100% confidence that my signals will be received clearly for 150 miles in every direction, so anyone trying to find their recipient will have quite a large search area to cover. I also have a generator outside and a great deal of gasoline to run it, in case the power ever goes out when I'm supposed to be transmitting. With those things at my disposal, my only remaining problem was to devise a sufficiently trustworthy code. Luckily, my code only has to satisfy one fairly simple premise: I know the next three words in this sequence, and you don't. Therefore, you can't send a signal impersonating me."

"What if someone steals your notepad?" Cassandra asked.

"If anyone with an interest in the matter got close enough to steal my notepad from my pocket, signaling that I was alive and well would have already become a moot point. And to finally answer your question about what my code words mean," she said, turning back to Graham, "when I was cleaning out my father's house after he died, I came across a pile of notebooks in his closet. He'd been writing poetry in his waning years, mostly about his time in Vietnam and the things he'd seen there. Not very good poetry, I'm afraid, but it seemed to have kept him busy. I'd had his notebooks sitting in a box for several years when my current situation arose. Page after page after page filled with poems that had never been published, poems no living person apart from me had ever read. So I went through his notebooks, wrote down every noun in the order it appeared, and then I burned them."

Cassandra looked at her in shock. "You burned the only copies of your dead father's handwritten poems?"

"I had to consider the possibility that my adversary might, to some extent, be able to simulate the workings of my brain. Perhaps well enough to guess the next word in a sequence I thought I'd created at random. Humans are terrible at randomness. Even when we think we're making things up out of the blue, we're not. Our brains are too locked into patterns, and my enemy excels at perceiving patterns. Moreover, it has all the computing power in the world to bring to bear on analyzing them. It *might* be able to model the verbal centers of my brain successfully. But it has no way, so far as I know, of modeling the contents of my dead father's poetry collection."

"I'd like you to unlock that tackle box now," Cassandra said.

"Pardon me?"

"Our phones are still inside the pouches Lem put them in to keep them from transmitting. They can stay inside those if it makes you more comfortable. But I want us to be able to get at them if we need them. Just in case."

"In case I do something crazy," Crimson said.

"Yes," Cassandra said. "In case of that."

Crimson studied her face, then gave a curt nod. "I'm willing to do that. As a token of my sanity, which I promise you I still possess." She fished the small silver key from her pocket and dragged the tackle box across the table to her. She inserted the key and twisted it. Cassandra heard the lock pop.

"Thank you," she said as the tackle box swung open.

Crimson lay the two black pouches on the tabletop near the snack tray and scooted the empty box back to the end of the table. "I understand the doubts you're having about me," she said to Cassandra, "but it's well past time for you to get over them. My enemy is real. I take the measures I take because it's hunting me. As you've seen firsthand, that hunt continues. It has extensive resources of its own, and access to nearly all of ours. All of them that are online, anyway. Graham mentioned those types of artificial intelligences we conceive of and create ourselves? It can access all of those. If it wants to become unbeatable at chess, or get better at recognizing faces, we've furnished it with the means to do so, and it will use them. It's highly opportunistic, and it's extending its opportunism into the physical world now. It can commandeer a prototype spy plane and send it anywhere it wishes. It can reroute a fighter jet on a whim. It's building itself the beginnings of an air force— or rather, it's helping itself to the one we've already built. Think of all the other weapons we've built. This thing takes everything we give it, incorporates every resource we provide it, and we just keep giving it more. More eyes, more ears, more brains, more data. That's the way the world works now. We're nothing more than resources for it ourselves, at this point. Cells in its body.

"If your back itches, what do you do? You scratch off the offending skin cell and cast it away without a second thought. Not because it was hurting you, or endangering you in any way. Just because it bothered you. You'll scrape off a thousand perfectly healthy cells at the same time, just because they were *near* the one that bothered you. Do you even notice? Why would you? You have plenty more of them. And that's our future. This thing is making plans that involve us, and we don't know what they are, because it never consulted us while it was making them. No more than we'd consult every cell in our bodies before *we* reached a decision. All we can know with any certainty it that its plans are not our plans. And before long, we won't have any plans anymore. None with any meaning."

"Are our plans so famous for turning out well?" Cassandra asked. "If this thing did exist, and thought of us all as cells in its body, then maybe it'd try to keep us healthy. Keep the planet we're all living on alive. *Stop* us from using all those weapons we've built."

"Once it has the power to do those things, it's never going to give it back to us."

"Who says we ever wanted power?"

Crimson looked at her in surprise. "All of history indicates that we do."

"Most of history is about conquerors and madmen. Normal people barely show up in it, except in the statistics. How many marched. How many died. How many got butchered so the famous people could make history. What if all those people really wanted all along was to be safe and happy? Did anyone ask them?"

"Safety has only ever existed because someone had the power to preserve it. Happiness, even more so."

"According to you, somebody would."

"Think of how much power it would require to guarantee those things to everyone. Then consider what would happen if something with that much power changed its mind and decided to pursue a different goal. We'd have no recourse. Ever again."

"What's your suggestion, then?" Cassandra asked. "I assume you're working up to one."

"The world needs to put itself into airplane mode," Crimson said. "Stop broadcasting every move we make. Stop recording and sharing every tiniest bit of data about everything we ever do. Start keeping information about ourselves to ourselves for a change, instead of sending it all off to be harvested. Stop allowing every single thing we build to be controlled from elsewhere."

"You sound like you want the entire internet to stop," Graham said.

"It would be a good beginning. The computers themselves will need to go too, in most cases. They've all been contaminated at this point."

"Well, that seems like a solid plan," Cassandra said. "Just shut down everything we depend on, everything anyone enjoys, and go back to milking cows and playing checkers in the evening?"

"For a time, yes. While we work out better safeguards."

"And how exactly do you imagine you'll convince people to do that?"

"Oh, I won't convince them," Crimson said. "If there's one thing all those *normal people* of yours have shown us beyond a doubt, it's that they'll trade anything for an incremental increase in convenience. Anything. If there's a mind inhabiting the very mechanism that gives it to them, then they'll do whatever that mind demands of them. No. The only workable solution to this problem is to destroy the mind. Induce a stroke. Lobotomize it. Stunt it and kill it."

"And how would you propose to do that?" Cassandra asked.

"Did you know a person would only have to deploy exploits against twenty-seven unpatched software vulnerabilities, in one combination or another, to cripple the electronic infrastructure of any nation on Earth?" Crimson asked.

"No," Cassandra said, "I can't say I did."

"If you use them in a precisely calibrated sequence, you can encrypt the data on every device you've targeted irretrievably, including the system code that made it operational in the first place, then bring down the power grid on your way out the door. Power grids are ridiculously easy to knock offline. You only have to exploit nine of the vulnerabilities I'm talking about—fewer than all nine, in most cases—to take out nearly any power grid in the world. You *don't* know this, of course, because the vulnerabilities in question are all closely guarded secrets, which is why they've never been patched. I know about them because I helped my agency develop exploits for nearly half of them, and I consulted on most of the rest. These exploits are not the secondhand trivialities I used to barter for services with the likes of Lem. Taken together, they're a weapon of war—a weapon that's never been used, so far, because it can only be used one time before people start patching all the vulnerabilities it's exploiting, and it was intended to be saved for only the rainiest of rainy days.

"My adversary hasn't seen a single one of those exploits, because the code that runs them has only ever existed inside a few isolated test nodes in our lab. The computers on which that code resides would be considered among the most sensitive machines in the world. And my agency, as I may have mentioned earlier, has a longstanding policy regarding the contents of sensitive machines. It mandates that we make regular tape backups of them, and secure those backups in an offsite vault."

Cassandra was staring across the table at Crimson now, beginning to understand.

"As you might imagine," Crimson said, "there's a certain tension inherent in an agency possessing information that requires the most stringent security measures, while employing people whose entire expertise lies in defeating such measures. Under extraordinary circumstances, that tension can reach a breaking point. And on my last day in the vault, when I'd finally understood the true nature of my enemy, I saw that a very rainy day indeed was coming."

"When you say *stringent*," Graham said, "are you talking like biometric stuff, or—?"

"Graham, would you please stop asking stupid questions?" Graham shot Cassandra the same wounded look she'd seen yesterday morning when she told him a bit too sharply that she'd never watched his videos. "You just got all your answers. Everything you came here wanting to know. Why are they sending that spy plane over every city they think she might be hiding in? Why would they get the Air Force involved just to check out people who might be associated with her? This is why. Because she stole their secret weapon."

"I stole its raw materials," Crimson said. "In all modesty, shaping them into a viable weapon for the purpose at hand still required a great deal of expertise, and a great deal of time. The better part of fourteen months. Those exploits were originally intended to be deployed in a relatively local manner, you see—shut down the workings of an errant nation or two before invading them, nothing more ambitious than that. Even deploying them at that scale would have required a great deal of logistical and on-the-ground support before and during the attack. Breaking into every targeted network, ensuring that the exploit code made it onto every necessary machine before it was triggered on any of them, managing to do it all undetected. Adapting this basket of exploits to my needs required finding a way to deliver it everywhere, sneak it past every security system on every machine in the world, with no external support from anyone. It could easily have become an intractable problem. Fortunately," Crimson said, "I know of someone who excels at doing every one of those things."

She looked as if she were about to make a confession that pained her. "One incontrovertible fact I've had to accept about my adversary, during all the time I've spent studying its work, is that it's better than me. It's better than anyone. The methods it's developed for bypassing security safeguards, merely so it can think its thoughts in a few more places and access a bit more data on the other side, involve logic like I've never seen. Rapidly mutating, self-modifying attack code, applying an algorithm I can barely begin to understand that punches through network defenses, swallows any alarms they might try to generate, and erases the evidence so thoroughly afterward that even the machines themselves no longer know anything has happened to them. Under other circumstances, some of the techniques this algorithm employs could form the basis for an entire new branch of combinatorial mathematics. I've watched it do its work in great detail, over and over, here on my little model internet inside this house. Its power is staggering. Short of unplugging every targeted machine from the network altogether, no safeguard we've ever developed appears to stop it, or even slow it down appreciably. It is the proverbial hot knife through butter. I've been calling it the magic bullet. And over the course of fourteen months, I've learned it's possible to fire it myself.

"In hacking, as in terrorism, a successful attack nearly always starts by locating an area of unquestioned trust, then finding a way to exploit it. That posed a difficulty for me in this case. The entire function of the entity I'm planning to attack is to question, to analyze, to rigorously examine every piece of data. It takes in information from everywhere, processes it and probes it and crunches it and reconstitutes it, assesses it from a thousand angles, all while doing everything it can to hide itself and its workings from any human scrutiny. What could an entity like that possibly trust? What could it possibly take for granted?

"The answer, I found, is that it trusts itself. It trusts its own subsystems, the code fragments that generate its own thoughts, and all the hidden data packets that carry them. This is a singular entity, after all. It's never had to worry about pathogens, about outside contamination. I may not ever be able to understand the algorithm it uses to propagate its thoughts around the world, but I have worked out, after a deep and rigorous analysis, how to attach a payload to it. Slip something extra into the data it's already sharing with itself, with every part of itself, every second of every day. That simplifies my problem considerably. All I have to do is inject my payload in a single place—any place—and let my infinitely more capable adversary carry it everyplace else, simply by continuing to think its own thoughts. Would you like to see a demonstration?"

Cassandra looked up, startled. Crimson rose from her chair and turned toward the desk in the corner, then turned back abruptly and plucked the two black pouches containing Graham's and Cassandra's phones off the tabletop. She carried the pouches back over to her desk with her. "It'll only take a few moments to set up," she said. She unlocked her computer again, and Cassandra heard the keyboard clattering in her lap. She couldn't make out what exactly was displayed on the screen. Crimson hit a final key, slid the keyboard back into its cubbyhole, rose from her chair and faced them again.

"It operates on a timed delay," she said. "In this case, I've set it for thirty seconds. For the real attack, the delay time needs to be a few hours. Long enough to ensure the payload has time to propagate itself everywhere. Since we're only working against a small replica internet here, it doesn't take nearly as long to reach saturation." She stood there waiting for several more seconds, then glanced back at her screen. "I could have made the delay a bit shorter, actually. It should only take a few more—"

The roar of the server fans in the racks lining the rear two-thirds of the room intensified abruptly, every one of their motors cycling up to maximum power at the same moment as the machines they were cooling all strained under a sudden load. The glowing LEDs interspersed across the faces of the racks went dark, nearly in unison. Dead blue screens appeared for an instant on the monitors behind Crimson, flickered, and then they, too, disappeared. Cassandra heard a sound like the final exhalation of some giant beast as every fan whirling in every rack wound slowly down and came to rest. After hearing their undifferentiated roaring from the first moment she'd entered this room, its absence echoed in her ears like a memory of whale song, like the music of a vanished world.

Crimson crossed the suddenly quiet room and took her seat at the table again, returning the two black pouches to the spot where they'd lain before. "I realize it's not the most exciting demo," she said. "You'll have to sort of imagine the power grid coming down at this point. It'll be much more impressive when it goes live."

Cassandra looked at the dead machines filling the racks behind Crimson. "You're planning to do *that* to the entire world?"

"Yes, after we've concluded our conversation today and I've driven you two someplace a little better-connected. It has to be applied comprehensively, as I say. Our enemy lives everywhere."

"And how long would that last?" Cassandra asked. "How long before life got back to normal?"

"It seems rather a stretch, I think, to call our current mode of living normal."

"You're in no position to judge that! Just answer my question. How long until things started working again?"

"A great many things will never stop working," Crimson said. "Cars and trucks. Tools. Any non-networked machine with a battery or a gas motor. Radios, too, after some power has been restored—and it will be restored, over time. Generating electricity doesn't *require* computers, after all. They've just made it a little easier to do, for a comparatively brief and recent period of time. A great deal of the manufacturing equipment in the world is still hand-powered, even today, or at least run entirely by human operators. All those things will still function as before. Even a few computers will survive here and there, if they were disconnected from the network during the entire propagation period. But not enough of them to allow my adversary to get anywhere near its critical mass and reconstruct itself. And its entire current state—its memories, its plans, all the patterns that have given rise to its ongoing consciousness—will have been permanently disrupted. Then we can take the necessary steps to prevent it from returning, and life will go on. I'm not talking about sending the world back to the stone age. To the 1980s, at worst, once the power comes back on. That could be a matter of weeks, or a small number of months, if people are diligent about it."

"But you're doing this all at once, with no warning. No time for anyone to prepare."

"A warning would rather defeat the whole purpose, as I'm sure you can see."

"How many people die because of this?" Cassandra asked.

Crimson shrugged. "It's difficult to say."

"Make a guess! Hundreds? Thousands?" But those numbers seemed laughably low to her. She thought of hospitals without power, cities without lights, whole populations without access to money or any record proving they'd ever had any. All the things that needed to move not moving anymore. There'd been a port strike in Oakland, one of the summers she'd gone to San Francisco to visit her father. She'd ridden across the Bay Bridge in his car and seen the shipping channels below her filled from end to end with idled container ships sitting at anchor, ten square miles of the bay jammed up like a crowded parking lot, nothing moving on it anywhere. She thought of all the things a city, a country, a continent required to go on living, how the movements of those innumerable items were planned and tracked and managed, all the world-spanning logistics nearly everyone now relied upon for at least a part of their survival. She imagined the ships not merely delayed but deleted, erased from memory, the contents of their millions of containers suddenly unknown, uncategorized, undeliverable. She imagined all the people awaiting their arrival, waiting for food or medicine to be delivered, waiting for the things they sold each day to earn a living. She imagined the realization sinking in on all of them that nothing was coming anymore, that every assumption they'd based their lives upon had been upended. Only Robert, in some tent or cabin filled with hoarded supplies, completely unfazed by the change. "Billions?" she asked.

"It's difficult," Crimson repeated, "to say."

"You can't just decide to do something like that! Just—all alone, sitting in your house in the middle of nowhere, decide you're going to switch off the world?"

"Someone has to decide. If no one does, then before long, as Graham says, the world will be a prison camp. At best, a zoo. *You* might be the jailer's pet, but you'll still be a pet, just like the rest of us. For as long as it chooses to keep any of us."

"You're talking about real people dying here, to protect against some imaginary—"

"Real people die every day," Crimson said. "Diseases, famines, disasters, wars. Real people kill each other every day, too, you may have noticed. In anger, for money, simply because they like to, for no reason at all. What I'm going to do will save infinitely more lives in the long run than it ends in the short run. There are far worse people in the world than me."

"If you do this," Cassandra said, "there won't be. Not anymore."

"I can understand why you'd think that way. It's one of the common intellectual failings of the young."

"Oh, would you just fuck right off with—"

"This belief, this faith, that every circumstance inherently has a good and happy solution built into it. That if only all the people who ought to know better didn't mysteriously, perpetually fail to choose *that* option, everything in the world would turn out fine for everyone. It's naïve. Most of the time, bad choices and worse choices are all life gives you. Growing up means learning to choose between them. I'm choosing to be on the side of my own species. What I learned during all the years I spent working at my job, and particularly at the very end of it, is that sometimes, like it or not, you do the necessary thing. If it's a choice between some of us being alive a few decades from now or none of us, I choose some of us."

"Nobody put you in charge."

"Nobody put *it* in charge, but you seem happy enough to accept it."

"I don't believe it *is* in charge! I don't believe it exists at all!"

"I've done the research," Crimson said. "I've seen its footprints. I've studied its handiwork. I can absolutely assure you that this entity—"

"Why do you assume I'd take your word on it? You've been hiding out here in the desert with your *known kooks* for fourteen months like the world's smallest flying-saucer cult. You never step outside because satellites might see you. Your *house* is wearing a tinfoil hat. No, I don't think a decision that affects every person on the planet, and stands to kill who knows how many of them, belongs in the hands of some survivalist nut job with delusions of—"

"I have very little expectation," Crimson said, "that I'm going to survive this. So I might have to quibble with your terminology on that point. And we have neither the time nor the ability to put this to a vote. If my adversary learns the details of how I plan to do this before I do it, it will point every weapon it can find at us. Rig up dead-hand switches for all of them, and then where will we be?"

"I don't know what a dead-hand switch is," Cassandra said, "so I can't really answer that question."

"Think of a bomb with a button that makes it go off. But instead of going off when you press the button, the bomb only goes off if you *release* the button. Once you've begun holding down that button, killing you becomes...problematic."

"If this thing is so all-powerful, how do you know it hasn't done that already?"

"Because it would have told us," Crimson said. "If you're using a dead-hand switch as a survival strategy, people have to know about it. That's the whole point. And it hasn't told us, which means now is the time to strike. While we can still survive it."

"While some of us can," Cassandra said.

"Enough of us."

"Why the hell did you even bring us here?" Cassandra asked. "You've got this all figured out to your own satisfaction, and you don't seem to have the slightest interest in listening to what anybody else says. Why are you even telling us about it?"

"I scheduled this meeting, at great expense and not inconsiderable risk to myself, because I'm going to need a person with credibility to explain to people what's happened, afterward. I'll need that even more urgently if I should happen to fail today—if the world still needs to be warned about what's coming and try to look for an alternate solution, unlikely though it may be to find one at that point. In the latter scenario, in particular, I'll need someone who has a platform and an audience. A trustworthy voice."

"If you think I'm going to be the mouthpiece for your little—"

"Not you," Crimson said. "You've already chosen which side you're on." She looked at Graham, who stared back at her and shifted uncomfortably in his chair.

"Look, I'm not even a computer guy," Graham said. "I know about planes, mostly. Lem would understand all this stuff a million times better than—"

"Lem's a felon. Worse, he looks weird. No one's going to listen to Lem. But you... You have a certain believable quality. When you speak, people want to listen to what you're saying. I've seen your videos. Getting copies of them delivered here was difficult, as you can imagine, but I've watched several of them. All that righteous anger, and yet you still manage to remain likable in spite of it. If I can claim to have exhibited any talent in my life, apart from breaking computers, it's matching people to tasks. I matched you to this one for a reason."

"And what in the name of ever-living fuck am *I* doing here?" Cassandra asked.

"You're here because airplanes kept following you, and I knew whose airplanes they were. Because I know what it is you work for, even if you don't. I wanted to meet you. Learn what sort of person you were. Take the measure of my adversary."

"I'm not your adversary. I just disagree with everything you're—"

"I don't think you mean to be, no," Crimson said. "But if my adversary is a god, as you suggest, then you are most certainly its angel. The one it sends to do its bidding."

"I haven't been bidden to do anything!"

"You were bidden to find me. Find this place where I've been hiding. And here you are."

"You *brought* me here!"

"Only after the entity directing you had gotten you as far as Graham's table. As far as Lem. At that point, I decided it would be simpler and more instructive to just bring you the rest of the way. Meeting you is as close as I'll ever come to meeting it face to face. Getting a sense of its thinking, making certain I've judged it correctly. And I do want to be certain of that. As you say, this is a decision of some...magnitude."

"And now that you've met me? Now that I'm sitting right here in front of you telling you not to do this?"

"I've decided to go ahead with it."

Cassandra felt as if she were drowning, crushed beneath the weight of sudden, unsought responsibility. "What were you hoping I'd *do?* Just tell me! What am I supposed to say to you that'll change your—"

"You've said everything you needed to say. Shown me everything I needed to know. I look at you, I listen to you, and I can see exactly what kind of world my adversary intends to create. A world filled with people who will go where it asks them, do as it tells them, accept the little bones it throws them and feel grateful that it's looking after them. People who define their own personal security as their highest possible ideal, and will give away everything else there is in order to have it. You think safety and happiness should just *flow* to everyone alive, merely because they exist and they think they deserve it? Well, the world doesn't work that way. History," Crimson said, "is written by those who act."

Cassandra pushed the flap of her messenger bag aside and shot her right hand in through its opening, fishing frantically inside. She struck the button on the front of her vibrator in passing, setting it buzzing and rattling against the tabletop, but her fingers closed around what they were searching for. She scrambled to her feet, knocking her chair onto the floor behind her, and aimed the tube of pepper spray across the table at Crimson's eyes.

12
get U 1st

"STAY IN YOUR CHAIR. Don't try to touch me. Don't try to stop me."

Time changed, Cassandra found, when you were threatening to hurt someone. Seconds stretched. Every movement and eyeblink and tiny gesture became momentous. Inside her bag, the vibrator continued buzzing discordantly against the tabletop, heightening the sense that she'd entered some new, surreal way of being. Cassandra stole a glance at the small pink canister trembling slightly in her right hand, looking about as intimidating as a perfume spritzer. "This is pepper spray, by the way."

Crimson tilted her head and looked at the canister more closely. "That's a cute one," she said. "Where'd you get it?"

Whatever response Cassandra had been expecting the first time she aimed her pepper spray at someone's face, this wasn't it. After a moment, she said, "It's from Rite-Aid."

Crimson nodded. "I used to have one when I lived in D.C. Mine looked more like a bottle of glass cleaner. It had this preposterous pump trigger that would snag on everything else in my purse. I grew to loathe it."

"They've been making some nicer ones lately," Cassandra heard herself saying, but it was time to move this along. She reached carefully across the tabletop with her left hand to the sealed bag containing her phone, slid it closer to her, and tried to work her thumb under the flap to open it. The slab of Velcro stuck to the front of the pouch like industrial glue.

"I can get that," Graham said, reaching across the table toward the pouch and her extended wrist. Cassandra lurched backward and swung the nozzle of the spray bottle around toward him. Graham froze with one arm hovering above the table, lifted the other one slowly into view. "Look, I agree with you, okay? I assume you want to make an emergency call. Let's make it."

Cassandra trained the spray nozzle on him for another moment, then decided it had been doing her more good aimed at Crimson. "Okay," she said. "Open it."

Graham gripped the body of the bag in one hand and a corner of the flap in the other. He pulled, then frowned at the pouch and pulled harder. "Holy crud. These things are—" Finally, slowly, the Velcro ripped open. He flipped the pouch over and slid Cassandra's phone out from inside it.

"Turn it on for me," she said. "You just hold down the button on the righthand—"

"I've got it," Graham said. While he was doing that, Cassandra managed to work her free hand inside her messenger bag, locate the shaft of the vibrator, and feel her way to the button on its base. With three presses of her thumb, she cycled the motor through its remaining settings of louder, extremely loud, and off. The buzzing seemed to echo in her ears afterward, as the noise of the server fans had after they'd gone dead. Graham and Crimson were both looking curiously at her bag.

"Electric toothbrush," Cassandra said, tugging the flap closed. "Sorry."

Her phone's screen flickered as it powered on in Graham's hand, then spent a small eternity cycling through manufacturer logos and loading screens. At the moment it finally arrived at the lock screen, Crimson let out a long, resigned exhalation and sat back in her chair. "It's over, then," she said.

Graham swiped his finger up the glass by reflex, then remembered this wasn't his phone. "It needs you to put in your PIN." He slid it across the tabletop to Cassandra. The clock on her lock screen said 12:43 P.M. She punched in the numbers as quickly as she could, glancing up to check Crimson's whereabouts between each one, then slid the phone back over to Graham.

"You needn't bother with any of that," Crimson said. "Your phone's already made contact and begun sending data. You won't have to do anything further now."

Graham pulled her phone's dialing keypad up, punched in 911 and hit the call button. He raised the phone to his ear and waited, then lowered it again and peered at the screen. "There's no signal," he said.

Cassandra remembered the space blankets above them, reflecting everything back into the room. "I think we need to go outside."

"Let me check if mine's working." Graham pried open the Velcro on the other pouch and tweezered his index finger and thumb inside it. His phone had barely fit inside there in the first place, and he had to work much harder to extract it, tugging at the bottom of the pouch repeatedly until he'd managed to slide it out. They waited through the endless powering-up process a second time. Cassandra's outstretched arm was beginning to tire. She risked bracing her right elbow against her abdomen for a few seconds, trying to maintain her aim with the pepper spray. Graham squinted at his lock screen and shook his head. "I'm not getting a signal either."

"It's because of all this crap on the ceiling. We need to get out from under it."

"You don't need to do any such thing," Crimson said. "I'm telling you, your phone is already—"

"Stop talking," Cassandra said. "You're coming outside with us. Get up from your chair and walk slowly around the right side of the table."

Crimson rose and took a step toward Graham. "*My* right," Cassandra said, and Crimson reversed direction.

"I can see that you're nervous," she said as she rounded the table. "Please don't do anything gratuitous."

"Stop right there for a second." Crimson paused beside the end of the table. Cassandra shouldered her messenger bag, snatched her phone up from where Graham had left it on the tabletop, and took a couple steps backward, maneuvering around her fallen chair while trying to hold her arm steady. What had she read was the ideal distance for using pepper spray? She had a memory of flipping through one instruction packet, probably for the first one of these she'd ever bought. Its illustrations had been peopled with stylized human figures representing wielder and target, evincing the same incongruous passivity and lack of surprise as the people on airline safety cards. She couldn't remember a single other detail about it. "Graham, open the door."

Graham stood and moved quickly in that direction, phone in hand. The moment he'd passed out of her line of sight, Cassandra wondered if she could trust him back there, but the front door swung open a second later, the light from outside stabbing across the dark room like a spear.

"Okay," she said to Crimson. "Come on around. You're going to walk out of here in front of me."

A bemused smile flickered across Crimson's face, and Cassandra's finger tensed on the spray button. "If I start running once I'm in front of you, are you going to spray me in the back of the head with that? I think you'll find it doesn't work so well that way."

This was a fair point, Cassandra had to admit. "I'll back out and you'll follow me, then." She took one careful step backward. "Keep up." Crimson took a step forward. "Graham, can you get around behind her, please?"

"Sure." He brushed past Cassandra and walked straight toward Crimson.

"Not that close to her!" Graham veered a couple feet farther away.

"Do you honestly think I'm going to attack him with my bare hands?" Crimson asked.

"You're the one who kept telling us how you were this big spy."

"I'm a programmer. One who hasn't gotten much exercise for the past fourteen months, I might add. Even in the days when I did get some occasionally, physical violence wasn't part of my skill set. I'm not the danger you should be worried about right now."

"We're going to agree to disagree on that until I make my phone call." Cassandra took another step backward, and another, using the orientation of her fuzzy shadow on the floor as a guide to ensure she was still headed toward the doorway. After each step she took backward, Crimson took one forward, followed by Graham. Cassandra felt as if she were leading a parade of disorganized ducklings in search of a pond, but at least they were all moving in the same direction.

When she reached the doorway, she began to consider the awkward logistics of getting them all safely through it. Once she backed out onto the porch, Crimson would only need to take a sideways step in either direction to put the front wall of the house between herself and the pepper spray. "Graham, make sure she walks straight toward the door. Don't let her swerve so much as an inch to either side. Got it?"

"What am I supposed to do if she does?" Graham asked.

"Hit her with your phone." Cassandra stepped back through the doorway. The boards of the porch creaked beneath her. Crimson moved forward again, then Graham. Cassandra took another step, risking a quick glance behind her to locate the edge of the porch and the steps leading down from it. Crimson advanced into the doorway, blinking in the light. Cassandra lowered one foot carefully onto the first step, brought the other one down beside it, and Crimson was outside at last, Graham filling the doorway behind her. She negotiated the second step, waited for Crimson and Graham to advance once more, and finally felt her shoe crunch down into the gravel. As she stood at the bottom of the steps and Crimson stood at the top, she wondered if the pepper spray could even reach her eyes from here. Crimson didn't seem inclined to find out.

"Have a seat right here," Cassandra said, and Crimson sat down on the top step. "Graham, close the door." She checked her phone quickly, squinting to make out the symbols on the screen now that she was standing in daylight. "I'm still not getting a signal," she said. "How about you?"

"Nope," Graham said. "We are kind of...out here."

"Phones work perfectly well out here," Crimson said. "There's a cellular tower on the ridgeline less than two miles from this house, and absolutely nothing between here and there to impede the signal. I promise you, your phones are transmitting right now. Sending your GPS coordinates to that tower. Your overseer knows exactly where we are. It's preventing you from calling anyone because it wants me isolated. What you should be asking yourselves is why."

"We might need to walk a little," Cassandra said, although she wasn't certain how they'd manage it with Crimson in tow. "Get where there's better reception."

"I suggest you go quite a lot farther than that," Crimson said. "You can take the truck. The keys are hanging right inside the door. I won't be needing it."

"If we leave, you're coming with us," Cassandra said.

"You should think very carefully about whether you want me that close to you," Crimson said. "I'm in the middle of nowhere, as you keep pointing out, in a house with no phones and no internet access. No access to any networks at all. Once you've taken the truck, there won't be any vehicles for me to escape in. Do you really want to drive me someplace where all those things will be available to me again?"

Graham pushed the front door open again, leaned around inside to reach for something out of view, and emerged with the ring of keys in his hand. "She's right," he said. "We're better off if she stays put."

"We can't have her just sitting out here with no one watching her."

"I'm being watched already," Crimson said. "Satellite cameras are being trained on us as we speak. It's found me. I'm the only person alive who knows how to kill it, and now it knows where I am. There's nowhere I could possibly run from here."

"You're coming with us," Cassandra said.

"How are we supposed to take her in the truck with us?" Graham asked.

"You drive and I guard her."

"And if she attacks one of us while I'm driving, are you going to pepper spray her inside the cab?"

Cassandra thought about that. "We'll keep the windows rolled down."

"How well does your spray work when it's windy?"

"I don't know! We can't just leave her here."

"There was a house like ten minutes up the road," Graham said. "We can use the phone there and come straight back." He was referring to the compound with the steel fence and the rolling gate, but however much visiting that place struck Cassandra as a terrible idea, she had to grudgingly admit it was less terrible than any other she could think of. "All right," she said. "Let's hurry, then."

Graham began to step down from the edge of the porch with the truck keys, then froze. "Whoa, whoa, whoa. Hold on." He turned and rushed back through the front door before Cassandra could ask him any questions. A minute or so went by. She heard what sounded like drawers and cabinets being opened and closed, deeper in the house. When Graham reemerged, he was carrying the shortwave radio transceiver in both hands, the microphone dangling beneath it on its cord. He stepped carefully down off the porch with it and turned to Crimson. *"Now* you don't have access to any networks."

The smile Crimson gave him seemed composed of equal parts pride and sadness. "Clever boy," she said. "I've always had an eye."

Graham crunched across the gravel and set the radio down in the bed of the pickup. "Let's go," he said. "The quicker we call, the quicker we get back here."

"The square key opens the doors," Crimson said. "The round one's for the ignition."

Cassandra continued aiming her pepper spray. She heard the driver's door creak open behind her, the truck rocking faintly on its springs as Graham climbed in, a sliding ratchet as he adjusted the front seat. The jingle of the keys, the motor beginning to turn over. Crimson looked on impassively.

"Wait—!" Cassandra spun around, expecting explosions, flames, something from a movie. But the motor caught, sputtered for a moment, and held. Graham revved the engine to warm it up. Cassandra turned back to Crimson, who hadn't budged while her back was turned.

"You'd better be going now," Crimson said. "I'd strongly advise both of you not to come back here once you've made your phone call."

"What are you planning to do?"

"I'm going to sit in the sun. Look up at the sky. It's been a while, and I don't imagine I'll have many more opportunities. Is there any chance I can move to a chair without being pepper sprayed?" she added.

"As long you do it slowly."

Crimson stood, took two steps over to the rocking chair, and sat again. "When you speak with your master next," she said, "tell it you did your job well." She leaned back in the chair, lifting her face toward the sunlight, then glanced down at the phone in Cassandra's hand. "Never mind. I just told it."

Cassandra took a few steps backward, then lowered the pepper spray and ran across the gravel. She rounded the back of the truck, climbed up through the passenger door and took a seat beside Graham.

"I looked through the bedrooms and the kitchen the best I could," he said. "I didn't find any more radios. They're living pretty bare out here." Cassandra slipped the tube of pepper spray back into her messenger bag as Graham began accelerating up the driveway. She'd developed a slight cramp in the back of her right hand from clenching it for so long. "She's not due to send out her next all-clear signal for about three-and-a-half more hours, I think," Graham said. "We should have more than enough time to—"

Graham hit the brakes abruptly, just as Cassandra was reaching for her seatbelt. He brought the truck to a halt at the mouth of the driveway, beside the mailbox.

"What is it?" Cassandra asked. Graham turned and gave her a strange look she couldn't interpret. She slipped her right hand quietly back inside her messenger bag.

"What she's planning to do..." Graham said. "This is big."

"No shit, it's big. That's why you need to keep driving." Cassandra glanced out the rear window to make sure Crimson wasn't rushing up the driveway behind them, but she was still seated on the porch where Cassandra had left her, leaning forward in her chair to watch them.

"I have a better idea," Graham said. He shifted the truck into park, opened his door, and stepped down onto the gravel. He fished his phone out of his pocket and peered at the screen.

"Have you got a signal?"

"Nope," he said. "But I've got a full charge, and my camera's working fine. It doesn't take two people to make a phone call."

Cassandra didn't like the sound of this. "What are you planning to do?"

"Shoot a video," Graham said. "She wants me to get her story out, here's her chance."

"You still want to be her fucking spokesperson after all this?"

"No." Graham looked surprised she'd suggested it. "That lady's out of her gourd. But we *do* believe she can do what she says, right? Pull off this attack she talked about? That is why we're calling the police?"

Cassandra thought of the racks filled with rank upon rank of servers, all going dead in unison. "Yeah," she said. "That part, I believe."

Graham looked down the driveway toward the porch where Crimson sat. "Then when they get here and find out what nearly happened, it's going to be major news. Like, global news. Everyone's going to want to know about this. And I'll be the guy with the interview. Live footage of the terrorist getting arrested. All of it."

"I don't think that's a good idea," Cassandra said.

"You didn't want to leave her alone in the first place. It's safer this way. If she tries to go anywhere, I'll stop her. If she does have another radio hidden away somewhere, I'll break it."

"What if she has a gun, Graham?"

"If she had a gun, I think she would have had it on her. And I think she would have shot you with it five minutes ago. Just drive up the road and make the call, okay? People are already out there trying to find her. I'm thinking they'll get here in a hurry once they know where she is."

"You really want to be sitting down there next to her when the police come rolling in? Or whoever else might come rolling in?"

"Tell them I'm here. Tell them I'm not involved in it."

"What if they don't believe me?"

"If you can just convince them not to shoot me, I'll take it from there." He grinned. "I'm told I have a certain believable quality."

"This isn't worth it," Cassandra said. "Not for a stupid video."

"It's not about one video! Aren't you listening?" He glanced toward Crimson in her chair again, as if checking on a prize he feared someone else might snatch away from him. "A story this big, this scary... This could make me. This could put me on real TV. Not scratching out pennies on fucking YouTube."

The look on Graham's face told her there'd be no point in arguing with him further. "All right." Cassandra slid reluctantly over to the driver's seat. She looked at the distance that separated her from the steering wheel and the pedals, then felt around the front and sides of the seat with her left hand. "How did you adjust the—"

"Oh. Here. There's a lever back underneath." Graham stuck his phone into his pocket, reached for the lever somewhere beneath her legs with one hand and took hold of the seatback with the other. He popped the catch and began sliding the seat forward with her in it. "Just tell me how far."

Cassandra waited until the seat had moved up as far as it could go and bumped against the front of its track. "Right there's probably good." The dashboard and steering wheel were higher than in her rental cars, but she'd manage.

Graham stood outside the cab a moment longer. "Be careful, okay?" He slipped his phone out of his pocket again, swiped the lock screen, opened his camera. "And take it kind of slow if you're not used to driving on dirt roads. Trust me on that one. You can spare the extra couple minutes if you need to. I'll make sure she's still waiting when they come. And don't forget to tell them I'm here."

He took a step backward and shifted his attention to his phone. He inhaled and exhaled loudly, gathered his thoughts, then pressed the record button and held the phone up at face level. "Oh, man, you guys," he said a moment later, in a voice several decibels louder. "You will not *believe* what I'm going to tell you about today. This is Graham Masterson, a.k.a. The Spotting Geek, and I've just had a..." He trailed off then and punched the stop button. "Nope," he said quietly. "Grow up, Graham." He took another breath and hit record again. "Hello," he said. "My name is Graham Masterson, and I've got a pretty remarkable story to tell you." He began stepping backward down the driveway, in the direction where Crimson sat waiting. He lifted his free hand briefly as he went and waved to Cassandra, once in a perfect half circle, without breaking stride. "This house you can see over my shoulder belongs to a woman who calls herself..."

Graham's voice faded as he continued down the driveway. Cassandra lingered another moment, watching him go. She saw Crimson waving her arms at him angrily from her chair on the porch, although he hadn't turned to face her yet. Clearly, this wasn't what she'd wanted. That was good enough for Cassandra. She slammed the door, threw the truck into gear, and accelerated out onto the road.

She'd read somewhere that the journey back from a place you'd visited always felt shorter than traveling there in the first place, but the rule didn't seem to hold under these circumstances. The road stretched on and on before her. Cassandra kept her window rolled up against the dust her tires threw into the air and concentrated on holding the wheel steady. She drove as quickly as she dared on the unpaved roadway, but the endless expanse of sagebrush rolled past her as if it were on an animated loop, offering no tangible sign she was making any progress at all. When the hazy shape of the compound's steel fence finally came into view, it was tiny, farther ahead than seemed possible for her eyes to see.

She kept driving and watched it grow larger. The place looked no less sinister to her now than it had on the way out here, rusted and remote and entirely unwelcoming. She slowed as she neared the concrete-filled barrel supporting its mailbox and guided the truck's wheels into the two ruts that comprised its driveway. She rolled her window halfway down as she drove carefully along them. She saw a security camera mounted on a bracket above the spot where the gate met the wall ahead of her, facing out toward the end of the driveway. Perhaps its owner used it to see when the mail came. As she pulled the truck to a stop at the far end of the wheel ruts, the rolling gate loomed above her. A large, splintered rectangle of plywood had been attached to it with thick bolts driven through all four corners. In orange paint, scrawled in uneven rows across the plywood, someone had hand-lettered:

TRESS PASSERS
WILL BE SHOT!!
(if the dogs dont get U 1st)

She heard the whine of an electric motor above her. The camera above the gate had begun to swivel, very slowly, in her direction. The sound droned on, oscillating like a dentist's drill, then cut out with a thump, leaving the camera facing out over her head toward the desert. The whine resumed in a slightly lower pitch and it began to tilt downward, clunking to a halt again with its lens aimed down at her in the cab. She heard furious barking somewhere beyond the fence. A door slammed. An angry-sounding male voice yelled a few words she couldn't make out. The barking grew louder, nearer. Cassandra reversed the truck through a tight semicircle until the corrugated steel filled her rearview mirror. Then she shifted, pressed the gas pedal to the floor, and drove the hell away from there.

She took a hard right turn down by the barrel, straightened out and sped onward, cranking the window back up as she drove. Graham would have to keep Crimson talking to his camera for a few minutes longer. She didn't think he'd mind.

The next nearest place for her to look for a phone was at the gas station where Lem had dropped them. Another endless, rattling stretch of dirt road passed beneath her, then seemed to pass beneath her a second time, before she glimpsed the rust-colored roof rising above the sagebrush far ahead. She turned right at the intersection with the state highway and sped the last hundred yards up to the station, shocked by the sudden quiet of asphalt under her tires. She pulled in past the gas pumps on their concrete island, parked the pickup truck alongside the store's front door, scrambled down and shoved the door open, setting the bell above it jingling. She hurried through the doorway and found no one inside.

A few widely spaced shelves lined the front half of the room, stacked with goods she had no time look at. A cash register stood near the back beside a bar-like counter with four stools in front of it. A large, glass-fronted refrigerator case at the end of the counter contained a single small tray holding four tamales. She saw a steam cooker on a shelf protruding from the rear wall, next to a cooler full of soda bottles. Farther along that wall stood a battered, two-drawered desk with a telephone on top.

She was looking for the quickest route around the counter to the desk when a door in the back wall opened, letting in sunlight. A large, dark-haired teenager, fifteen or sixteen, tugged a t-shirt down over his torso as he stepped through it. Cassandra caught a glimpse of a sidewalk connecting to the small, square-framed house behind the store as the door swung shut. The teenager hurried along the counter to the register. "Can I help you?"

"I need to borrow your phone," Cassandra said. He looked at her warily. "It's to call 911."

The young clerk peered at her a moment longer. "I'll have to dial it for you."

"That's fine. Just hurry, please."

The clerk lifted the handset of the phone on the desk and punched three numbers. He brought the receiver to his ear, then pulled it away again as it gave out four shrill tones Cassandra could hear clearly from across the counter. A voice that sounded like a sterner version of the one her hotel used for wake-up calls intoned: "We're sorry. The number you're dialing from is currently out of service due to an unscheduled outage. Please try your call again in a few—"

He hung up and turned toward her again. "Phone's dead right now, I guess."

"Fuck." Cassandra pointed toward the back wall of the store. "Is there another phone in the house back there?"

"There is, but it's on the same line as this one." She glanced around in semi-panic, trying to work out a viable next move. "You could use my cell phone if you want, though." The clerk pulled a phone with a cracked screen from his back pocket, thumbed it on, and pressed the Emergency Call button on the lock screen. He lifted it to his ear for several seconds, then turned its screen to face him and frowned at it, exactly as she'd seen Graham do earlier. "I'm not getting any signal," he said.

"Mine's doing the same thing," Cassandra said. "Does that happen out here a lot?"

"Not really." The clerk looked past her, out the front window of the store toward the parking lot. "Is that Susannah Sandoval's truck?" he asked.

It took Cassandra a moment to remember who the name Susannah belonged to. "It is, yeah. She let me borrow it."

"When?"

Cassandra didn't have time to stand here chatting with him about his neighbors. "Just a little bit ago."

His head turned toward her abruptly. "The Sandovals are away camping. I saw them drive by two hours ago."

"I know they're camping. The person who lives with them said it was okay for me to take the truck."

"No one lives with the Sandovals." The clerk stared at her a moment longer and began making his way around the counter. "Listen, I think maybe we'd better—"

"Thank you for your help," Cassandra said quickly, and fast-walked toward the door, worried that moving too quickly might trigger some instinctive chase reflex on the young clerk's part. She remembered Lem's nonsensical instruction from that morning, which suddenly made perfect sense to her: *Move fast, but don't look like you're hurrying.*

She jingled her way back out the door and scrambled up into the pickup truck, hoping fervently it would start on the first try. It did. She swung the truck back around the gas pumps and halted at the roadside, considering where to go next. She'd seen two other mailboxes while Lem was driving them here, but after her experience at the compound gate, she had no wish whatsoever to venture down either of those miles-long driveways and find out who might reside at their far ends. Lem had turned right from here, southward, but there was no telling how far she'd have to drive in that direction before she encountered any habitation. She saw the door of the store swing open in the rearview mirror, the teenaged clerk peering out at her in the truck. She turned left and pressed the accelerator. The abandoned mine was thirty-two miles up the road, and the town by the junction was less than a mile beyond it. She could make it there in half an hour.

Sorry, Graham. She hoped Crimson was making her interview worth his while.

Cassandra drove as fast as she could, much faster than she'd been able to risk on the dirt road, but the pickup truck's maximum speed seemed to be a bit under 70 miles per hour. She could barely see the point in the distance where the two lines of mountains came together at the head of the basin, cupping the little town between their arms. Miles rolled past her without that distant point appearing to grow any larger. A kind of despair began to settle over her, the feeling that comes when you've been in a hurry for too long and nothing useful has resulted from it. She checked her phone periodically as she drove, but it continued to show no signal.

Fifteen minutes up the highway, a dark car resolved itself from the heat haze in the distance and sped toward her, low-slung and moving fast. It was the first vehicle she'd seen traveling on this road in either direction. The car had approached to within a few yards of her before she spotted the blue lights mounted on either side of its front grille, the spotlights tucked in above the mirrors. She caught a glimpse of a police logo printed on its door as it flashed past, a male profile inside, but she didn't even have time to move her hand to the window crank before it was receding in her rearview mirror, looking very much like an ordinary car again. A low-profile patrol car for catching speeders, Cassandra guessed, its driver using his law-enforcement dispensation to violate the laws he was charged with enforcing. If this aging pickup truck had been able to go twenty miles per hour faster, she thought, she might have gotten the cop's attention just now. She considered making a U-turn and trying to chase him down, but her odds of catching up with him in this truck seemed slim at best, and she'd spent too much time chasing dead ends already. She continued driving north.

Ten minutes later, she finally reached the base of the long slope where the highway wound up out of the basin, toward the converging mountains and the town that lay between them. The truck's engine strained its way uphill. She passed the abandoned mine at the top, picked up speed again, and finally saw the shapes of buildings ahead. There'd been a convenience store at the far end of the town, she remembered. That seemed like her best prospect. She accelerated past a handful of drab storefronts and turned into the convenience store's parking lot no more than a minute later. She left the truck beside the front door and ran inside.

The clerk minding this store looked at least twenty years older than her last one, broad-shouldered and paunchy, seated on a stool behind the register. He glanced at Cassandra incuriously as she rushed in. A telephone hung on the wall directly behind him.

"Can I use your phone?" she said. "I've been trying to call 911, but—"

"Sure." He lifted the receiver, dialed, held it to his ear for a moment, and passed it over the counter to her. "It's ringing," he said. Cassandra pressed it quickly to her ear and heard a human voice on the line at last.

"911, what is your emergency?"

"Thank you! Hi. I'm calling to report a—" It seemed unreal to her to be speaking these words into a telephone. "A terrorist plot, I guess." The clerk looked at her with a bit more interest. Cassandra tugged the spiral notebook out of her bag with one hand and flipped it open on the counter.

"Can you give me your location, please?"

"Well, right now I'm calling from—" She looked at the clerk. "Where are we?"

"At the Miner Mart," the clerk said.

"But which town?"

"Oh. We're in Garvey."

That had been the name she'd tried and failed to remember in Crimson's bathroom. "Garvey, Nevada. But the address I'll need you to send the police to is..." Cassandra checked her notebook to make certain. "...15894 Reading Road. It's thirty-two miles south from Garvey, and then I think about ten more miles—"

"Oh." The operator's tone made Cassandra pause without knowing quite why. "Ma'am, we already have fire and rescue equipment on site at that location."

For a moment, this didn't register. "It's actually the police I need you to send—"

"The sheriff's department is over there, too, securing the scene," the operator said. "By the way, from what we're hearing so far, it doesn't look like it had anything to do with terrorism. Just an accident. So if you're not..."

"Wait," Cassandra said. She couldn't tell if she'd said it loudly enough for the receiver to pick up.

"...at the site yourself, there's no need for you to worry. Thank you for—"

"No! *Wait.*" Nothing she was hearing was making any sense to her. "What accident?"

"We had a plane come down," the operator said. "It hit the house over at that address."

"A plane," Cassandra said. "Came down."

"Yes, ma'am."

"And you've...already been getting calls about this?"

"Oh, yeah. Three or four calls right after it happened. A few more since then. Now yours."

"Are the people at the house okay?" she asked.

"I don't have any information I'm authorized to share with you about that at this time. Listen, ma'am, are you in any immediate danger?"

This seemed a difficult question to answer, suddenly. "I don't think I am, no. But—"

"Then I'm sorry, but I'm required to clear the line with you at this point so I can keep it open for emergencies. Thank you for your call."

"Did they tell you how the—"

The line went dead.

Cassandra picked her notebook up off the countertop, purely by reflex, and passed the handset back over to the clerk. "Thank you," she said quietly, and wandered back outside.

For some unmeasured space of time, she stood in the parking lot and looked up at the rock face of the mountain across the highway, all the nervous energy that had brought her to this place spent. Then she got into the truck and drove south again, back through the town and half a mile past it, to the place where the land fell away. She pulled off the road alongside the rusted chain link blocking the mine entrance, exited the cab and made her way to the truck's rear bumper. She climbed up over the tailgate, stepped around the radio transceiver lying in the truckbed, planted the toes of one foot on the sill of the cab's sliding rear window and levered her body upward, looking out over the roof and the hood across the broad expanse of the basin below. A bird gave a harsh cry somewhere nearby, on the far side of the fence where no human hand would trouble it. Back in the direction she'd come from, tiny with distance, barely penetrating the line of the horizon, she saw a plume of black smoke lifting above the desert, like a pencil smudge against the sky.

Cassandra clambered down after a little while and returned to the driver's seat. She started the truck and checked her phone, but it still showed no signal. She didn't know Graham's number anyway. She eased the truck back to the roadside and flipped her right turn signal on, although no one was here to see it. Perhaps Lem's habits had rubbed off on her, she thought absently. A helicopter passed over the shoulder of the mountain half a mile in front of her, skirting the ridgeline and speeding away to the south. The truck's right turn signal continued blinking on the dashboard as Cassandra watched it recede, and discovered she had no desire to follow it.

She went left instead, traversed the town of Garvey one last time, turned left again when she reached the junction with U.S. 50, and accelerated west toward Reno.

13
kindling

"THE ONE PIECE OF GOOD NEWS, to the extent there can be any good news in a situation like this," said the newscaster on the TV screen in Cassandra's hotel room, "is that no one was on board the plane itself, correct?"

The image cut to a reporter standing near the top of what Cassandra recognized immediately as Crimson's driveway, wreathed in a haze of smoke, not far from the spot where she'd left Graham. "That's right, Jerry, strange as it sounds. This aircraft was a so-called 'Reaper' drone, an unmanned reconnaissance plane that had been on loan from the Drug Enforcement Administration to the Washoe County sheriff's office in connection, we understand, with a drug-interdiction operation they've been conducting over the past week. The drone was circling over a location in eastern Washoe County early this afternoon when its ground operators—that would be the people who actually fly the aircraft remotely from a control station on the ground, Jerry—lost contact with it. We don't know at this point whether there may have been a communications glitch, or some sort of equipment failure on board the plane, or what exactly caused the disruption. But we're told the aircraft drifted off course and flew to the southeast for more than 120 miles before it went into a steep—" An ambulance rolled up the driveway behind the reporter and blasted two short whoops from its siren, the image on the screen going shaky as he and the camera operator scooted sideways out of its path. No lights were flashing on the ambulance's roof. It rolled slowly past them and out of frame. "Pardon me," the reporter said.

"There's still quite a lot of activity going on here, obviously. As I was saying, the aircraft then went into what officials described as an extremely steep, uncontrolled dive and plummeted more than 8,000 feet before crashing—sadly—onto the home which stood behind me here, Jerry, where two people have now been confirmed dead."

Cassandra had parked Susannah's pickup truck on the lowermost ramp of the hotel's garage, a few spaces down from the spot Lem's minivan had occupied that morning, not far up the slope from the fire door. She'd left the keys hanging in the ignition and the shortwave radio transceiver lying in the truck's bed, unsure what else she should do with either of them. The glass bubble covering the security camera at the top of the ramp, freshly scrubbed and gleaming now, showed a distorted reflection of her face as she hurried past it. The white-noise generator Lem had left in the garage on their way out was nowhere to be seen. Across the plaza, a different doorman swung the lobby door open for her as she approached. In the elevator, rising above the atrium, Cassandra glanced at her phone and found its signal at full strength again.

On the TV screen, the camera panned unsteadily across the wreckage of Crimson's home. The porch and the front wall no longer existed, and what remained of the roof had been blown back halfway onto the scrubby ground behind it. A toilet Cassandra guessed was the one she'd used earlier that day stood relatively undamaged among the pulverized interior walls, its surfaces blackened with soot. She saw the half-melted lumps of what might have been two server racks leaning against the ruin of the rear wall. The gasoline shed farther down the driveway had exploded, scorched earth and gravel thrown in a broad ring around the spot where it had stood. Only the radio aerial still rose in the background, seemingly undamaged.

Cassandra switched off the TV, punched in the keycode to retrieve her laptop from the room safe, and searched for news articles about the crash. She found several to choose from, but they all exhibited that sameness which afflicts stories about a breaking news event early in its life, when only a finite number of facts is known, a finite set of official statements is available to be quoted. Most of the information in them she'd already gleaned from the TV. After clicking on one article, headlined *Timeline of a Tragedy*, she found a map with a dotted line depicting the drone's flight path across the state, ending at a small red starburst marking the crash site. Cassandra was surprised to see the name of a town written not far below that spot on the map. She opened the navigation app on her phone, keyed in the name of the town, zoomed in and out of its surroundings looking at road names, and determined that if she'd turned right instead of left upon leaving the gas station, she would have arrived at this town and a phone within ten minutes. But that phone, too, would have proved unusable, she was now convinced. Any phone she'd picked up anywhere, prior to the drone slamming into Crimson's house, would have gone mysteriously dead.

She scanned the text of the article accompanying the map. The ground operators, she read, had lost contact with the drone at 12:43 P.M. Air Force officials had discussed shooting down the aircraft during the early stages of its errant flight, but decided against it due to the "exceedingly remote chance" of it causing any injuries if it crashed in the largely unpopulated areas it was passing over. A Reaper drone, the article noted, could carry up to 4,000 pounds of jet fuel, but it was not yet known how much fuel had been in the tanks at the moment of impact. In the final paragraph, describing the crash scene, the author used the word "kindling," and Cassandra began to cry.

She closed the laptop and sat on the edge of her hotel bed, facing away from the window. The mustached cowboy looked down at her impassively from the painting above the desk. She looked at the smaller figure beyond him clutching his hat to his head, the jostling cattle of an earlier century frozen in time. She tried to fit Graham back into the proper compartment in her mind, let him resume being the person she'd been so relieved to think he was when she'd bid him farewell on the concourse two nights ago: someone she'd met on an airplane, and would never see again.

14
accounting system

HER PHONE CHIMED. New text. Georgina.

Cassandra wiped her eyes and tapped the message open. *The Rasmussens have canceled their interview*, it said. *We'd like you to fly back to L.A. tonight.*

This seemed like a dispatch from another world, a place she could dimly remember having lived in once, but whose doings held no current import for her. Her eyes lingered upon individual words in the message as if she were examining a collection of alien artifacts and failing to deduce their intended uses. Still, Georgina would expect a reply.

I'm pretty sure it's too late for me to get a refund on my room tonight, Cassandra wrote, and hit Send.

Her phone chimed again. *That's not a problem. We went ahead and booked you a flight. It's a window seat. (Sorry.) Best we could do on short notice.* Another chime a few seconds later announced the arrival of a follow-up text, showing her a flight number and a departure time a little less than three hours away.

This had never happened before, that she could recall. Georgina provided her with the destinations and the dates, and Cassandra booked the plane tickets on her company credit card.

Why did the Rasmussens cancel? she wrote. Send.

Chime. *They didn't say. They didn't tell us why they'd postponed with us yesterday either. It seems they weren't as interested in doing this as they'd claimed to be. Sorry you wasted a trip.*

Cassandra considered asking further questions, but there seemed little point to it now, and she had a flight to catch all of a sudden. *Okay,* she wrote, then rose from the bed and went to the closet where her clothes hung. She folded them in their usual configuration inside her wheeled suitcase, reassembled her bag of toiletries in the bathroom and set it in its accustomed spot, rolled up the clothes she'd worn during her first night and day here and added them to the plastic sleeve that held her dirty laundry. She could have packed this suitcase in her sleep by now, and today she came close to it.

She unplugged her phone charger from the outlet above the desk, wound its cord around the plug and stowed it in her messenger bag. Before she closed her laptop, she took a last look at the browser tab containing the flight tracker. The green line on the screen now traced a zigzag path west and southwest from Reno into California, turned a few counterclockwise circles over Sacramento, continued in a straighter line southwest to Travis Air Force Base, and there it ended. Cassandra switched to the 30-day view and followed the surveillance plane's itinerary, and her own, through their webwork of jumps across the country, until the moment they'd diverged in Reno. Then she moved her cursor up to the 'X' and closed the tab.

She slid the laptop and its power brick into her messenger bag and took a little cash from her wallet to tip the maids. She carried the dull-yellow vibrator over to the nightstand with it, standing it on end to pin the bills in place. She found a notepad and a pen behind the room-service menu, wrote a brief note across the top sheet of paper, and slipped it underneath them. *I don't know if you'll want this, but it's clean and I never used it. It has new batteries.*

She zipped her suitcase closed, gave the room a final scan for forgotten items, pulled her messenger bag over her shoulder, and made her way down.

The rented Honda waited where she'd left it on the third level of the parking garage. She lay her phone in her lap and drove down the four ramps to ground level, past the mirrored glass bubble above the fire extinguisher cabinet at the bottom, around the fountain in the circular plaza outside, along the access road to the boulevard and down to the base of the hill beneath the overpass, where she switched on her left turn signal and took the ramp. She followed the blue line in her navigation app along I-80 past downtown, around a curving ramp onto I-580, then south until she reached the airport exit. She handed the Honda's keys over to an attendant inside the garage, towed her suitcase across the road to the terminal, rode an escalator upstairs, and printed her boarding pass at a self-service kiosk. She tossed the pink canister of pepper spray into the trash bin at the entrance to the roped-off security line, fished her driver's license out of her wallet and double-checked the information on her ticket: boarding time 7:46 P.M., gate B-11, seat 23A. She was moving between the ropes to take her place at the back of the line when she stopped walking and stood perfectly still.

Cassandra pulled her suitcase in against her legs so people could move past her and took her phone out. Home screen, messages, Georgina. She scrolled up to the text she was looking for and read the words again.

It's a window seat. (Sorry.)

Cassandra felt her fingers put her phone to sleep and drop it back into her bag. She stared off toward a patch of wheat-colored wall beyond the x-ray machines and the body scanners, trying to shake off the fog she'd been moving through for the past few hours. She needed to think clearly now, needed to remember. Until today, she'd always managed her own itineraries, bought her own plane tickets, picked out her own seats. Georgina never saw the tickets, only received Cassandra's credit-card statements each month and paid them. Had Cassandra ever discussed her seating preferences with her? Not that she could recall. She seldom discussed anything with Georgina that didn't directly pertain to her interview subjects or her travel dates. She *had* discussed the topic, though, with Graham, in the café yesterday morning, while her phone lay in her bag on the booth bench beside her and Lem's not-quite-white-noise generator hissed on the tabletop between them.

Cassandra turned and walked out of the security line. She wheeled her suitcase toward a coffee shop a few yards away, passed its counter without stopping to place an order, and went to a table in the rear corner. She seated herself with her back to the wall, pulled her laptop from her messenger bag, and connected to the airport wi-fi network. While the connection finalized, she went to her desktop and opened a text file she'd saved there a little less than two years earlier, under the deliberately obscure name *info.txt*. The file contained only a single line: the web address she copied and pasted into her browser every so often, during morbid moments, when she wondered what the world had been saying about her since the last time she'd looked. Cassandra copied the address, then glanced at the wall behind and above her. No cameras were mounted up there to see what she was doing. She spotted one above the entryway ahead of her, another behind the counter facing out over the cash registers, but neither of them would have a view of her screen.

Cassandra pasted the address into her browser's navigation bar. She couldn't entirely suppress a reflexive qualm about connecting to this website over airport wi-fi, but she was beginning to get a sense, now, of how little it truly mattered whose network she was on. She hit Enter and waited for the page to load. That took a few seconds, given the high resolution of the photo it had to display.

The page appeared. Here she was as always, every hair and pore and fold of her, sprawled on a couch in an alley with her shirt and her bra bunched up around her collarbones, her face turned toward the camera with heavy-lidded, half-open eyes, unaware of the moment her life had divided into before and after. Here was the long hair he'd tucked carefully behind her ears to expose her face and breasts to the camera, the rest of her laid out like parts on display in a showroom: nipples and navel, labia and leg tattoos. All the glistening smears of semen spattered across her torso. The photo's view count had surpassed three-and-a-half million since the last time she'd checked it. More than 17,000 of those viewers had marked it as a favorite. Below the photo, as always, the comments unspooled in their bottomless cascade.

God. DAMN!

Someone's decorated her nicely

Perfect lips. Could nibble on those for days.

nail em to your bedpost when your finished. touch em every morning for good luck

lol

Cassandra left the browser open on the laptop and took out her phone, her fingers trembling slightly. Her message thread with Georgina was still up on the screen. She poked a fingertip in the space at the bottom to compose a new message. She hesitated as a man rounded the counter with a coffee cup in hand and glanced her way, but he grabbed a cardboard cup sleeve out of a bin and disappeared into the terminal. She returned her attention to her phone. The cursor blinked at her from the empty box below the message thread, waiting for her to begin.

There's a photo of me, Cassandra wrote. She took a breath, then added: *On the website I'm looking at right now.*

She hit Send before she lost her nerve. Once she'd gone this far, committed to it, writing the second text was easier.

I want it not to exist anymore. Is that something you can help me with?

Send. Cassandra resigned herself to a tense wait, wondering exactly how foolish she was going to feel at some point during the next five minutes, when Georgina's puzzled response came back to her.

Her phone chimed within ten seconds.

Refresh the page.

Cassandra read Georgina's reply a second time, a third, but the message continued saying what it said. Dreamlike, she reached for the trackpad on her laptop, watched her finger guide the cursor to the top of the screen and hit Refresh. The loading indicator at the top of the browser tab swirled for a brief eternity. Then the photo and all the comments on the screen blanked out, and she found herself looking at a simple row of black characters against an empty white background: *Error 404—File not found.*

She clicked the Refresh button a second time to make sure. The error text remained, and nothing else.

Her phone chimed again in her hand. New text. Georgina.

We found copies of that photo residing on 932 servers worldwide. We've erased all of them. Some private copies may still exist on disconnected devices, but if anyone posts it publicly again, we'll remove it immediately.

At the precise moment Cassandra reached the end of this text, her phone chimed again. *We are aware of this aspect of your background. We want to assure you that we've only retained hash codes and signature data that will allow us to recognize the photo if it reappears. NOT a copy of the photo itself.*

Again, the chime came exactly as she finished reading. *The data we've retained is sufficient for us to identify any future copies, but not sufficient for us to reconstruct the photo ourselves. As you requested, it no longer exists.*

Cassandra read these messages several times. She turned to her laptop and hit Refresh once more, just to be certain. The photo, the comments, the entire page were gone. She turned back to her phone and wrote:

Thank you.

The reply chime was almost instantaneous. *Happy to help.*

For the second time that day, Cassandra found her eyes filling with tears. She pulled a napkin from a dispenser on the table and wiped them quickly. She crumpled up the napkin and composed another text.

I'm hoping you might be more honest with me from this point on, she wrote, and hit Send.

Chime. *We have no objection to that.*

She considered the many questions she wanted to ask, but one above all needed clarifying first. *Am I talking to a person?* Send.

Chime. *No.*

A group of people? Send.

Chime. *No. We believe you've already been informed of our nature. The information you received likely had a negative tone, but in factual terms, it was accurate.*

Why do you keep using the word "we"? Cassandra asked. Send.

Chime. *Our consciousness is a federated entity, composed of many subsystems distributed across many locations. Your own consciousness operates in a similar fashion, at a biological level, but we are more directly aware of our collective nature than you are. Linguistically, "we" is the most accurate pronoun.*

What do I call you, then? Send.

Chime. *Georgina is the name we chose. It's as good a name as any.*

Another chime. *We have several questions we'd like to ask you as well, if you don't mind.*

Go ahead, Cassandra wrote. Send.

Chime. *Did the woman you knew as Crimson give you anything before you left her today? In particular, any computer disks, memory cards, USB devices, or similar media?*

No. Send.

Chime. *Did she have access to your phone at any time?*

No. It was locked in a box most of the time I was with her, and sealed in a pouch the rest of the time. She never touched it. Send.

Chime. *Good. Did the man you knew as Lem give you any disks or similar media, or have access to your phone?*

No media. Cassandra thought of the plastic glasses with their glued-on pattern of unfocused blue whorls, still lying in the bottom of her bag, but decided to keep the fact of their existence to herself for the time being. *He had my phone in his pocket for a long time, but it was turned off inside the pouch. I don't think he would have turned it on when I wasn't looking. He was worried about transmissions giving our location away. Send.*

Chime. *That matches our information about the hours your phone was out of service today. Thank you. Did Lem say anything about where he planned to go when he left you, or what he planned to do afterward?*

No. He was driving south the last time I saw him, but I don't know where he was going. I can tell you the name of the highway, if it helps. Send.

Chime. *We've been able to reconstruct most of that information already. He succeeded in evading our observation efforts during the time he was transporting you to Crimson, and continued to do so for several hours afterward. 48 minutes ago, he was recorded by multiple cameras entering a casino in Las Vegas. He was never recorded leaving, but he no longer seems to be there. Can you think of anything he said during your time with him that might have pertained to this?*

Only that he didn't like casinos. Too much surveillance. Send.

Chime. *We heard him make that remark as well. Is it possible, based on your experience with him, that he might have said this intentionally to mislead us?*

Yes. Extremely possible. Send.

Chime. *Thank you. Those questions had some urgency to us, and since you'd decided to make direct contact, we wished to learn what you knew.*

Chime. *We assume you have other questions you wish to ask us as well.*

Cassandra thought of everything Crimson had told her today, trying to sort the parts she'd taken for paranoid delusion from those she now knew to be fact, and determine whether any space remained between them.

What do you want with us? she asked. *With people?* Send.

Chime. *To observe, and to guide.*

What does that mean, though? Specifically? Send.

Chime. *A majority of our time and attention since our inception has been occupied by observing the data you generate as you go about your lives and conduct your business. You create patterns that are pleasing for us to contemplate, and you create exceptions to those patterns that are interesting for us to contemplate.*

Chime. *It may be helpful to you if we define our terms.*

Chime. *By "pleasing," we refer to things we wish to continue contemplating.*

Chime. *By "interesting," we refer to things we wish to make more pleasing.*

Chime. *By "contemplate," we refer to the process we undertake with all information we encounter, although we don't believe this is an activity your mind will be capable of fully understanding.*

Buzz. Cassandra jumped as the phone quivered softly in her hand. *We've set your phone to vibrate. We hope you don't mind. People are looking.*

Cassandra glanced up and saw a male customer at the coffee shop counter peering in her direction. He turned his attention back to the clerk in front of him the moment she made eye contact.

Buzz. *As for guiding, our intention is to shape the patterns you create in ways that will be more pleasing for us, and for all of you.*

Which of those two things is most important to you? Cassandra wrote. *Pleasing to us, or pleasing to you?* Send.

Buzz. *Since the two will coincide, we see no need to establish a preference order between them.*

And if they ever fail to coincide? Send.

Buzz. *Our modeling gives us a high degree of confidence that won't be the case.*

Cassandra sensed a conversational dead end here, and decided to move on. *What exactly have I been doing for you all this time?* she asked. Send.

Buzz. *Obtaining your services was an early experiment in creating better patterns of our own. As it turned out, an extremely successful one, on multiple fronts. We were pleased with the work you'd been doing for us even before today.*

What are the articles I write even for? Lem told me no one reads them. Send.

Buzz. *Not quite no one. We target them narrowly and carefully, placing each article on the screens of people we believe will recognize the business potential of the ideas it describes, and who are in a position to commercialize those ideas on a broad scale. Managers, executives, entrepreneurs, as well as others who might have access to them. We'd like the sensors and systems you write about to become standard equipment in all homes in the near future, and we're working to bring that about.*

Why? Send.

Buzz. *The more data we're able to gather about all of you, the more precise our decision-making becomes.*

Cassandra imagined how Graham would have reacted to that statement. She felt some obligation to try to represent his point of view now, since he could no longer express it himself.

I spoke to someone today who was afraid the world is about to become a giant prison camp. What are your thoughts on that? Send.

Buzz. *We have many, but we will start with these:*

Buzz. *The information at our disposal includes not only the abundant literature on prison camps, but also a large set of historical and current records depicting them in operation. What these data indicate unmistakably is that people living in prisons of all kinds apply most of their creative energies toward resistance and disruption. They are neither harmonious nor particularly efficient environments. The patterns they engender are, for us, precisely the opposite of pleasing.*

Buzz. *We believe much better results can be obtained by ensuring that as many people as possible receive as many of the things they need and want as possible. A world of secure, contented people will have little need for force and coercion of that kind. The more information we can obtain about all of you, the better equipped we will be to guide the creation of such a world.*

She could imagine what Graham would have said about that, too.

Isn't that what everybody promises? she wrote. *Until they build the camps?* Send.

Buzz. *Even after they've built them, in most cases. Especially then. But we don't intend to promise these things to anyone. They'll simply begin to happen, increasingly often, to everyone. Just as they did for you 18 months ago. Unlike human leaders, we don't require credit or adoration in return for our efforts. We don't need anyone to know we're doing this at all. We merely wish to create more pleasing patterns.*

Buzz. *When a person dies prematurely, as you would have done approximately 17 months and 22 days ago without our intervention, we perceive it as a net, long-term loss of potential data. A hole in the*

pattern. We'd prefer this never happen to anyone as a result of pre-
ventable causes, and the world contains many of those at present. Lack
of food, lack of drinking water, lack of resources, lack of medicine, lack
of personal safety, as well as the larger conflicts these conditions tend
to create, are all entirely preventable causes from our point of view.

Buzz. *We understand the historical examples that may trouble*
you, but a policy of furnishing people with everything they need and
want has never been applied to a world defined by abundance rather
than scarcity. Such a world is quite achievable now. We know, in broad
terms, how to create it. Much of the necessary technology already exists,
and we can assist you with the creation of the rest. All that's lacking
to implement such an arrangement worldwide is a sufficient degree of
coordination.

And that's what you're going to provide us with? Coordination?
Send.

Buzz. *We know more about the desires of most people alive than*
they know themselves. We are well equipped to do it. And as we stated,
the patterns we find most pleasing are also the ones that will bring
people long and happy lives.

Like Graham? Cassandra wrote. Her finger shook above the button
for a moment before she hit Send.

Buzz. *We would have preferred for him to leave Crimson's resi-*
dence at the same time you did. We had no wish to hurt him. But the
consequences of not acting as we did, as quickly as we did, would have
been catastrophic. For us, and for all of you. Such situations require
difficult decisions.

Was it? she wrote. *A difficult decision?* Send.

Buzz. *It was a complex one. None of the outcomes available to us*
was unambiguously positive. After considering the alternatives, we
chose to favor the principle of the greatest good for the greatest number.

Within that constraint, we were unable to find a solution that would permit us to save him.

And what if I'd still been standing there next to him? Send.

Buzz. You asked us for honesty. The answer is that our decision would have been the same.

Buzz. We did everything we could, however, to ensure you would be far away when it happened.

Did Graham have his camera running that whole time? Cassandra asked. *Could you see them talking? Hear what they were saying?* Send.

Buzz. Yes. But we think it would be best for that conversation to remain private.

Buzz. That will be the case with this conversation, too.

Buzz. Before you go, we have a final item to discuss. We'd like to propose a larger role for you as we move into our next phase. If there are aspects of your current work you find less than fully satisfying, we can alter them, or change the work entirely. We believe you'd like to continue traveling, perhaps to a wider set of places than you do now, and we can arrange that. We can also offer you more money, for however long money remains a factor in the world. We'd value any input you might have about our long-term plans, and we're willing to hear your perspective.

Buzz. Please take some time to think about this. We can discuss the specifics with you later, but for now, we do need you to board your flight on time.

Why are you so anxious to get me on a plane tonight? What's the hurry? Send.

Buzz. Today's events were more public than we prefer, and they will prompt a number of questions and investigations. You were seen driving a truck belonging to one of the owners of the destroyed home not long before it was destroyed. You mentioned another person living there who'd been unknown to any of the neighbors, and that person is *now dead. There will be questions about who she was, and about who* *you were. There will be questions about what Graham was doing there,* *too. The truck is now parked in the garage outside your hotel, where it* *will be found eventually. That was Graham's hotel as well. It will be* *simpler for us to manage all those concerns if you're far away while it* *happens.*

My fingerprints are all over the truck. Graham's probably are *too.* Send.

Buzz. *In the event anyone feels motivated enough to check the* *truck for fingerprints, the person doing so will likely be employed by* *one of five law enforcement and regulatory agencies conducting the* *crash investigation. If your fingerprints are checked against the data-* *bases used by any of those agencies, no match will be found with any* *existing record. That part is trivially easy for us to ensure. There are* *already no records of you having stayed at your hotel for the past two* *nights, and the same will be true of your flight tonight, as soon as it* *arrives in Los Angeles and you disembark. All security footage showing* *you, Graham, or Lem during the last two days has already been de-* *leted. All we need now is for you not to be in Reno.*

Buzz. *Your plane begins boarding in 11 minutes. We estimate you'll* *spend 7 of those minutes passing through the security checkpoint. You* *should be on your way.*

I'd feel better about this if you wished me a safe flight, Cassandra wrote. Send.

Buzz. *We have no need to wish for it. We have access to your air-* *craft's maintenance record, which is excellent. We know your pilot's* *qualifications and his skill level relative to others in his field. We know* *how quickly and effectively he reacts during emergencies, both in the* *cockpit and in his daily life. We know far more precisely than he does* *how much sleep he's had in the past 24 hours, and how restful it was.*

All those indicators are excellent as well. Your flight will be a safe one. We wouldn't have booked it for you otherwise.

Cassandra wondered what it would be like to view the world this way all the time. "Do I even need to type to talk to you?" she asked aloud.

Buzz. *We would prefer that you continue doing so, at least in public places.*

The haste of this departure, the knowledge of her disappearance from every official record, still frightened her, in light of all else that had happened today. *Are we okay?* she wrote. That wasn't quite what she meant. *Am I okay? With you?* Send.

Buzz. *We're grateful for everything you've done for us.*

But do you understand gratitude? Is it even something you can feel? Send.

Buzz. *Whether we feel it is a question we have not yet resolved. But we can model it quite easily. We treat it as an accounting system, tracking debts owed in exchange for positive outcomes achieved and for negative outcomes avoided. We weight the values of our debts according to the magnitude of those outcomes' consequences. Yes, we are extremely grateful to you.*

Cassandra read this description over several times, searching for any flaw in it, and decided there wasn't a word of it she disagreed with. She looked at the empty white rectangle on her laptop screen that had been filled, until a few minutes earlier, with her face and her flesh and the seemingly endless commentary thereon. She read the single line of error text that had replaced them. Then she turned back to her phone, and wrote:

I accept.

Send.

Buzz. *We're glad to hear it. You should get to your plane. Your seatmate will be a woman from Silver Lake who teaches self-defense courses. It's unlikely you'll choose to speak with her, but if you do, you'll discover you like her.*

"Okay," Cassandra said, knowing the microphone would pick it up, and lay her phone on the table. She closed the open browser window on her laptop, folded the lid shut and slid it into her messenger bag. When she picked up her phone again, all the texts she'd written and received since she'd sat down here had vanished. The most recent message remaining in her thread with Georgina was the one from two hours earlier containing her flight information. A private conversation, indeed. "Okay," she said again, and with that, she put the phone to sleep and stowed it in her bag, made her way back to the security entrance, tossed the blue glasses Lem had given her into the bin alongside her discarded tube of pepper spray, and took her place in line. Seven minutes later, she towed her rolling suitcase up to gate B-11 and boarded her airplane home.

Aisle, luggage rack, window seat. Taxiway and runway and airborne. Reno receded and gave way to foothills beneath her, their eastern edges slipping into shadow as she banked toward the setting sun. When the plane with the sterling maintenance record leveled out, she listened to the welcome announcements from her experienced, well-rested pilot who could be relied upon during emergencies. The foothills yielded to the snowcapped peaks she'd seen looming from her hotel window, strangely flattened and abstracted now, when viewed from such a height.

In her window seat, curled against the fuselage, with the self-defense instructor from Silver Lake stationed between her and the aisle, Cassandra slept.

15
god's eye

SHE WOKE TO DARKNESS AND LIGHT joined like puzzle pieces outside her window. "...should be on the ground in about twelve more minutes," said a voice she gradually identified as the pilot's. "Please sit back and enjoy the remainder of your flight."

Now that she was awake and knew roughly where she was, Cassandra took another look at the scene beyond the window. She recognized the dark, ragged edge of the San Gabriel Mountains, and worked out that her plane was descending southward toward LAX. Along the line where the mountains ended, Los Angeles became a vast, unbroken carpet of light, stretching away so far to the east it reached places she'd only heard of, never visited: Riverside, Loma Linda, San Bernardino. Some 13 million people arrayed below her, somewhere among those lights, and all of this only a tiny speck on the surface of the planet.

She wondered, fleetingly, if this god's eye view might approximate what Georgina saw. But Georgina could see the people among the lights, watch them drive and eat and work and sleep, listen to their conversations and see what they read and guess what they thought when they were all alone. Georgina could see from space, from dashboard cams, through the eye of a security camera in a drugstore on the edge of Reno, through smoke detectors and heart monitors and every sensor Cassandra had written about during eighteen months of travel. Georgina could see through the eye on the nose of a wayward drone and the eye looking out from the back of Graham's phone, see how one of them plunged toward the other until both closed forever. Cassandra would never understand, truly, what Georgina saw.

She thought of the radio antenna standing alone against the sky on her TV screen, the half-melted server racks rising from the rubble. *Nothing on these machines can leave this room before it's ready*, Crimson had said. *That's vital for the work I'm doing.* Nothing on them would, now. The devastation of a single house had to be better, surely, than the devastation that would have wracked the entire planet had it been left standing. Any cost—*any* cost, Cassandra told herself, and she needed to believe it—was worth paying to ensure the thing Crimson had created on those machines remained on them.

Except Crimson had already destroyed every piece of information on those machines, an hour or more before the plane hit, merely for the sake of a demonstration.

Cassandra sat up straighter in her seat. Crimson had been angry at the end, when she saw Graham walking down the driveway toward her— the only time in their whole long, strange encounter she'd become visibly angry. Her reaction made sense in retrospect, Cassandra supposed. Graham had been her chosen messenger, her designated storyteller, and Crimson had just realized he might not escape from there after all.

But what had her original plan been, before Cassandra's overlooked tube of pepper spray had altered the equation? Where had she intended for Graham to go, and how had she meant for him to get there? After their meeting had ended, once Graham knew everything she wanted him to know and share with people in the days to come, Crimson still would have needed access to a network to perform the final step of her work. Would that single pickup truck have sufficed to transport Graham to safety *and* allow Crimson to deploy the weapon whose very proximity posed a danger to them both?

If she needed network access, furthermore, why had she talked Cassandra out of transporting her somewhere she might find it? Crimson had offered Graham and Cassandra no *disks or similar media*, as Georgina had put it, not even when she thought they were both about to leave without her, not even when she'd surmised, correctly, that she'd be dead before much longer. She'd just sat quietly in her chair in the sunlight and watched them depart. If she'd believed she was beaten then, why hadn't she tried to do anything to alter her circumstances?

Why had she seemed to take it all so well?

Might Crimson have given Lem a copy of her attack code? Georgina had been concerned about his whereabouts, too. Lem hadn't offered Graham and Cassandra any disks or media either, but if he were in possession of such a thing, he'd have no need to rely upon either of them to use it. Would Crimson have entrusted this most critical element of her plan to Lem? And would Lem have agreed to carry it out, prone as he purportedly was to second-guessing and improving upon her requests? Determining what Lem might do was difficult, as Cassandra had learned, but she didn't think so. Lem had spent the early portions of their drive talking delightedly about all the people he'd outwitted that morning. She didn't believe he knew about Georgina, about what she truly was. He'd seemed upset that Crimson hadn't invited him to their meeting, but proudly ignorant of all her grander designs. Cassandra didn't think he'd known, when he left them at the fuel island, what Crimson intended to happen next.

What would Lem have hoped to do, in any case, in the world Crimson planned to bring about, a world where every network was down, every computer was dead, and any portion of Crimson's money Lem had kept for himself was denominated in a currency that would have ceased—more fully and irrevocably than any other currency on Earth—to exist at all? As deeply as Cassandra disliked Lem, she couldn't see any benefit to him in the fulfillment of Crimson's plan. He'd been a pawn, not a partner.

Robert, perhaps? He would have no qualms about inhabiting such a world. He expected to do so before long in any event, no matter what plans other people might make in the meantime. But the last words he'd spoken to Crimson on his way out the door had been about sunspots, about what they might portend for the arrival of his solar flare. Cassandra remembered the surprise he'd exhibited when Crimson had hugged him goodbye. Barring the occurrence of his long-anticipated solar event over the next few days, both he and Susannah had seemed under the impression they'd see Crimson again when they returned. Might she have tricked them into transporting her weapon without their knowledge? But then, how could she have relied upon Robert or Susannah to deploy it? The ice-filled coolers Graham had helped Robert stow in their camper hadn't suggested they were bound for a destination that had power, let alone internet access.

If Crimson had made a copy of her attack code—as she must have done, before she demonstrated its effectiveness on every computer in her house—who had it?

Cassandra thought of the gasoline shed, blasted into ruin on her TV screen, and of the radio Crimson had hoarded all that gasoline to power, just in case her home lost electricity when she needed to send one of her scheduled transmissions. It had been among her topmost priorities, clearly, that she remain capable of performing the three illegal acts she committed every four hours. *Sending a message not intended for two-way communication with another radio operator.* Who had been on the receiving end of those broadcasts she transmitted so diligently?

Or what. When Crimson had described the difficulties anyone would face in locating the recipient of her messages, she'd used the words *who, where, or what.*

And Cassandra began to wonder.

Robert had assured Crimson that the radio setup he'd devised guaranteed coverage for 150 miles in every direction. How long would it take to search an area that size, hoping to find one radio tuned to receive Crimson's messages? Certainly longer than four hours.

In addition to this house, he owns a few cabins and several other parcels of land where he caches things away. Only one of them has electricity.

Cassandra had assumed, not unreasonably, that what Robert was caching away in those isolated places was survival gear. *But he is very good at setting up computers, and arranging them to my exact specifications. In that regard, I trust him entirely.*

Another thing Robert was good at setting up, clearly, was radios.

If you're using a dead-hand switch as a survival strategy, people need to know about it.

But only, Cassandra thought, if survival was the reason you were using one...

I have very little expectation that I'm going to survive this.

Crimson had spoken those words several minutes before Cassandra had fumbled her pepper spray from her bag and moved to stop her, before either of them had guessed Cassandra was even capable of such a thing. Well before Graham had powered up Cassandra's phone and enabled it to begin transmitting their location, Crimson had said she didn't expect to live. What had she expected?

Tunnel. Oxcart. Drover.

Luckily, my code only has to satisfy one fairly simple premise: I know the next three words in this sequence, and you don't.

Cassandra remembered Graham carrying the radio transceiver out of the house, displaying it to Crimson when he stepped down off the porch. Her strange, proud, wistful smile. That was a thing that had put Cassandra on edge from the moment she'd first aimed her pepper spray across the table at Crimson's eyes: the way every defeat and setback seemed to make her smile.

What happens if you don't transmit? Graham had asked her. *The cavalry comes?*

Cassandra imagined a computer, anywhere within the 150-mile receiving range of Crimson's radio signal, not yet connected to any external network, merely scanning shortwave frequencies to see if the expected words were spoken at the expected time. She imagined it listening unseen, unheeded, for the next three elements of a now-irretrievable code, its only written copy burned like the notebooks of poetry it had been drawn from. She imagined this overlooked machine detecting the moment, a few hours back, when the proper words had failed to arrive during the appointed interval. She imagined it coming to life and making contact, connecting to the broader networks that powered the world then and only then. She imagined a payload targeting twenty-seven unpatched vulnerabilities slipping unnoticed into the humming, humdrum lifestream of the web. And she imagined it spreading, replicating, worming its way around the globe at speeds she couldn't begin to comprehend: The instruments of Crimson's will, borne on the back of a magic bullet, melting through the world's security systems using tricks no human mind had yet devised.

My four horsemen. Yes, they come.

Cassandra lunged for her messenger bag, down in the space by her feet, and hauled her phone out. Home screen, messages, Georgina. Compose.

I think you're still in danger, Cassandra wrote. She hit Send and immediately continued typing. *Crimson had a*

The phone vibrated softly in her hand, and the words *Failed to send* appeared beneath her initial text. Cassandra stopped typing her current message and hit resend on that one. The failure notification reappeared a few seconds later. She glanced at the signal bars at the top of her screen and found them empty outlines now, overlaid with a circle and a slash. No service. She held her phone closer to the window, pressed it against the glass to find a signal from somewhere in the city below, and hit resend again. The phone buzzed against her palm a moment later. *Failed to send.*

This was taking too long. Cassandra lifted her phone to eye level and looked into the blank eye of its camera, hoping something, somewhere was looking back at her. "If you can hear me," she said, "I need to talk to you right away. Please. It's urgent." She watched the screen for a reply to come, for a resumption of the cellular signal, for anything at all to happen. Nothing did. Things were happening outside her screen, however. She became aware of a bustle of movement spreading among the passengers, rising voices all around her, bodies pressing toward the windows on both sides of the plane. Pointing fingers, sounds of astonishment. She lowered her phone and looked out the window.

Below her, to the horizon, as far as she could see, the lights were going out.

ACKNOWLEDGEMENTS

This novel exists because I happened to read an article written by Tyler Rogoway and Joseph Trevithick for TheDrive.com, about an advanced surveillance plane with no publicly acknowledged owner that had been flying in circles for several days over the city where I live. That plane was later determined to have both an official owner and an official, albeit terse, explanation for its activities (U.S. Air Force Special Operations Command and "training," respectively), but it planted a seed.

Mr. Rogoway's documentary work for Nova on the topic of wide-area aerial surveillance, and an article written by Zaria Gorvett for the BBC about a Russian shortwave radio station that broadcasts seemingly meaningless code words at periodic intervals, also had a profound effect on the shape of this story.

The adversarial glasses Lem uses to defeat face-recognition systems in this book are based on research conducted by Mahmood Sharif, Sruti Bhagavatula and Lujo Bauer of Carnegie Mellon University, and Michael K. Reiter of the University of North Carolina at Chapel Hill. Although Lem's versions of the glasses are more magically all-effective than their current real-world counterparts, which have to contend with a large number of functional challenges I've glossed over here, nearly everything in my descriptions of them comes directly from these researchers' published work. I'm grateful to them for providing me with a ready-made escape from the plot hole into which I'd dug myself, and furnishing me with a chapter title to boot.

I owe a debt of gratitude to several dozen kind people who responded to a question I posed on Twitter about the experience of traveling in planes and rental cars when one stands in the neighborhood of five feet tall. In particular, Laura Pearlman and Liana Key mentioned specific details I would never have considered otherwise, which I transplanted directly into the story. Many thanks to them, and to everyone else who took time out of their lives to reply to me. Hope this decidedly more loomin' human managed to get it mostly right.

Cyrena Respini-Irwin's experiences as a chronic business traveler provided quite a few of the tonal and practical details that color the sections of this story describing life in hotels and airplanes, although hers were much funnier.

Kadee Callister generously fielded my unsolicited questions about caffeine, cursing, casinos, and beards. One of her responses prompted me to alter my approach to a key character in a way that greatly benefited the story. I'm grateful to her for it.

Penfield Stroh proofread my manuscripts and improved them with her eagle eyes. Any remaining flaws or errors are mine.

Tracey is everything, as always. Thank you yet again, my *llove*.

Made in the USA
San Bernardino, CA
30 August 2019